Hush, Little Baby
Judith Arnold

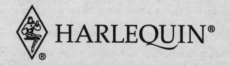

HARLEQUIN®

TORONTO • NEW YORK • LONDON
AMSTERDAM • PARIS • SYDNEY • HAMBURG
STOCKHOLM • ATHENS • TOKYO • MILAN • MADRID
PRAGUE • WARSAW • BUDAPEST • AUCKLAND

ISBN 0-373-70979-X

HUSH, LITTLE BABY

Visit us at www.eHarlequin.com

Printed in U.S.A.

This book is dedicated to Yehuda,
who reminds me of what a joy baby boys can be.

PROLOGUE

THE LAST TIME he'd been here, Ruth had brought him. "It's my absolute favorite place in the whole world," she'd rhapsodized, and although she'd often resorted to hyperbole, in this case he could see her point.

The bluff was one of a long row of palisades looming high above the Pacific Ocean. Rock broke through the dry grass, and the trees—small, gnarled evergreens stunted by the wind and the lack of soil—were nothing like the trees back in Connecticut. A slope of scrub-covered stones and ledges descended from the bluff to a beach so narrow it looked like a seam of glossy shells and white sand separating the ocean from the earth.

He recalled sitting on the bluff's straw-brown grass last June, feeling the salty wind tug at his hair as he gazed out at an uninterrupted horizon of sea and sky. Ruth was beside him, her legs crossed and her long, dark braid unraveling in the breeze. The sun dipped in and out of a misty haze, but her eyes glowed enough to brighten the afternoon. "Isn't this place gorgeous?" she said.

Levi nodded.

"I hike up here whenever I want to think, when I want to plan things out." She plucked a strand of grass from the ground and twirled it around her finger. "I have to tell you something."

"I'm listening."

"I'm pregnant."

Pregnant. His baby sister. All right, so she hadn't been a baby for a long time. In her midtwenties, she'd reached an excellent age to get pregnant. But he couldn't picture her handling such a huge responsibility. She was a weaver, for crying out loud, unmarried, footloose and carefree, sharing a ramshackle house with three other artisans.

"Who's the father?" he asked delicately.

She laughed and a sharp gust of wind scattered the sound. "Oh, don't worry about him."

He immediately began to worry. "Why? Who is he?"

"He isn't around anymore. He's from L.A. He was up here for a couple of months on business."

"What kind of business?" In Mendocino County, the biggest business seemed to be agriculture, the major crop marijuana. Crafts were another popular industry in the region; Ruth and her housemates earned their livings by selling their creations at craft shows and in boutiques, pooling their resources to save money. Among the four of them, they usually had one functioning car, and their meals consisted mostly of grains and greens. But they did all right for themselves.

Still, Levi struggled to imagine his sister having an affair with a businessman just passing through.

"He works for a film company. He was scouting locations for a movie. He was here for a couple of months, but he ended up deciding they'd be better off filming in British Columbia." She smiled placidly. "It's really perfect, Levi, because I don't want him in my life. We weren't in love or anything. Don't get me wrong—he was a nice guy. Good-looking, too. This baby is going to be beautiful.'' She rubbed her hand gently over her abdomen.

''Does he know you're pregnant?'' Whether or not Ruth wanted the man in her life, Levi thought she ought to be practical. Given her precarious finances, she couldn't afford to be so cavalier about child support. And in all fairness, the man deserved to be told. If Levi fathered a child, he'd want to know.

Ruth shrugged. ''It wasn't a great romance. Just a fling. I didn't plan this, but it happened and I'm thrilled. Be thrilled for me.''

Levi swore he was thrilled.

In late January, Ruth gave birth to Darren. A big, strapping, healthy boy—and Levi *was* thrilled. He couldn't get away from work at the time, but he promised Ruth he'd take his annual June trip to California. He'd spend a week with her and her new son and develop his skills as a doting uncle.

It wasn't June. It was May 1, but there he was, on the bluff overlooking the Pacific. Ruth had brought him to this place again.

He stood apart from her small circle of friends as they tossed her ashes into the air at the edge of the cliff. He didn't want to see if the ashes would fall all the way down to the water, if they'd get caught on the narrow ledges en route or a sea breeze would curl around them and carry them away. He didn't want to know.

Ruth was dead. His sister. Twenty-six years old, an aneurysm, and now she was dead.

Sandy, a potter and one of Ruth's housemates, wept silently while Doug, a leather worker and another housemate, sang ''Amazing Grace.'' Ruth had loved that song, but it was too unbearably sad. Levi clenched his hands and his jaw and kept his gaze on the horizon, dreaming that Ruth might live on in the shimmer of golden sunlight dancing along the waves, that her spirit would soar in the wind. Several other friends of Ruth's held hands and sang along with Doug. The baby dozed in a carrier someone had lugged up the steep path to this spot.

Levi wished he could disappear, be somewhere else, go to a place where none of this had happened, none of it was real. Ruth. His baby sister. He didn't want to believe she was gone.

Sandy sidled over to him, dabbing at her face with a crumpled tissue. "We have to talk," she murmured.

"Okay." He sounded wooden to himself, numb.

"Ruth wasn't as much of a flake as you might think," Sandy said, a faint smile fighting through her tears. "When Darren was born, she wrote a will."

Levi tried not to snort. Ruth didn't exactly have a substantial estate to dispose of. Most of the time, she'd been close to broke. He used to send her money when she was facing a particularly lean stretch.

"She's left you the baby," Sandy said.

"What?"

"She left you Darren."

He'd only met his nephew for the first time yesterday, when he'd driven up to Ruth's house from the airport in San Francisco. He'd been in no mood to bond with a strange infant. His sister had just died. He could hardly think, let alone get excited about her baby.

"She wrote it in her will," Sandy explained. "She signed it in front of witnesses. It's all legal."

"I thought—my parents—"

"You know she'd never trust your parents to raise her son."

Levi nodded reluctantly. Ruth had been estranged from their parents for years. Levi himself had little to do with them.

"Then why not you?" he asked. "You lived with her. You saw how she was raising him. You would know what she'd want."

"What she wants is you, Levi. She wants you to be a father for her son." Sandy pressed her hand to his. "She wants you to do this for her. You will, won't you?"

He closed his eyes. How could he? He was a bachelor with a demanding career and a busy life back in Connecticut. He'd just lost his beloved sister. He didn't even know how to change a diaper.

She wants you to do this for her.

"Okay," he heard himself say. In his heart he knew he had no choice. "I'll do it."

CHAPTER ONE

CORINNE WORE her gray suit. Gray was last year's color, or maybe the year before's, but she didn't care. She liked the way it made her feel: cool, composed and invincible. She was about to enter into combat with Levi Holt, and she didn't want to be emotional about it. The gray suit contained her emotions very nicely.

Straightening her shoulders, she entered the barn-shaped building that housed Arlington Architectural Associates. From the outside, the building on the eastern edge of Newcombe Street was boxy and bland. But inside she found a brightly lit hub of desks and drafting tables, jingling phones and staffers chattering and scurrying about. One young woman wore stretchy black capri pants and a loud pink blouse; one young man wore a silver eyebrow ring. A stairway at the far end of the room led up to an open second-floor hallway lined with doors. Private offices, Corinne guessed. Levi Holt was probably behind one of those doors.

She'd never met him, and she didn't know much about him. All Gerald had told her was that the man was brilliant and talented. "Just do what you think is best," Gerald had advised her. "Take care of it."

Of course, that was what Gerald always told her. That was why he'd hired her. That was why he was

desperately in need of her and half in love with her:
because she took care of everything.

The fellow with the eyebrow ring moseyed over to
her. A pencil was wedged behind one of his ears and
a slightly mangled roll of paper protruded from a hip
pocket of his jeans. In her tailored suit and low-heeled
black pumps, Corinne felt a generation older than
him, even though they were probably no more than a
few years apart in age.

"Can I help you?" he asked, smiling congenially.

"I have a nine-thirty appointment with Levi Holt."

"Oh." He glanced over his shoulder, as if searching the room for support. With a shrug, he turned
back to her. "Levi's having kind of a rough morning.
You might want to come back later."

"I don't think so." She didn't care how brilliant
and talented Holt was, or how rough his morning was.
She'd driven to Arlington last night, checked into a
hotel and awakened at seven-thirty that morning, just
so she'd get here on time. She was *not* going to come
back later.

"Well..." The young man shrugged again. "It's
up to you. He's in his office." He pointed to the walkway above. "Take the stairs, hang a right, and it's
the second door. I'd show you up there, but—" he
pulled the tube of paper from his pocket and rapped
it importantly against his palm "—I've got stuff to
do."

"No problem. I'll find it." She gave the man a
frosty smile, smoothed the straps of her leather tote
bag over her shoulder and stalked through the maze
of desks and drafting tables to the stairs.

The air smelled of gourmet coffee. A phone on
a desk near the stairs rang, chirping like a hungry

parakeet. The stairs themselves were open backed, floating up to the second story. It occurred to Corinne that this building might very well have been a real barn years ago, before the town had grown big enough to swallow all the farmland around it, and that the architects who worked here could have redesigned it, turning the loft into second-floor offices, opening skylights in the sloping roof, hanging large, bright lamps from the rafters on braided steel cables.

Overall, the effect wasn't bad. Overall, Levi Holt's design for Gerald's house wasn't bad, either. But it did have some flaws, and the flaws needed to be dealt with. Gerald shouldn't have signed the contract before he'd discussed the plans with Corinne, but he had. Now she was going to have to make things right.

Upstairs, she turned right and knocked on the door the man downstairs had indicated. After a moment's silence, she knocked again.

It swung open while her hand was still raised. Startled, she fell back a step and gazed up at Levi Holt.

Gerald hadn't mentioned that Holt was well over six feet tall and sinfully handsome. Of course, that wasn't the sort of thing Gerald would have noticed— the handsome part, anyway. Gerald himself was short enough that, beyond a certain point, *everyone* seemed extraordinarily tall to him.

Corinne took a moment to gather her wits. At five-foot-nine, she wasn't used to men towering over her. Nor was she used to being stared at with such intensity. Levi Holt's eyes were dark and sharp, his gaze boring into her like a precision drill. He had chiseled cheeks, a sensitive mouth and a jaw that looked stone hard.

He also had a baby on his shoulder.

She turned her attention from his eyes to the baby. It lay silent and motionless on top of a cloth draped over Holt's shoulder. It was dressed in a fuzzy yellow one-piece outfit. Fine, dark curls of hair swirled across its scalp, and its face was flushed.

"Don't say a word," Levi Holt whispered, backing away from the door.

Well, that was a great way to get this meeting started.

She remained in the doorway, watching as he moved in measured steps to a stroller in a corner of his office. Bending at the knees, he kept one hand firmly on the baby while he released the stroller's back with the other, then lowered it into a reclining position. Very, very slowly, he eased the baby off his shoulder and into the stroller. He hunched over the stroller for a moment, poised as if expecting something awful to happen, and then straightened up. The cloth, a square of white cotton, remained on his shoulder.

It was a diaper, Corinne realized.

She had traveled all the way to Arlington, Connecticut, to revise the design for the dream house her boss was going to have built on the four-acre parcel he'd bought in the western part of town, and the architect on the project had a diaper on his shoulder.

Wonderful.

"Look, Mr. Holt—"

He held his hand up to silence her and gave her a stern glare before he pivoted to check on the baby. Satisfied that she hadn't awakened it, he crossed to the door, his footsteps muffled by the carpet. "I've just spent the past half hour getting him to fall asleep," he said. "If you wake him, there'll be hell to pay."

She sensed his threat: if there was hell to pay, *she'd* be the one picking up the tab. She considered that possibility completely unreasonable, though. She hadn't brought the baby into the situation. She wasn't going to let Levi Holt hold her responsible for the success or failure of his son's nap.

All right. He was a new father. Evidently he'd suffered some sort of child care snafu that morning. The baby-sitter had called in sick, the mother was in Chicago on business—whatever the reason, Dad had gotten stuck with primary parenting duties today. And being a new parent—and a man—he was probably a bit anxious about fulfilling those duties.

Maybe if Corinne offered sympathy for his plight, he would accept all her requests for changes in the design without making a big fuss. They could both be nice to each other. Niceness as a strategy: it could work.

He didn't look nice, though. He looked…intense, every nerve in his body tuned a half-step sharp. There was an edge to him, an alertness, as if he were prepared to explode into action at the most subtle signal.

"I'm Corinne Lanier," she whispered, shooting a quick glimpse at the stroller across the room to make sure her voice was soft enough not to rouse the child. "I work with Gerald Mosley, and—"

"Gerald Mosley." He raked a hand through his hair. He had large hands, she noticed, perfectly proportioned to his large body. And longer hair than she'd realized at first, given the way it was combed back from his face. It was thick, walnut brown and wavy, and the ends brushed against the diaper on his shoulder. Beneath that diaper he wore an ordinary blue business shirt, a loosened tie featuring a busy pattern of blue and brown splotches, and pleated brown trousers that emphasized the length of his legs. He was built like a basketball player—a college player, not a pro with pumped-up muscles but a lanky athlete, someone who would rely on finesse rather than power to score.

"Gerald Mosley," she repeated. "He signed a contract to have you design and build a house for him. However, he and I have reviewed the plans, and—"

Levi held his hand up to silence her again. She thought she'd kept her voice muted, but he shot another anxious look at the stroller. Maybe he was going to use the baby to shut her up. Maybe this was a ploy to keep her from making demands and negotiating effectively. Maybe the baby wasn't even real; it was a lifelike doll that Holt whipped out when he was expecting a difficult meeting with a client.

A faint whimper from the stroller convinced her it wasn't a doll. Holt continued to stare at the stroller, as if he could will the child back to sleep. Apparently he could. After a moment, the whimpering faded away.

Nodding, he joined Corinne in the doorway. Not exactly a suitable place to hold a meeting. "I'm sorry," he murmured, slightly louder than a whisper. "This appointment slipped my mind."

"Well, I'm here."

"Yes." He glanced behind him, let out a long breath and shook his head. "Again, I apologize. Things just didn't work out the way I expected."

She felt a pang of genuine sympathy for him, and it startled her. He'd screwed up, he was jeopardizing the success of this meeting, he might very well refuse to make the changes in Gerald's house without charging exorbitant fees—and he was insufferably handsome, to boot. With or without a diaper on his arm, Levi Holt wasn't someone for whom she ought to be feeling sorry.

She lifted her chin and met his gaze. "I traveled all the way from New York City so we could resolve this."

"Resolve what?"

When she'd set up this meeting last week, she'd explained the reason to the woman who had answered the phone—Holt's secretary, Corinne assumed. Surely if the secretary had told him about the meeting, she would have told him what it was about.

Then again, with his child care problems, he probably couldn't remember any conversations from a week ago.

She suppressed an exasperated sigh. "The design needs to be reworked a bit," she said. "I know Gerald signed a contract with you, but after reconsideration, he realized that some changes have to be made." She directed her gaze to Levi's cheekbones. Any lower and she'd be distracted by the diaper on his shoulder. Any higher and she'd be trapped by his dark, soulful eyes.

He raked his hand through his hair again. The motion of his arm jostled the diaper, which slid down his arm. Frowning, he caught it in midair as it floated toward the floor. He stared at it for a moment, as if not quite sure why it was there, then spun around and tossed it into his office. It landed squarely on his desk.

Turning back, he said, "We've already broken

ground on that project. The changes Mosley wants had better not be extensive.''

''You've already broken ground? So soon?'' Gerald had signed the contract with Arlington Architectural Associates barely a month ago. ''I thought construction projects always had all kinds of delays.''

''We're one of those rare firms that actually gets things done on time and on budget.'' He dug his hands into his pockets and slouched against the door frame, looking arrogantly proud of his firm's performance. ''If the changes Mosley's asking for are significant, we'll have to rethink the budget and the completion date.''

This was the reaction she'd anticipated: that as soon as she started enumerating the changes, he was going to ratchet up the price of the house. He'd probably want to inflate the price even more because construction on the project was already under way. She didn't know enough about the construction business to understand all the ramifications of ''breaking ground,'' but she could guess that the further along the project was, the more expensive it would be to make changes.

''Gerald would really like to hold the price to what was contracted. I know the construction company on this project was hired through you—it's all one set price for the whole house. And it's a big price. A very big price.'' Not that Gerald couldn't afford it, but still, there was no reason he should have to pay twice as much as the house was worth, simply because he asked for a few alterations.

''We went to contract, Ms.—what was it?''

She tried not to frown. If he couldn't remember

their appointment, she shouldn't expect him to remember her name. "Corinne Lanier."

"Ms. Lanier. If you want changes in the design, you're going to get changes in the contract. That's only fair."

True enough. Her mission was to maximize the changes in the design and minimize the changes in the contract.

Levi Holt was no fool. In spite of his rough morning, in spite of his diaper and his baby and his failure to remember this meeting or Corinne's name, he was going to bargain hard, to try to make Gerald pay for the privilege of turning a bizarre house into a livable one.

Gerald should never have agreed to the design without running it past Corinne first. Men had no idea how to design a practical house. Multilevel rooms were dramatic, but not if you had to drag a vacuum cleaner up and down the steps, and not if guests who'd consumed too many martinis tripped and broke their ankles when they wandered from room to room. Elevated nooks and beams were eye catching—but spiders could reside in them for generations because no one could possibly dust them. Changing the bulbs in the two-story entry's elegant chandelier would be impossible without a thirty-foot ladder or perhaps some scaffolding. To have such a large house with only three full bathrooms was ridiculous. The fireplace in the master bedroom consumed the only wall where one could place a triple dresser.

And the kitchen was a disaster. Gerald's concept of cooking was can openers and microwaves; what did he know about kitchens? The one in his new home lacked adequate counter and storage space because

Gerald was infatuated with an ostentatious wall of glass—which would suck all the heat out of the room in the winter and let all the heat in during the summer, when the sun struck it. And that wine cellar cabinet? It shouldn't be taking up valuable pantry space. It ought to go in the basement. That was why it was called a wine *cellar.*

Women understood these things. Men—even architects—didn't. They liked flash, special effects, the house equivalent of mag wheels and racing stripes. They were willing to blow a million dollars on a house with soaring glass and multilevel living, and give little thought to the functionality of the place.

"Some of the design changes shouldn't cost any extra money," she told Levi Holt, hopeful that "breaking ground" meant nothing more than digging a hole in the middle of the lot. "And some are so obvious, they should never even have become issues in the first place."

His gaze changed, losing some of its intensity and becoming speculative and vaguely amused. His mouth didn't move, his jaw shifted only the slightest bit, but the light in his eyes, the angle of his gaze, the deliberation with which he regarded her...

His eyes were almost hypnotic. Maybe that was how he'd gotten Gerald to agree to include only three full baths and locate that stupid wine cellar in the kitchen pantry: he'd hypnotized him.

"I've written a list of the changes we want," she said briskly, sliding her bag from her shoulder and pulling out her file of notes. She was good at this, she reminded herself—good at being prepared, good at having her documents organized in a neatly marked folder. Good at having everything where it was supposed to be, which was why, once this situation was straightened out, she would have the wine cellar in the basement.

His eyes still glimmering with what could pass for amusement, he took the folder from her and opened it. She watched him skim the first page, and the glimmer faded. In its place she detected skepticism. "Gerald Mosley specifically requested a fireplace in the master suite," he said.

"You must have misunderstood him."

Levi raised his eyes from the folder. They'd gone cold. "No. I didn't misunderstand him."

"Well, maybe he misunderstood himself," she said, backtracking. "He didn't think through all the implications of having that fireplace there. He got caught up in the razzle-dazzle."

"He specifically said he wanted a fireplace in the master bedroom. I suggested it and he said yes."

She checked herself before retorting that no one could sleep with a fire burning right across the room—it would be too bright and too hot. As for lending the room a romantic atmosphere, well, Corinne thought a roaring fire in the hearth was something of a cliché. And there was a fireplace in the family room, if a burning log was really necessary.

Gerald wasn't the kind of guy who went for fireplace seductions, anyway. He was cerebral and nerdy, the sort who would find innovative software far more of a turn-on than a blaze crackling in a bedroom fireplace.

She steeled herself for battle. "Assuming Gerald did say he wanted the fireplace, did you point out to him how much wall space he would be sacrificing?"

Levi studied her for a long moment. "He's not an idiot. He could see that for himself."

"You were the expert. You showed him designs, suggested ideas—yet you didn't point out that if he had a fireplace on one wall, and the glass sliders to the upstairs deck on another wall, and the doors to the dressing room and bathroom on a third wall, there would be only one wall available for both his bed and a triple dresser. This isn't the sort of problem that would occur to a lay person like Gerald."

"It occurred to you," Levi noted. "Aren't you a lay person?"

His eyes unnerved her. They didn't seem so cool anymore. In fact, they were smoldering. With anger? she wondered. Resentment?

"I'm a woman," she said, smiling in the hope of deflecting his apparent hostility. "I notice details that Gerald misses."

"So you think the fireplace is a detail." Levi Holt glanced at the folder in his hands, then met her gaze again. His expression was disdainful.

"Getting rid of it should actually reduce the price, not increase it," she noted hopefully.

He appeared unpersuaded, but before he could flip the page, the baby began to whimper again. He cursed, a low hiss of sound, and stalked back into his office.

She hesitated on the threshold, evaluating how things had gone so far. Not badly, she decided. Not well, but not disastrously. If only Holt had normal eyes, eyes that didn't seem to cut right through her, things would be going better. If he were about eight inches shorter and had a potbelly, things would be going better yet. Attractive men rarely rattled her; but this man was different. He was just so damned...*big*.

She ventured into his office. Her gaze circled the room—the broad windows letting in early June sunlight, the austere teak desk neat except for the diaper heaped on it, the drafting table with a jointed light arching over it, the corkboard on the wall, with various sketches pinned to it. The swivel chair behind the desk, the swivel stool in front of the drafting table...and the stroller tucked into the dimmest, but currently the noisiest, corner of the room.

She watched while he eased the baby out of the stroller. Its tiny arms flailed and its sobs grew louder. His large hands cradled the child gently, almost hesitantly, one hand cupped around the baby's body and one protecting its head as he carried it over to his desk and grabbed for the diaper. Once it was draped over his shirt, he lifted the baby onto his shoulder.

"Shh." He sighed, swaying slightly. "Come on, D.J. Be a sport. Shh."

"Deejay?" Who would give a child a name like that?

Still swaying and cradling the baby's head in his palm, he turned to her. "His initials. D.J." He bowed his head to the child's and whispered, "Shh."

Corinne wasn't sure what she was supposed to do. Watch him lull the baby back to sleep? Offer her assistance? She'd never dealt with infants, but she figured this one could be crying because he was hungry or wet. What else did babies weep over?

Levi wasn't asking her for help, but if she offered some she might win points in their negotiation. "Perhaps he's hungry," she said. "Does he have a bottle I could get for him?"

"He just ate. He's not hungry."

"Then maybe—" she tried not to wrinkle her nose "—he needs a dry diaper. If you tell me where I could find one for you—"

"He's fine." Levi rocked the child. Despite their wide contrast in size, or maybe because of it, they looked right together, a father and his son doing a magical dance. For a moment, Corinne was transfixed by the sight. Then she shook her head clear. Babies didn't melt her heart. Neither did fathers. She could think of no reason Levi Holt would look so magnificent trying to soothe his fussing child.

"Maybe he has a tummy ache," she suggested, wishing she could fix this problem the way she fixed so many others.

"He's fine." Levi seemed to be saying it more to himself than to her. More to himself and to the baby. "You're all right, buddy, aren't you? There you go, D.J. That's my pal. There you go. Shh."

The baby had grown quiet. One tiny pink hand clutched at Levi's shirt and the other found its way to his own mouth. He snuffled, hiccupped and burrowed his face into Levi's shoulder. Levi continued to rock him, slowly, slowly.

"I'm sorry," he mouthed to Corinne.

"That's all right." The more accommodating she was, the more accommodating he'd be. And really, he did look sweet soothing his baby that way.

"He's teething," he explained.

"How old is he?"

"Almost six months. His doctor says that's what's going on with him." He settled against his desk, apparently not planning to put the baby back in his stroller. Instead, he stroked the baby's back.

His hands mesmerized her.

Again she shook her head clear. She had to stay focused, had to get through this negotiation, pull Gerald's butt out of the fire and make sure he was getting a livable house for his money. She had to remain ingratiating with Levi Holt—but not fall under his spell. As if a man stroking a baby's back could cast a spell on her.

"What happened? Did your baby-sitter call in sick today?"

"I just hired someone last week. She's terrific, the best by far out of all the nannies I interviewed. But she can't start work until next Monday. I'm juggling things until then."

"You and your wife are taking turns?"

His eyes flashed, dark and mysterious. "No," he said, so tersely she knew there was a whole lot more than *no* to it.

Had his wife left him? Abandoned him and the baby? Run off with someone else? Or had she died tragically? In childbirth, maybe. That had happened on an episode of *Mercy Hospital* a couple of seasons ago, such a depressing episode Corinne had stopped watching the show.

Levi's *no* hung in the air, a warning, a challenge. She stored it away, figuring she'd pull it back out and analyze it later. "What do the *D* and the *J* stand for?"

"Darren Justice."

"What an unusual name." She liked it. It had a lilting rhythm to it.

"It's too fancy for a little baby," Levi said. "D.J. fits him better."

"So, what does one do to comfort a teething child?"

"He's got toys he can bite on. And there are ointments. They don't seem to work that well with him, though. According to Dr. Cole, some kids have a harder time getting through it than others. He spiked a fever the other night, just from the teething."

Levi was talking to her as if she were an expert on child rearing, someone who understood these things, a fellow parent at the playground or in the pediatrician's waiting room. She wished she could contribute some wise advice—rub ice on the baby's gums, or give him a shot of tequila, or hold him upside down and count to ten.

"I'm real sorry about this meeting," Levi said. "Why don't you leave your notes with me? I'll review the changes Mosley wants, and then we can talk about how much they'll cost you."

That was exactly what Corinne didn't want. As long as she was present, she could argue against cost increases. But if she left him alone with her list of changes, he could pull out a calculator and start hitting the plus button. And he might not even understand how some of the changes should be made, or why they were necessary.

But she couldn't hang around his office for hours while he consoled his anguished son.

"Are you staying in town?" he asked. "I could get back to you."

"I've got a room at the Arlington Inn, but—"

"Great. Give me a little time with this stuff, and maybe I can twist some arms and get someone to watch D.J. for an hour while we figure out what exactly Mosley wants me to do. Would that be all right?"

She couldn't refuse without seeming unreasonable.

All he was asking for was a little time. While he reviewed her list, she could drive out to Gerald's property and see just what "breaking ground" entailed. That would give her a clearer idea of how difficult it would be to make changes, and then she'd know if Levi Holt was being reasonable or ripping Gerald off.

"Fine," she said, managing a bright smile. "I'm going to drive around town for a bit, but I'll be back in my room by eleven. You can call me any time after that."

"Thanks." He stood, careful not to jostle the baby. "I appreciate it, Ms. Lanier. This is not the way I usually conduct business, but—"

"That's okay. We'll talk later." Oh, yes, she could be accommodating and charming and terribly flexible. How could he be a bastard about amending the contract when she was accepting this inconvenience with such equanimity?

"I mean it. I appreciate it," he whispered, walking her to the door. She stepped out into the hall, and he gave her a farewell nod. A few paces down the hall, she glanced back and saw him bowing his head and touching a kiss to the baby's downy hair.

A man kissing his son. Who would have thought it would be the most beautiful sight in the world?

HE'D HEARD her voice. A woman's voice, just a whisper, but it made him think of his mother.

He missed her. He wanted her so much. When was she coming back?

At least he had the man. The man had a good shoulder, big and hard and strong, and his neck was warm and smelled sweet. When he was on the man's shoul-

der his mouth didn't hurt so much. Sometimes it felt as if someone were reaching inside his face and stretching the bones apart. It hurt all the way into his cheeks and his chin and he could only cry and cry and wish his mother would come back.

But the man was good. His hands were big, and when he held D.J. against his shoulder, D.J. felt better.

And he'd heard that woman's voice. Soft like cotton balls, a light, gentle voice. He imagined it puffy and white, brushing against his skin.

If only he could ask the man who she was.

If only he could ask the man where his mother was and when she was coming back. She would make the pain go away. He knew she would.

Maybe this other woman could make the pain go away, too. Maybe she could be soft and round like his mother, with her body full of milk and lullabies on her lips.

He nestled closer to the man and wished the pain would go away.

CHAPTER TWO

D.J. WAS MAKING a burbly sound. Levi recognized the soft vocalizing; it meant the baby was winding down, not yet comforted but too weary to cry.

It amazed Levi that he'd learned to interpret D.J.'s vocabulary of noises. He actually understood what the kid was trying to tell him...sometimes.

It amazed him even more, at that particular moment, that long after Corinne Lanier's departure, he was still thinking about her.

Before D.J. had entered his life, he used to think about women all the time. He liked women. He admired them. More than once, he'd felt something for a woman deep enough to qualify as love. But ever since that overcast Tuesday in May when he'd stood on a bluff overlooking the Pacific Ocean and said goodbye to his sister, he hadn't thought about women at all.

Not the way he was thinking about Corinne.

Since he'd brought D.J. home to Arlington, everything in his life had changed: his sleep patterns, his mealtimes, the disorder of his house, the smell of it. Brightly colored plastic objects—dolls, blocks, balls, trucks—currently occupied his living room like a conquering army. Sacks of disposable diapers lined a wall of the spare bedroom, and a crib stood next to the oak futon. Kitchen cabinets that used to hold boxes of pasta and jars of jam now held cans of formula and individual-size portions of strained peas. D.J. was crazy about strained peas.

Dr. Cole had assured Levi that D.J. couldn't possibly overdose on all that pureed green glop. And that was another change in Levi's house: the office number, emergency number and pager number of a pediatrician were on prominent display, fastened to the refrigerator with a magnet.

In spite of all the changes, Levi was grateful for the tiny child in his arms. Without D.J., Levi would have had too much time to mourn for Ruth, to rage at the senselessness of her death. Twenty-six-year-old women weren't supposed to die from aneurysms—especially twenty-six-year-old women who had just become mothers, who had so much to live for, so much to give.

Levi couldn't afford to lose himself in grief, not with D.J. demanding his attention. Sometimes he wondered whether Ruth had known, when she'd written her simple will, that by naming Levi her son's guardian she'd be denying him the opportunity to fall apart if she died.

He hadn't fallen apart. He couldn't. He was too busy giving D.J. his baths, leafing through picture books with him, rubbing ointment on his tender gums and trying to calm him down when he wailed.

But right then, with D.J. losing steam and growing limp against his shoulder, he wasn't too busy to think about Corinne Lanier. "She's bad news," he murmured into D.J.'s dark, corn silk hair. "She's asking the impossible. She may not realize it yet, but there's no way in hell I'm making big changes in the Mosley project.'' He sighed. "Even so…a man's allowed to look, isn't he?''

D.J.'s quiet snuffle sounded like agreement to Levi. And why shouldn't he agree? Corinne was definitely worth looking at. Levi's eyes, his body, his mind and soul were stirring awake, noticing an attractive woman and relishing the experience as if it were something he'd never done before.

It felt weird to let someone who wasn't twenty-eight inches long and incontinent occupy his mind; to think about a woman who wasn't Ruth, to think about that woman in terms other than sorrow.

She was tall. Given his own lanky height, he liked tall women. Corinne Lanier was statuesque enough to be a fashion model, but she had too much flesh on her for that, thank God. Levi had noticed the muscular curves of her calves below the hem of her skirt, the feminine swells of her hips and bosom in her tapered jacket. Her hair was chin length and blunt, styled to proclaim that she wanted to be taken seriously, but its rich brown shade shimmered with playful red highlights.

He wondered what her official position was. Gerald Mosley's assistant? His vice president? His consigliere? Whoever she was, as attractive as her clear hazel eyes, narrow nose and delicate lips were, she was crazy if she thought Levi was going to overhaul a magnificent architectural design just because she'd asked him to.

Gerald Mosley had fallen in love with Levi's blueprint for his country house on a pricey swath of land on the west side of town, where all the rich New Yorkers had their weekend retreats. Mosley was a rich New Yorker—very rich, given that he'd been able to afford such a desirable lot and arrange the financing for the house without popping a single bead of sweat. As Levi recalled, he was one of those dot-com guys, awash in new money and eager to spend it.

He'd had grandiose ideas for a house when he'd approached Arlington Architectural Associates last winter. Levi had actually toned down Mosley's initial concepts—and Mosley had been enthusiastic about the ultimate design Levi had presented to him. He'd liked the daring lines of the house, the unique shape of it, the flow of the space, the rivers of sunlight that would spill through different rooms at different times of day. "I want it to be majorly cool," he'd told Levi, and Levi had designed a majorly cool house.

Now, according to Mosley's pretty agent of doom, the boss wanted everything redone. Levi wondered if Corinne was the engine behind Mosley's sudden change of heart.

D.J. had drifted off. He breathed heavily, not quite a snore but a sibilant exhalation through his mouth. "Okay, kid," Levi whispered. "Are you going to stay quiet long enough for me to do my work today? I've got partners here who think I ought to be pulling my weight. How about it, buddy? Are you going to let me do that?"

D.J. sighed deeply.

Levi carried him back to his stroller. Next Monday, Martina Lopes would take over as D.J.'s nanny and Levi's life would be easier. In the past few weeks, though, he'd gotten used to having the baby in his office. He'd grown accustomed to working in spurts, conducting meetings with his colleagues while balancing D.J. on his shoulder, brainstorming while feeding him bottles. What would it be like to work with two hands again?

Levi had lived thirty-two years without D.J. in his life and only five weeks with D.J. in it. And somehow, he could no longer remember what those first thirty-two years were like.

D.J. *was* his life now.

But for the next ten minutes or so, Levi had both hands free. He used them to pick up the folder Corinne had given him, so he could peruse her requested changes and decide just how ludicrous they were.

THE ONLY GROUND BROKEN, as far as she could tell, was under a few orange stakes that had been hammered into the dirt to mark the outer edges of the house's foundation.

She'd driven across town to Gerald's lot, a prime piece of real estate nestled among gentleman's farms and country manors on winding country roads lined with thick shade trees. The predominant color was green: green grass, green foliage and the lush green of fir trees covering the hills that formed a backdrop to the area. Living in Manhattan, Corinne couldn't surround herself with so much natural green even if she stood smack in the middle of Central Park.

Gerald's four-acre parcel of land seemed a bit excessive. But he could afford it, so why not? Corinne wouldn't mind having a weekend retreat in a place like Arlington. She could get used to the peace that settled like a smooth blanket over this tiny corner of Connecticut, the minty tang of the air, the twittering of sparrows, robins and wrens, the tranquillity so pervasive that she could hear the leaves rubbing against one another when a breeze wafted through the trees.

She'd never been a big fan of city living. She'd moved to New York because she'd needed work and because it was two thousand miles away from her parents. Pure luck had enabled her to cross paths with Gerald. He'd needed someone with a level head and business skills, and there she'd been, exactly what he was looking for. She'd soon become his right hand, his adviser, his confidante. When his company had been bought last year, she'd gotten rich—not as rich as he was, not rich enough to *feel* rich, but rich enough not to have to hesitate before choosing gourmet ice cream over the store brand.

The long driveway to what would someday be Gerald's country home was for now just a packed dirt path that cut neatly through a small grove of trees she'd urged Gerald to preserve when he'd brought her to see the lot last fall. None of the trees had been touched, even though knocking them down would make it easier for the construction trucks to reach the building site. The trees were fenced off by strips of mesh fabric the same glow-in-the-dark orange as the paint on the wooden stakes. Thick tire treads had left imprints in the dirt, but no trucks or workers were present.

So much for the ground being broken, she thought with a sniff. Levi Holt must have said that only to intimidate her.

She wasn't easily intimidated. Just because Levi was tall and had enchanting eyes, just because that sweet little baby fit against his shoulder so well...

She reminded herself that Levi's baby wasn't sweet. He'd wailed and howled and made a general nuisance of himself most of the time she'd been at Levi's office.

As she strolled around the perimeter of the foundation—or at least her estimate of the foundation, based on the painted stakes—she rummaged in her tote bag for her cell phone. She punched the preprogrammed button for Gerald's private line and listened to the phone ring on the other end. After a couple of rings, he answered.

"Gerald Mosley."

"Hi, it's me."

"Hey," he said, his voice losing its formal chill. "Are you still in Arlington?"

"Yes."

"Any luck with Levi Holt?"

"We haven't exactly had our meeting yet," she said, avoiding muddy-looking patches around the foundation's outline, so she wouldn't ruin her shoes. "He seems to be stuck baby-sitting this morning."

"Baby-sitting?"

"He had his infant son in his office with him. The kid is going through a traumatic teething experience, apparently."

"His son?" Gerald said nothing for a minute. "I didn't know he had a son."

"I'm not making this up."

Gerald chuckled. "Did I call you a liar? Don't get defensive on me, Corey."

She relented with a smile. "Well, I'm telling you, he's got a baby. D.J. It stands for Darren Justice."

"Darren Justice? What a stupid name!"

Corinne had thought it was a beautiful name. But she wasn't going to argue with Gerald about it.

"He just didn't seem like the daddy type to me," Gerald added.

Of course, the first time Gerald had visited Arlington Architectural Associates, last December, Levi Holt wouldn't have been a father yet. They'd met a couple of times since then, mostly in New York. No doubt they'd talked about nothing but the house. Levi wouldn't have had any reason to mention his newborn son. If his child care arrangements hadn't fallen apart, he wouldn't have mentioned his son today, either.

"Be that as it may, I think I've developed a certain rapport with him," Corinne informed Gerald, putting a highly optimistic spin on her brief meeting with Levi. "He's going to review my notes and get together with me to discuss them once his kid isn't in the way."

"So, his initial reaction was…?"

Extremely negative. "Not too bad," she fibbed. "We've barely gotten started."

"I'm already committed to a huge expenditure on this house," Gerald reminded her unnecessarily. "I don't want the price to skyrocket."

"I'll do my best."

"You don't have to say it," Gerald assured her. "Doing your best is what you do. I've got to go, babe. Keep me posted, okay?"

"Sure. Bye." She turned off the phone, tucked it into her tote and grinned. When Gerald called her "babe," it meant one of two things: he thought she was wonderful, or he was so distracted her name temporarily slipped his mind.

She finished her circuit around the painted stakes. It really was going to be an enormous house. Much too big for Gerald to live in alone, even if he used it only on weekends. She was as great a fan of solitude as anyone, but surely he couldn't have custom-ordered this house just for himself. He must have had in mind that he would be sharing it in some way.

She wondered whom he'd want to share it with. He had friends, but he didn't date much. She couldn't imagine him bringing a blushing bride to this house, sweeping her into his arms and carrying her over the threshold. Corinne was the only woman in his life.

All she knew was that if she were the woman he swept into his arms and carried over the threshold, she'd want more bathrooms and a sane kitchen. And no silly fireplace in the master bedroom.

SHARON AGREED to watch D.J. for an hour. "Not one minute more," she warned.

"I won't need a minute more," Levi assured her. What he intended to say to Corinne, after reading everything in her folder, could be said in less than an hour.

Less than thirty seconds, actually. "No. None of these changes. No way." Fifteen seconds, max.

He reminded himself, as he'd told Sharon, that a job was on the line. Gerald Mosley's house was the last original design he'd completed before Ruth died. It was the last project he'd tackled as a childless architect, the only hefty commission he'd brought into the firm in months—and likely the only one he'd bring in for the next few months, too. He wasn't working at full strength. His partners understood and forgave him, but this commission was vitally important. Not just for the firm but for Levi. It proved he was still a functioning professional, something he'd come to doubt more than once since D.J. entered his life.

His design for Mosley's house was brilliant. To

save the contract and all the income it would bring, Levi could force himself to make a few minor adjustments. Clients always wanted minor adjustments. But the big stuff—removing the glass wall in the kitchen, leveling the first floor, adding bathrooms and subtracting that gorgeous brick fireplace in the bedroom—

No. None of these changes. No way.

His partners would encourage him to be flexible and open-minded. Levi could be flexible and open-minded about a lot of things, but not a project as daring and inspired as this one.

Mosley *had* loved the house Levi had designed for him. He wondered what had changed, what had made his client abruptly think a traditional mudroom with a laundry area made more sense than a small solarium connecting the garage to the kitchen. What had made him decide in the past few weeks that he wouldn't be able to fit his furniture into the master suite? Hell, he could work with an interior decorator on that. The basic design—that romantic fireplace—had to stay.

This meeting with Corinne Lanier wasn't going to take long at all.

Still, he didn't have time to waste. He cruised across town to the Arlington Inn, enjoying the rare minutes of privacy the trip afforded him. He'd gotten so used to strapping D.J. into his car seat in back, listening to him fuss and jabber and being unable to make eye contact with him as he drove, unable to help him or touch him if he started crying. The silence of his ten-minute solo drive to Corinne Lanier's hotel was a treat.

The Arlington Inn was 180 years old and overflowing with atmosphere. Its main building epitomized

New England architecture—white clapboard, black shutters, a solid symmetry beneath the slate-tiled roof. In a nod to modern times and competition, the owners had added two new wings and a pavilion that housed a pool and health club; one of Levi's partners had designed the updates ten years ago, before Levi had joined Arlington Architectural Associates. Bill had done a fine job on them, too. Unlike Levi, his talent lay in contemporizing historical buildings without destroying their essence.

Levi specialized in modern design. He'd grown up stifled by tradition, and just as his sister had rebelled by running off to California and becoming a weaver, he rebelled by creating stark, disconcerting buildings of glass, stone and raw wood. Residential sculptures, he called them. Gerald Mosley had grasped the spirit of Levi's style; it was why he'd hired Levi to design his dream house.

Levi pulled into a parking space, grabbed his leather portfolio and entered the inn. The colonial flavor of the lobby was so strong he could practically taste it: patterned rugs over wide-plank pine floors, ladder back chairs, stodgy paintings hanging on walls papered in a floral pattern. He strode to the massive oak reception counter and said, "Can you ring Corinne Lanier, please?"

The clerk turned to a console and hooked up to Corinne's room. He listened on his headset for a minute, then shook his head. "She's not in. Would you care to leave a message?"

Damn. "No, thanks," Levi said, turning from the counter. Unsure how to make the best use of his hour without D.J., he wandered toward the French doors overlooking the pool patio behind the lobby. Al-

though it was only early June, a few hearty souls were
lounging in the chairs around the pool, which glittered
bright blue beneath the midday sun.

Levi wondered what Corinne would look like in a
swimsuit. A bikini cut high on the sides to show off
her long legs, her skin golden and glistening with water from the pool. He grinned. It felt good to be thinking about something other than whether D.J. needed
a bottle or a bath. It felt very good.

Turning from the glass doors, he surveyed the
lobby once more. She'd said she would be at the inn
by eleven, and it was now 11:15. His smile faded as
he considered his shrinking baby-sitter time.

The front door swung open and in she walked, the
answer to a prayer. How pathetic that his prayer was
about maximizing his child-free time rather than enjoying the company of a strikingly attractive woman.

Her gaze intersected with his and she halted, apparently startled. He noticed the flicker of caution in
her eyes. It vanished almost instantly, replaced by a
cordial smile that struck him as less than genuine.

He reminded himself that he couldn't jeopardize
the project by being intransigent. For the firm, for his
own sanity, for the proof it offered that his identity
hadn't been entirely swallowed by D.J., he had to
make this house happen.

"Hi," she said pleasantly, sliding the strap of her
tote bag off her shoulder and wrapping her fingers
around it. "I didn't know you were going to be coming here."

"I had a few minutes."

"Where's your son?"

It still pained him, like a sharp jab in the gut, when
someone referred to D.J. as his son—not because he

was appalled by the idea but because it negated Ruth. D.J. was her son and always would be.

But he wasn't about to straighten Corinne out about D.J.'s lineage. It was hard enough explaining the situation to friends, who invariably turned gloomy and maudlin when he told them his sister was dead. He saw no reason to go through all that with a near stranger.

"Someone's watching him for a while," he said. "I don't have much time, though, so we should probably get right down to business." He lifted his portfolio.

She circled the lobby with her gaze. An antique-looking camelback sofa stood in one corner, facing a wingback chair. Neither seat looked particularly comfortable, but they'd do for a quiet one-on-one.

"Actually, I'm kind of thirsty. Why don't we get something to drink." She started toward the dining room off the lobby.

He checked his watch again. Only a drink, he resolved. He didn't have time to eat.

The dining room was nearly empty—it was a little early for lunch. Corinne passed it for the taproom to one side. Was she planning to hit the booze? Wouldn't that make for a fun meeting, he thought grimly.

The taproom was darker than the dining room, its decor a cliché of paneling, intimate tables, amber lighting and a long mahogany bar. A single bartender stood behind it, lazily drying glasses and standing them upside down on a shelf. The room felt sleepy, almost dead.

At their entrance, the bartender lowered his dishrag

and stared at them, mildly curious. "Do you have iced tea?" Corinne asked him.

"Sure."

Corinne peered at Levi. "Two iced teas," he ordered, then gestured toward the nearest table.

As soon as they were settled, the bartender brought over two frosted tumblers of iced tea garnished with lemon. "You want any pretzels or anything?" he asked.

Corinne glanced at Levi again. Her eyes were truly extraordinary, the irises a mix of gray and gold, the lashes unusually long and thick and devoid of mascara. Her mouth seemed at war with itself, soft yet determined to express her words firmly, without ambiguity.

"No pretzels for me," he said.

She sent the bartender away with a thank-you, then lifted a packet of sugar, shook it and tore it open. He watched her hands, smooth and long fingered, the nails glinting with a clear polish. In her severely tailored suit and conservative shoes, she seemed to be screaming to the world, *Take me seriously!*

No reason anyone *wouldn't* take her seriously, Levi thought. She was Gerald Mosley's representative. No matter how flaky Mosley was, only a fool would ignore his newly minted Internet millions—or his second in command.

He sipped his unsweetened tea and settled back in the captain's chair. It wasn't big enough for his long body, but he was used to that. She fit well in her chair, her skirt riding up a couple of inches above her knees.

Nice knees. Very nice legs.

And he'd better take her seriously, or that delectable mouth of hers was going to spew invective.

"I've looked through your notes," he said as she stirred the sugar into her tea, "and the answer is no."

"No?"

"No."

"What's the question?"

For a moment, one dangerous, disconcerting instant when his gaze slid from her knees to the delicate indentation in her upper lip, he couldn't remember the question. Then it came to him: "Will I make all the changes you've requested to the design? No. This house was conceived as a unified, organic whole. Every detail was put there for a reason. The design is exactly what it should be."

She must have heard the fervor underlining his calm words. He couldn't hide it; if he didn't feel passionate about a design, the design didn't leave his drafting table. If she and her boss had wanted an architect who didn't care about his work, who didn't invest himself heart and soul in it, they could have hired someone else. Mosley had come to Levi and Arlington Architectural because he'd wanted an architect who cared.

"Gerald doesn't think the design is exactly what it should be," Corinne said gently, as if she didn't want to hurt his feelings.

His feelings had nothing to do with it. His ego wasn't involved. It was a matter of design, of lines and angles coming together, of stone and glass marrying and creating a home. "A month ago, Gerald knew this design was perfect."

"He hadn't thought it through. Now that he has, he realizes that there are certain impractical aspects to it."

"Impractical?" Levi swore his ego wasn't involved, but really—she didn't know what the hell she was talking about. If she was simply quoting Gerald, *he* didn't know what the hell he was talking about, either.

"For example," she said, "the kitchen."

"The kitchen." The kitchen was the heart of the house. It beat, it pulsed, it sent life pumping through the rest of the building. She didn't seem to have a clue about what made a house come alive. Rather than point out her ignorance, however, he only shifted in his chair, took another swig of iced tea and waited for her to justify what couldn't be justified.

"Yes, the kitchen," she said cheerfully. "First of all, the counter space."

"What about it?"

"There's not enough. You lose one entire wall to that glass—"

"The glass wall is the most essential element of the room." He stated it as irrefutable fact.

"The glass wall not only means losing a whole lot of work and storage space, but it'll make the room impossible to heat in the winter."

"The kitchen is traditionally the warmest room in the house. This kitchen shares a two-sided fireplace with the family room, it's got radiant heating in the slate floor and the glass wall will actually add warmth to the room. We'll be using triple-glazed thermopanes."

"If the glass wall adds warmth to the room in the winter, it's going to add warmth to the room in the summer, too. It'll be unbearably hot in July and August."

"The panes can be covered with shades. Look, Corinne—can I call you Corinne?" At her faint nod, he continued. "I know what I'm doing, okay? I know how to design a house that will hold its temperature. Everything is insulated to the maximum level. I've designed commercial buildings and private residences, and no one has ever complained that the interior temperature can't be kept stable. The builders' work is guaranteed—"

"The builders can't guarantee that there's enough counter space, because there isn't. And taking up half the pantry with that wine cellar—"

"My clients love mini wine cellars in their kitchens. Your boss was really enthusiastic about it."

"It reduces the storage space in the pantry."

"And saves him from having to hike up and down the stairs whenever he wants a bottle of wine."

"Speaking of stairs—"

He cut her off before she could speak. He knew what was coming next—he'd read all her notes in the folder. "Gerald loved the concept of multilevel rooms. It breaks the monotony. It skews sight lines and gives the house energy."

"Oh, for heaven's sake," she muttered, then took a quick sip of her iced tea as if she needed to cool off before erupting in anger. "Who cares about skewed sight lines? Gerald hired you to design a house for him. He's the client. It's your job to listen to what your clients want."

"Gerald Mosley is my client, but right now I'm listening to you."

"Good," she said, a smile teasing her lips. "That's exactly what I was hoping you'd do."

He didn't mean to smile back. The woman was being a pain in the ass. She was wrong about the house, wrong about what it should be, wrong about everything in her stupid folder. Yet she'd tripped him up on his own words, and her eyes glowed with pleasure. He couldn't *not* smile back.

Smiling weakened his resolve. It nudged him into remembering that Mosley's house was a big job with a big paycheck attached to it, and that ever since he'd gained custody of D.J. he hadn't been doing his fair share at the firm. He couldn't dismiss the woman. He had to listen to her, to keep this project alive.

Smiling also tweaked his awareness of her beauty—the gentle curve of her lips, her chin tilting slightly, her eyes warming in the reflection of her own smile. It felt so *normal* to be smiling with an attractive woman in a dimly lit tavern—even if it wasn't yet noon and they were sipping iced tea. Gazing into a woman's eyes, talking to her, *listening* to her—it was the sort of thing he used to do quite often, before he'd lost a sister and gained a son.

He missed it. He missed taking the time to admire women, to get to know them, to contemplate the possibilities with them. Did acknowledging how much his life had changed in the past few weeks make him a bad person? It wasn't D.J.'s fault that he'd landed in Levi's lap and turned his existence inside out, but for the first time since Ruth's death, Levi found himself resenting the baby and all the uninvited responsibility that came with him.

"The way I figure it," Corinne was saying, "the changes Gerald wants shouldn't add to the expense of the house. Well, some of them, maybe—the additional bathrooms. But removing the fireplace, and converting that glass wall into a regular wall with a few windows and some counter and cabinet space below—these improvements would actually bring the cost of the house down, wouldn't they?''

"They're not improvements,'' he said quietly, sifting all emotion from his voice. He didn't want to antagonize her. He just wanted to convince her that her "improvements'' would turn the house from a masterpiece into something mundane and boring.

Which would still give him a nice payday, a small voice at the back of his head needled him.

Which would go against all his aesthetic instincts, another voice nattered.

"The bathrooms I can do,'' he relented, figuring that if he let her win that round she might concede on the more important issues. "I have no idea what a single man needs with more than three full baths on top of the half bath downstairs and the stall shower and lavatory in the pool house. But I can probably carve a bathroom out of one of the bedrooms and pair the plumbing up with the master bath. A fifth full bath—I don't know what we'll have to lose to make room for that, but I might be able to figure something out.''

"Maybe four bathrooms would be enough,'' she said generously.

Lucky Gerald, he thought, trying not to smirk. How fortunate the guy was to have an assistant eager to guarantee him variety when he had to take a leak.

Corinne seemed to read his mind. "I'm anticipating that he'll be entertaining guests at the house. That's what the extra bathrooms are for—so each guest could have his or her own bathroom.''

"Okay.'' He nodded, hoping to prove to her that he could be reasonable. "If he's entertaining, I'll bet his guests will be spending a lot more time in the kitchen and family room than in the upstairs bathrooms. So I think you ought to let the kitchen remain the focal point it is. As I've designed it, it's the kind of room where Gerald's guests will walk in and gasp with delight.''

''But it will be harder to cook big meals for those guests. The room needs more counter space.''

''It's got acres of counter space.'' He decided that sounded too combative and softened his voice. ''Don't forget, the dining area of the room is enormous.'' *And fronted by all that spectacular glass,* he almost said, but she hated the glass, so he chose not to mention it. ''It'll take a huge table to fill that area. I assume that's what Gerald's planning. The table will increase his work space significantly.''

''You can't assume that the table is going to be work space. Most people have clutter on their kitchen tables—newspapers, the car keys, dirty coffee mugs, whatever. Kitchen tables don't count as work areas.''

Somehow, Levi didn't see the amount of counter space as a significant concern of Gerald Mosley's. He couldn't imagine Mosley rolling out dough for pie crusts or preparing an in-house luau complete with a stuffed whole pig. The kitchen Levi had designed for him was state-of-the-art, with more than adequate counter space for normal use. Normal use was what Gerald had described when they'd brainstormed about the house.

He wanted to remind her, again, that Gerald had loved the idea of the glass wall. He wanted to question her about when Gerald had undergone his change of heart, and under whose influence he'd undergone it. But before Levi could speak, his cell phone beeped.

With an apologetic smile, he pulled the phone out of his portfolio and clicked it on.

"Levi?" Sharon's voice cut through a faint hiss of static. "Your baby needs a clean diaper."

He inhaled deeply, using the moment to submerge his frustration. He couldn't ask Sharon to change D.J.'s diaper—but damn it, he was trying to salvage a project. Surely this interruption wasn't necessary.

"Leave it," he instructed her. "It won't kill him. I'll take care of it when I get back."

"But it—it smells, Levi. My work area stinks."

He ground his teeth together to keep from cursing, from pointing out that D.J. was a healthy child and healthy children emptied their intestines at semiregular intervals, and as he'd learned from recent experience, it was not such a big thing. "All right," he muttered. "I'll get there as soon as I can."

He disconnected before Sharon could complain any more. He couldn't blame her; she was an intern fresh out of graduate school, and her job description didn't include diapering babies.

Soon he'd have a full-time nanny. Soon D.J. would no longer be limiting his ability to perform his job. He'd be able to design projects and defend them without worrying about his cell phone breaking into the discussion, carrying dire news about D.J.'s digestive health.

"I've got to go," he told Corinne.

"Oh?"

"D.J. needs me. I'm sorry."

The elegant lines of her face and her clear, cool gaze made him realize how sorry he was. He didn't want to go. He didn't want to argue with her over Mosley's house, but he didn't want to leave her, either. He wanted to sit with her, drinking his iced tea and talking to her about what movies she'd seen recently, whether she was a Red Sox fan or a Yankees fan, whether she liked to ski or hike or garden—whether she was involved with anyone at the moment. Whether she was free for dinner.

"We could continue this discussion over dinner," he suggested.

Something sparked in her expression, bright and curious. "Tonight?"

"Were you planning to leave Arlington tonight?"

A slow smile traced her lips. "I'm planning to leave Arlington after I've gotten the design for Gerald's house fixed."

He accepted her words as the challenge they were, but he wasn't offended by them. The design for Gerald's house didn't need to be fixed. But Corinne Lanier was going to be in town until he convinced her of that.

Which meant she was going to be in town tonight.

"I'll pick you up around seven, all right?" He pushed away from the table and zipped his portfolio shut.

She seemed bewildered, a touch apprehensive. Did she think he was going to attempt to seduce her into viewing the house his way? Maybe that wasn't so far from the mark.

She didn't say no.

"Seven o'clock," he repeated, then smiled, gave her hand a shake that felt more like a caress and left the taproom.

CHAPTER THREE

SHE STARED at the mirror one last time, then ordered herself to stop obsessing about her appearance. However she looked would have to do.

She'd attended business dinners before, but never with a man whose parting handshake had caused a ribbon of heat to unfurl up her arm. The sensation had left her off balance. She'd spent the rest of the afternoon trying to regain her equilibrium.

Actually, she'd regained enough of her equilibrium to spend a few hours reviewing two reports Gerald had prepared. After selling his online graphics company to a much bigger competitor for millions of dollars, he'd become a consultant, and Corinne had remained with him. While he advised start-ups on the technical aspects of their companies, she advised them on the business aspects. Gerald related well to the computer geeks. They all spoke the same language. She was far from fluent in geek-ese, but she worked with the business people, the money people, people who communicated in sentences rather than bits and bytes. She'd thought she would get along just fine with the architect Gerald had commissioned to design his country house.

And she did get along fine with him, she assured herself, turning from the full-length mirror on the back of the bathroom door. She'd removed her stern gray suit, showered and donned a pair of tailored slacks and a silk shell blouse, then worried that she looked too casual, then worried that she looked too formal, then worried that if Levi shook her hand again that unnerving heat would return, spinning up her arm and spreading through her body.

The clock on the nightstand read five past seven. She caught another glimpse of herself in the mirror above the dresser and wondered whether the simple diamond posts in her ears appeared too elegant. Then she wondered why she cared so much about making the right impression on Levi Holt.

Because she wanted to get him to rework the design, she told herself—but she honestly didn't believe that that was all it was.

The phone rang as she was reaching for her gold hoop earrings. Abandoning her jewelry case, she crossed the room and answered. "Levi Holt is here for you," the desk clerk informed her.

"Thanks." *He's here for you.* What was wrong with her that even the clerk's innocuous statement unsettled her?

She stuffed her room key into her purse, stepped into her shoes and left the room, refusing to peek into any mirrors on her way.

She spotted Levi as soon as she entered the lobby. Given his height, he was hard to miss. He wore jeans that had been laundered a few times—not stiff but not faded, either—and a crisp white oxford shirt with the sleeves rolled up.

Her outfit was too dressy. He was probably planning to take her to a fast-food joint, where she'd look like a fool, eating a cheeseburger in her silk blouse and diamond earrings.

"I struck out with baby-sitters," he said, although his grin told her he wasn't terribly disappointed about this failure. "It's a school night. They're all doing homework."

"Then are we skipping dinner?"

"I was hoping you wouldn't mind coming to my house. I picked up some steaks and I can throw together a salad. Would you mind terribly?"

She wasn't sure. Going to his house for dinner as if they were friends didn't seem appropriate. But she wanted to resolve the situation with Gerald's house, and if they didn't get together this evening, who knew what Levi's baby-sitter problems would be tomorrow?

Unsure how much she ought to trust him, she peered into his eyes. They were so dark she saw her reflection in them. Trying to avoid mirrors, she'd found something far more dangerous: Levi Holt's eyes.

"All right," she relented, deciding she might as well get this meeting over with. If she was cooperative about the dinner arrangements, it might earn her some points in their negotiations.

He held the door open for her and she preceded him out into the mild evening. The sky still held plenty of light and a hint of warmth lingered in the air, even though the sun had set. He led her across the parking lot to a midnight-blue Porsche and unlocked the passenger door. As she got in, she noticed a baby car seat strapped to the narrow back seat behind her.

She didn't associate new fathers with Porsches. Expensive sports cars seemed like an indulgence intended for carefree bachelors or older fathers going through their second adolescence once their children were grown and gone. Porsches weren't what responsible parents drove.

The passenger seat was pushed forward in order to create a little extra room for the baby seat. The driver's seat was pushed way back to accommodate Levi's long legs. Even so, he seemed too close to her as he settled behind the wheel. When he shut his door, she caught a whiff of citrus and spice undercut with a hint of baby powder. The combination of fragrances was surprisingly sexy.

She pressed her lips together, and her knees. Ridiculous, thinking of Levi in terms of sexiness. Surely there was a wife somewhere in the picture, and given Levi's particular physical attributes, Corinne felt safe in assuming that wife would be equally sexy.

None of which was relevant to her. This was work, and he was her opponent.

"Do you usually conduct business by inviting people to your house for dinner?" she asked as he steered out of the parking lot and into the flow of traffic on Hauser Boulevard.

He shot her a quick look, then focused on the road. "I rarely have to go out of my way to convince a client that the design I came up with is great." His grin negated the arrogance in his words. "But no, this is unusual. D.J. has a way of complicating things."

A combination of curiosity and frustration—that they were going to his house rather than some nice, safe, public restaurant, that she'd linked him with sexiness in her mind—compelled her to ask, "Isn't D.J.'s mother available?"

"No." His voice was ice hard, his smile gone.

All right, then. Maybe there wasn't a sexy wife in the picture.

"She died," he added, as if aware he owed Corinne an explanation.

"I'm so sorry." A wave of guilt washed through her at having pushed him into discussing something that obviously brought him pain.

"Yeah. Well." He signaled and turned left, his gaze resolutely on the road. She had a feeling he wasn't going to glance her way for the rest of the ride. The poor man was clearly annoyed that she'd tapped into his sorrow. A widower with a baby—no wonder he was frazzled, overloaded, beleaguered by the demands of his career, the grief of his loss and the needs of his motherless son.

"I'm sorry," she said again.

At last he looked at her. "It's not your fault," he said, a faint smile vying with the sadness in his eyes.

"It's my fault that you're stuck dealing with me instead of your son tonight."

"He's not my son," Levi said.

She stared at him, utterly confused. D.J.'s mother was dead, and his father was—who? Where? Her own background had been complicated, but compared with Levi's domestic arrangement, her family seemed as conventional as one from a 1950s sit-com.

Before she could question him further—just as well, since she'd already asked too many questions regarding matters she shouldn't care about—he steered onto a rustic unpaved drive that wove around a cluster of flowering lilac bushes and ended in a circle in front of a stone house shaped in a geometric jumble. A Levi Holt design, she realized, more modest in size than what he intended to build for Gerald but just as daring and peculiar, with broken roof lines, oddly angled walls and lots of glass.

Levi yanked the parking brake, shut off the engine and smiled at her, as if to say he wanted to forget about D.J.'s dead mother and absent father for now, and simply have a pleasant and productive dinner.

She smiled back, hoping to communicate that she'd be happy to keep things pleasant and productive, too.

They walked together up to the tall oak double doors and he ushered her inside. The interior was as striking as the exterior. Although not huge, the house seemed spacious, the large room she entered airy and bright thanks to the evening light flooding in through the broad windows. A stairway divided the room into a parlor and a dining room. The furnishings in both rooms were sleek and casual. Colorful plastic toys littered the area rug covering the hardwood floor in the parlor, and a baby swing stood in the corner of the dining room.

From somewhere beyond the dining room came the sound of D.J. chirping. Corinne followed Levi past the long table and the baby swing and into the kitchen. A pretty blond teenager sat at the small table in a corner of the room, a notebook open before her and a pen wedged between two fingers. D.J. was ensconced in a contraption that featured a padded seat surrounded by a plastic table set on wheels. He pushed himself back and forth across the smooth tiles with his feet, which extended through leg holes in the seat and touched the floor.

"Thanks," Levi said, pulling out his wallet and handing the girl a five-dollar bill.

"No prob." She stuffed the money into the pocket of her stretch pants—not an easy feat, given how tightly they fit—and scooped up her notebook. "See ya!" Beaming a smile at Corinne, she pranced out of the kitchen. A quiet thump indicated that she'd let herself out the front door and closed it behind her.

Corinne surveyed the room. Levi's kitchen was much smaller than the kitchen he'd designed for Gerald's house, so she couldn't really compare counter space. She could see, though, that his kitchen didn't have a wasted wall of glass. Appliances and cabinets were arranged efficiently within the compact room. The recessed lights were well positioned, one wall held a rack of pans and pots and another contained a door that led out to a large deck, part of which was screened.

On the polished granite counter beside the sink sat a platter holding two steaks soaking in a dark, fragrant marinade. A head of lettuce awaited attention on the butcher block insert on the other side of the sink.

Levi was actually going to cook for her. The very idea confounded her. No one ever cooked for her, unless she was at a restaurant.

Not only was he going to cook for her, but he must have known she would say yes to his offer of dinner at his house. Otherwise, he wouldn't have gotten the steaks prepared.

D.J. scooted over in his wheeled chair. "Blee-lee-lee!" he shrieked. Evidently this was a happy sound; he gave her a big, toothless grin.

"Hey, there, buddy," Levi said, hunkering down to put himself at eye level with D.J. "Did Tara treat you well?"

"Lee-lee-lee-ba!" D.J. slapped the flat surface before him as if it was a tom-tom.

"I thought so." Levi straightened up and grinned at Corinne.

"What does that mean?"

"I think it means Tara treated him well."

She glanced at the steaks and tried to sort her thoughts. "Tara was the baby-sitter?"

He nodded and lowered the stainless steel door of the oven. Potatoes were baking inside. More proof that he'd expected her to agree to dine at his house.

"I thought you couldn't find a sitter."

"For the whole evening, no. Tara lives just across the street. She was willing to stay with D.J. while I picked you up."

"For five dollars? Not a bad wage to do your homework while the baby rolls around in that—" she had no idea what it was called "—thing."

"It's a walker," Levi told her, then shook his head. "Amazing how quickly you can become an expert on baby equipment. A month ago, I wouldn't have known about walkers, either."

She watched D.J. propel himself around the kitchen, pushing against the floor with his bare feet and babbling incoherently. His mood appeared greatly improved from that morning. Maybe his gums weren't bothering him. Or maybe he was just so over-joyed to be in his walker, he could bear the teething pain.

She glanced back at Levi, who was turning the steaks with a fork. "I thought it would be nice to eat out on the porch," he suggested.

"All right."

He abandoned the steaks for the refrigerator, from which he removed a bright-red tomato, a carrot and a stalk of celery. His movements were easy and graceful. He knew his way around a kitchen—at least, one that was created sanely, like this one.

"Is there anything I can do to help?" she offered.

"Change D.J.'s diaper. Just kidding." He sent her a quick smile. "Sit. Gather your forces. I'm sure you're going to want to enter into battle fully armed."

"Is this going to be a battle?" she asked, wariness alternating with amusement inside her. She didn't want to be amused. Amusing her could be Levi's most potent strategy: get her laughing, feeling comfortable and content, and before she knew it she'd be agreeing to a fireplace in every bedroom and a price fifty percent higher than the one Gerald had contracted for.

Levi eyed her over his shoulder, then got to work tearing lettuce into a ceramic bowl. "I hope it won't be too bloody. If you've got an open mind, I'm sure I can convince you that the design I came up with for Gerald's house is going to work."

"It's not my mind that has to be open," she pointed out, aware that she wasn't being entirely truthful. Without her, Gerald likely would have left the design as it was—and he would have been grossly disappointed when he tried to live in what would be a nearly unlivable house. In a way, she'd been the one to open *his* mind, to help him recognize that the design needed to be revised.

Levi shook the water off the tomato he'd just rinsed. "I want this house to happen," he told her. "Mosley wants it to happen. I think we'll be able to work something out."

He seemed a bit more conciliatory than he'd been earlier that day in the hotel's cocktail lounge. Maybe he felt bad that he'd had to cut that meeting short. Or maybe he was trying to soften her up, cooking for her and being a genial host. Maybe he only *sounded* reasonable because she was distracted by the graceful motions of his hands as he sliced the tomato, then chopped the carrot into chunks and added them to the bowl.

D.J. skidded across the floor and bumped into Levi's leg. "Da! Da! Da!"

"He's calling you Da," she observed, wondering if this meant the child was a precocious genius, already able to communicate in primitive English. Wondering if it meant he thought of Levi as his father.

"He's just exercising his vocal cords. I'll be right back." Levi lifted the salad bowl and strolled through the dining room and out to the screened portion of the deck.

She turned to D.J. He bounced on his toes, as if trying to escape the confines of his walker. Raising his hands toward the ceiling, he squealed. Corinne felt utterly at a loss. She had no experience in dealing with infants. No younger siblings, no baby-sitting jobs in her past. No children of her own.

He kept stretching toward the ceiling, jabbering and grinning, his chubby cheeks dimpling from his smile. He looked so cute she was tempted to pick him up— or at least enter into a conversation with him. Nothing he said sounded as close to actual speech as "Da" had, though.

She felt silly, watching him in tongue-tied helplessness. But to look away would be rude. "Tell Levi to change the design for Gerald's house," she urged D.J., feeling even sillier. "Tell him to make Gerald's house normal, like this house." No sunken living room here, she noted. A sunken living room would have been hazardous to D.J. when he cruised around in his walker. "Tell Levi I don't want to enter into battle with him tonight."

She peered out the door to the deck and saw that he had exited to the unscreened part to remove the grill cover. His rangy body was silhouetted against the twilight-pink sky. She hoped he wouldn't don an apron emblazoned with some goofy barbecue saying, like Kiss Me—I'm The Chef! She hoped he wouldn't cow her with pretentious commentary about which wine went best with his steaks.

Most of all, she hoped they could skip the battle. She didn't want to fight him. She wanted him to see things from her perspective, she wanted to make sure everything got fixed the way it should be—but she didn't want to go to war with Levi. What she wanted—

He draped the grill cover over a chair and leaned against the deck railing for a minute, staring out at his backyard, his face shadowed. What she wanted, she realized, was to get to know him better. To find out how he'd wound up with D.J., and when he'd designed and built his own house, and why a man like him didn't have a wife and children of his own.

What she wanted was to figure him out.

SHE WAS BACK. The sound of her voice made him happy. She had a good voice, a voice that gave him reason to believe everything was going to be okay.

She had good eyes, too. They weren't sad the way the man's were. They looked like morning, when he woke up and the world was full of light.

He tried to tell the woman he was glad she was

here, but she didn't understand him. So he just fol-
lowed the sound of her voice, the rhythm of it, the
hard, clicky noises and the smooth ones. Not a lullaby
like his mother's voice, but still a soothing sound.

He wished she would take him out of the walker so
he would know what she felt like. Her fingers had
shiny tips. Her hands would be soft, he knew.

He wondered if the man liked this woman. He could
never tell what the man was thinking from his face.
Only from his hands and the way his voice sounded,
from the way he stood and the way he held him. D.J.
could tell that the man felt tired sometimes, or
grumpy, or sad. Or happy, when his voice got shim-
mery bright and he called D.J. "buddy."

His mother used to call him Darren.

He wondered what this woman would call him.

FEEDING D.J. SOME applesauce and a bottle didn't
take Levi too long. D.J. tended to eat sparingly in the
evening, then wake up around ten-thirty at night for
a final snack to tide him over until breakfast. It
amazed Levi to think they'd fallen into a routine so
easily. Actually, it was Levi who had fallen into D.J.'s
routine. D.J. determined what happened when in this
house, in Levi's life. He was merely the baby's slave,
surviving from day to day.

On this day, he wanted more than to survive. He
had a great-looking woman in his kitchen, observing
him while he spooned the applesauce into D.J.'s
pudgy mouth. He wanted her to think he was competent and loving. He'd heard from friends that a certain type of woman was turned on by men who revealed their nurturing sides. He hadn't even known

he had a nurturing side, but if he had one and it turned Corinne on—

Hell, what was he thinking? She'd come to Arlington to duel with him over a project, not to melt into a puddle of sentimentality watching him wipe slobber off D.J.'s chin with a wad of paper towel.

She was damned attractive, though. Much more attractive than she'd looked in her prissy gray suit that morning. The rounded neckline of her blouse displayed her slender throat and the delicate hollow at its base where her collarbones met.

It felt good to be noticing such details. It felt normal. It felt as if the axis of Levi's world was straightening itself, the earth resuming its old, familiar rotation.

A good-looking woman was in his house. She was going to eat dinner with him. They'd talk, they'd get friendly, they'd…who knew? Test the waters, perhaps.

Sure. Then he'd suggest that she go back to her boss in New York City and tell him to drop to his knees and thank the gods of architecture that he had a visionary like Levi Holt designing his home for him.

The thought made him laugh. She gave him a curious glance and he busied himself wiping D.J.'s face. "I've got to bring him upstairs and put him in his crib," he said. "Can I get you a drink first? I have wine, beer, scotch—"

She gave the question a great deal of thought, her eyes flashing with doubt. Should he assure her that getting her drunk wasn't his plan?

After a few intense moments she said, "I'd like a glass of wine."

"Red or white? The red will go better with the steaks."

"Then red." Her smile seemed hesitant but game.

While D.J. played the tray of his high chair like bongos, Levi uncorked the bottle of Bordeaux he'd brought upstairs from the basement. Unlike Gerald Mosley's dream house, Levi's didn't have a wine cabinet in the kitchen. He lacked the space for one. But if he was serious about collecting wines—which he wasn't—he'd certainly enjoy the convenience.

He filled the bowl of a stemware glass halfway with wine and handed it to her. Then he hoisted D.J. into his arms. "I'll be right back," he promised, hoping the kid would oblige him by settling down quickly.

She nodded and cradled her wineglass in her hand without drinking. Giving D.J. a playful boost, he strode from the kitchen.

He rushed D.J. through his bedtime rituals—diaper change, face and finger wash, snapping the baby into a clean sleeper and whispering, "No bath tonight, buddy. I'll make it up to you tomorrow—you can have two baths if you want. Okay?"

"Da-da-da!" D.J. responded.

"Sounds like 'yes' in Russian." Levi closed the final snap and carried D.J. to his crib. "Now it's grown-up time. You know what that means? It means you let me be a grown-up for a while. Got it? No fussing, no barfing, no pain-in-the-butt stuff. Are we on the same page?"

"Da-lee-lee-lee!"

"Good. I've got to take care of business with Ms. Lanier downstairs. Don't screw things up for me any more than you already have. Now, here's your teddy bear—" he handed D.J. the stuffed bear Ruth's housemate Sandy had given him "—and I'll wind up your music box—" he did, and it began to play a tinkly version of "Twinkle, Twinkle, Little Star" "—and I'll turn on the walkie-talkie, so if you've got a real emergency you can summon me. Not a fake emergency, D.J., not one of those 'I'm bored and I want someone to play with me' whines, but a genuine 911 emergency. Got it?"

"Ba-ba-ba-ba."

"That's it. 'Baa-Baa Black Sheep.' It's the same melody as 'Twinkle, Twinkle, Little Star.' There are probably plagiarism issues involved." He scruffed his hand gently through D.J.'s downy hair and backed up to the doorway, where he switched on the night-light. Plenty of evening light brightened the room, but once night darkened the windows, D.J. would want the night-light on.

Levi tiptoed down the stairs, listening for a wail. Sometimes, when the realization struck D.J. that he'd been abandoned, he'd send up an outraged yell loud enough to shake Tara's house across the street. Other times he babbled contentedly for a few minutes and then drifted off to sleep. Levi prayed tonight would be one of those times.

He found Corinne gazing through the deck door, her wineglass still in her hand. She glanced over her shoulder at him as he entered the kitchen, and another shy smile flickered across her lips.

Shy. That was what she was. Levi tried to recall the last time he'd met a shy woman and drew a blank. Most of the women he worked with were brassy and assertive; most of the women he dated were up-front and in-his-face. He didn't mind. It was the way women were these days, and more power to them.

But Corinne… It wasn't just that her voice had a whispery edge, even when she was making demands. It was the reserve in her gaze, the stillness in her posture, the restraint in her smile.

He reminded himself that this was a business dinner. Her shyness meant nothing more than a possible weakness he could exploit once they got down to discussing the house design and the contract.

Still, he smiled back at her, once again feeling the urge to reassure her. "Let me get myself some wine, and we'll head out and put this meat on the grill."

"Is D.J. okay?"

For a moment, he thought she actually cared about D.J., but then he figured she was probably only asking if the kid was going to remain quietly out of sight long enough for them to eat and hash out the issues surrounding Mosley's house. "I've got an intercom," he said, displaying the portable receiver he'd brought downstairs. "If he's not okay, he'll let me know."

He poured himself a glass of wine, then carried it, the intercom and the platter of steaks to the door and edged it open with his hip. He motioned with his head for Corinne to accompany him outside, and she moved straight to the deck railing as he busied himself lighting the grill.

His backyard was small, but it bordered on conservation land, so beyond his little square of lawn stretched an untouched expanse of dense New England forest. In the mellow warmth of early June, the foliage was a dozen shades of green, ranging from the silvery pallor of poplars to the almost gloomy dark green of balsam fir. The slender trunks of birch trees stood out in slashes of white, as if someone had streaked the forest with paint.

"It's beautiful," she murmured.

He was pleased out of proportion that she liked it. "I wish I could say all this land was mine, but it's not."

"It doesn't matter." She sipped her wine. "Everything is so—so rural here."

He chuckled. "Arlington is a small city. I'd hardly call it rural."

"Compared with Manhattan it certainly is," she said, her smile a little less shy. "You designed this house, didn't you?"

He adjusted the burners on the grill, then joined her at the railing. "Yeah." He grinned. "You hate it, right?"

"No. It's striking. It seems more practical than the design you came up with for Gerald."

"His kitchen will have more counter space."

"His kitchen will be three times the size of yours. The ratio of counter space to total kitchen size is better in your kitchen." She must have realized how bizarre that sounded, because when he laughed, she did, too. "Anyway, I bet you don't have a fireplace in your bedroom."

As a matter of fact, he did. "Would you like to see?" he asked.

Her smile faded and she took a small step backward. He hadn't meant his invitation as a strategy to lure her upstairs and into his bedroom, but she seemed to take it that way—and the possibility obviously made her uncomfortable.

Okay. He'd shelve all thoughts about her collarbones, her long legs and her large hazel eyes. This was supposed to be a business dinner, and it would be. "What I meant," he explained, "was that if you'd like, I can give you a tour of the house after dinner so you can see how a Levi Holt design comes together. We'd have to wait until D.J. is sleeping, but then you could have a look around. I plan to do a lot more with Gerald's house—he has a lot more money to spend than I did when I built this place—but maybe you'll get an idea of what the finished product would be.''

Skepticism shadowed her gaze. Either she didn't want to see how well a fireplace could fit into a master bedroom, or she didn't trust his motives. Both possibilities made him smile.

He returned to the grill and laid on the steaks. They hissed against the hot metal and released a rich, meaty smell. His peripheral vision tracked her as she turned from the scenery and rested her hips against the railing. She looked—not relaxed but like someone trying hard to appear relaxed.

"When did you build this house?" she asked.

"Three years ago. I'd just gotten a huge commission, and the land wasn't too expensive—this isn't the west side of town, which is a lot pricier—and I grabbed it. I did a lot of the construction myself, and I have friends in the business who cut me some breaks. I could probably sell this place for twice what it cost me to build it." Enough. He wanted her to realize that a Levi Holt house was an excellent investment, but he didn't want to come across as pushy. "Do you like your steak red, pink or burned?"

"Pink, please." She sipped some wine. Her lips were soft and rosy. The wine darkened them slightly. He wished he hadn't noticed that.

"I'll be right back." He left her for the kitchen, took the baked potatoes out of the oven, stuck a loaf of sourdough bread in to warm, pulled a cruet of salad dressing and a tub of butter from the refrigerator and loaded everything on a tray. A glance through the door informed him that Corinne was back at the railing, gazing out at the woods.

Shy, or just guarded? If she was afraid of him, she had no reason to be. Even before D.J. entered his life, he'd never been a wolf. He liked women too much to treat them without respect. If a woman sent signals that she wasn't receptive, he was sensitive enough to pick up on them.

The thing was, the signals he was picking up from Corinne were erratic. She'd been clear about not wanting to see how he'd integrated a fireplace into his bedroom, but the way she gazed at him implied that she wanted to know him better, wanted to dig beneath his surface. Maybe she was so hardheaded her interest in him was only a means to renegotiate Mosley's contract with him from a position of strength.

But she didn't seem hardheaded. Smart, articulate, reserved, but vulnerable underneath. Not vulnerable to a seduction, alas, but not impervious, either.

He carried the tray through the dining room to the screened part of the porch. He'd set the table before driving to the Arlington Inn to pick her up, and it looked cozy and inviting. One of the few worthwhile concepts his mother had indoctrinated him in was the importance of cloth napkins that matched the tablecloth—or in this case, place mats. Napery had been a big thing with her.

He returned to the kitchen for the bread, arranged it in a basket and brought it to the table. Then he stepped out onto the deck and lifted the grill lid. Aromatic smoke wafted out.

"If you want pink, we're ready," he said.

She smiled again. Shy, but definitely something more. Something warm, aware, responsive—just possibly willing to take a chance.

CHAPTER FOUR

THE WINE WAS GOOD. The steak was tender, the bread crusty. The porch was dimly lit. At the center of the table, a candle inside a tinted blue glass augmented the waning evening light that seeped through the screened walls and the brighter light that poured through the glass slider to the dining room. Blue, gold and rusty pink played on Levi's face, painting mysterious shadows across his skin.

Corinne didn't want to be caught up in the mystery of Levi. She wanted to straighten out the problems with Gerald's house and go back to New York. Perhaps if the lighting was better, she'd be able to concentrate on her mission.

Maybe it wasn't the lighting that distracted her. Maybe it was the wine, or the filling food, or the summery scent of the air wafting in from the backyard. Maybe it was the faint, steady hiss of the intercom receiver, informing them that D.J. was sleeping peacefully upstairs.

Or maybe it was just Levi.

Whatever the reason, Corinne couldn't force herself to care about Gerald's dream house. Later, she'd care. Tomorrow morning. But not now.

"The house I grew up in was dark," he was saying, and as she lifted her glass for a sip she assured herself that listening to him describe the path that led to his career as an architect was actually relevant to the business she was supposed to be conducting. "It was an antique farmhouse, maybe 150 years old. The windows were small, and the surrounding trees blocked a lot of the light, too. It was awfully gloomy."

Was he talking about his childhood house or his childhood? "I don't know much about old houses," she said. "I grew up in Phoenix, where most buildings are pretty new. A hundred fifty years ago, Phoenix probably had a few adobe haciendas, but most of the houses have gone up in the past forty years or so."

"And they all look like adobe haciendas," he guessed.

She grinned. "They *try* to look like them. Everything is stucco, with red tile roofs. It's nothing like Arlington, Connecticut." The candle flickered. She saw the flame reflected in Levi's eyes, just as she'd seen herself reflected in them earlier. "Was your family's farmhouse in Connecticut?"

"Indiana," he told her.

"How did you wind up here?"

"I finished grad school and got a job offer." He pushed his chair back from the table so he could stretch his legs. Sliding down a bit in his chair, he rested the base of his wineglass against his belt.

His abdomen was board flat. She couldn't detect a hint of flab on him—not that she was ogling his body or anything, not that she had any particular interest in it, but she could certainly appreciate it in a dispassionate way.

"I liked the people at Arlington Architectural Associates when they brought me in for an interview," he continued. "It's a small enough firm that everyone depends on everyone else. People collaborate and bounce ideas off one another. No one acts like a prima donna. Even though all the partners have different styles and different strengths, there's a real respect and openness to other people's approaches. And we all agree on certain basic philosophies of building design.''

"What are those philosophies?'' she asked, silently commending herself for the fact that she and Levi *were* talking shop. Even if she was maybe ogling him just a teeny, tiny bit, she was also taking care of business, which made the ogling almost justifiable.

"Light,'' he said, then grinned. "That's our main philosophy. Buildings should be full of natural light. They should be open to the outside world, integrating the outdoors into the interior as much as possible.'' He sipped his wine. "Having grown up in a dark house, I want to design houses full of light.''

"In other words, houses with walls of glass,'' she muttered, although she smiled so he wouldn't sense any hostility in the comment.

"Walls of glass,'' he confirmed. "Skylights. Porches. Broad doors and windows. Whether we're designing an office building or a colonial reproduction or a postmodern private house, we try to open it up as much as possible. I like having all that light embracing a room. Or natural darkness. Not the kind of gloom caused by small windows and long eaves, but a night sky. With the right kind of windows, a room can be filled with the night.''

She tried to calculate how much wine she'd consumed. Certainly not enough to be thinking what she was thinking: that a room filled with the night sounded remarkably romantic.

The word *romantic* ought not to be a part of that evening's vocabulary. Just because she'd shared a candlelit dinner with a handsome man on his back porch—which had been filled with dusk and now was filling with night—didn't mean she was in a romantic mood.

If she were in a romantic mood, a room filled with night would be appropriate. But she wasn't, and this wasn't a room. And Levi Holt was not only her adversary but also some form of father to a baby, which was not the least bit romantic.

"Tell me more about the house you grew up in," she urged him, because even if she wasn't in a romantic mood, neither was she in the mood to argue about the application of his architectural philosophy in the context of Gerald's house. "You said it was a farmhouse. Did you grow up on a farm?"

"We had a pretty extensive garden," he said. "We grew a lot of the food we ate, and we also raised chickens. Nasty little beasts. They were always pecking and squawking. I didn't like them."

"It sounds wonderful," Corinne murmured, despite his negative attitude toward chickens. "I mean, the old house and the garden." She'd come of age in a variety of interchangeable suburban houses. For a few years she'd had a pet cat, but she'd had to give it to her father when her mother's second husband proved to be allergic to cats. And her father's wife at the time hadn't wanted the cat, so she'd given it to a neighbor who'd moved to Tucson. Corinne realized with a pang that she still missed Muffy.

"It wasn't wonderful," Levi told her, his smile lacking humor.

"Were the chickens really that bad?" she needled him.

"Not the chickens. The whole thing. The house wasn't just dark—it was drafty in the winter and sweltering in the summer. The plumbing and electricity were unreliable. Whenever anything broke, my father insisted on fixing it himself. He made my brothers and me help him. Our repairs were pitiful. He should have hired professionals, but he refused to."

"There's something to be said for doing things yourself." Corinne prided herself on her self-sufficiency. She might not be able to perform plumbing and electrical repairs any better than Levi's father, but she knew how to take care of herself. She'd learned that necessary skill at an early age. With her parents caught up in their own chronic melodramas, their marriages and divorces, passions and feuds, she couldn't count on them to take care of her. So she'd learned to launder her own clothes, write shopping lists, forge her parents' signatures on permission slips from school—whatever was necessary to keep her life on track.

She'd even done a few repairs in her day. Nothing elaborate, but by the time she was seven she knew how to pump air into her bicycle tires and change lightbulbs, and by the time she was ten she'd figured out how to set a circuit breaker and how, using a bent wire hanger, to clean a hair clog from the sink drain. Her mother probably still didn't know what a circuit breaker was.

"Self-sufficiency was a big thing with my parents," Levi said.

She imagined pioneers, backpackers camping beside a wilderness trail, sailors marooned on a desert island, rigging lean-tos on the beach and subsisting on coconuts and whatever fish they could catch. No, none of those images fit with Levi. She conjured another picture: old hippies trying to get back to the land. That one clicked. "Did your mother jar her own preserves?"

"You bet. She and my sisters did lots of canning."

"Wait a minute. The brothers did household repairs and the sisters did canning? What kind of a sexist division of labor was that?"

Although she'd said it in a joking way, Levi didn't smile. "It was very sexist. My parents are extremely conservative. They believe men and women each have their places." He shook his head, as if to dismiss the entire subject.

Corinne wasn't as willing to dismiss it. She'd seen Levi with his son—or whatever D.J. was to him. She'd seen him feed the baby and carry him and kiss his brow. Raising an infant—without a woman's help—struck her as extremely evolved, not the sort of role a man who'd been raised with such old-fashioned values would accept. "What do your parents think about you taking care of D.J.?" she asked.

He leveled a gaze at her. She realized her question had crossed a line, but she wasn't sure where the line was or what it marked. She felt the way she had in his car earlier that evening, when her questions had pushed him into revealing that D.J.'s mother was dead and that Levi wasn't his father. Perhaps she'd pushed him again. Perhaps he'd reveal some other interesting tidbit, something that would demystify him—or make him even more mysterious.

He had the option of not answering. But after scrutinizing her for a long time, his face shimmering in the golden light from the candle, he said, "My parents think I'm a fool."

The words held no self-pity, no plea for sympathy. He'd simply stated a fact.

"Your parents are obviously mistaken," she said—another simple fact, as far as she was concerned.

A smile whispered across his lips. He lifted his glass toward her, as if he was seconding her opinion by drinking to it.

Joining in the toast, she sipped some wine. Her gaze met his over the rim of her glass, a moment of connection between them, a silent bond that had nothing to do with houses or parents and everything to do with men and women and their places. Levi knew his place: it was in the kitchen, preparing a delicious dinner, and upstairs in a nursery putting a baby to sleep, and there was no question in Corinne's mind, no question at all, that he was one hundred percent man.

She lowered her eyes, suddenly uneasy at the direction her mind was journeying. Gerald had sent her to Arlington to get a job done, not to entertain erotic thoughts about the one hundred percent man who represented an obstacle to her accomplishing that job. She was here to rework a blueprint and a contract. The last thing she was looking for—with Levi or anyone—was an involvement that would complicate her life and tangle her emotions.

For some reason, she was absolutely certain that an involvement with Levi *would* tangle her emotions. He wasn't the sort of man a woman could expect to pass through her life without leaving things different from the way he'd found them. Her heart would be disordered by his wake, her soul smudged with his fingerprints. Merely exchanging looks with him over a glass of wine left her feeling altered somehow.

"I'm not sure we're going to get much work done tonight," she said, eyeing her watch. It was nearly ten. She ought to go back to the hotel and regain her perspective. Tomorrow, in a room filled with natural light instead of atmospheric night, she and Levi could fight their battle over the plans for Gerald's house.

He, too, checked his watch. "I hadn't realized it was so late. I guess we were less productive than we could have been." He sounded vaguely apologetic.

"We had good intentions," she said with a smile. He smiled back, and if she hadn't been feeling so warm and easy inside, she would have regretted how natural it was to share a smile with him. "Can we meet tomorrow?"

"Probably. Until the nanny starts work on Monday, my schedule is shot to hell—which means I'm pretty flexible."

As if on cue, a feeble cry threaded through the intercom speaker, high and tinny. "He wants his snack," Levi explained, obviously less than thrilled.

He gathered a couple of plates and led the way into the house. Corinne helped by carrying the wineglasses indoors. "Just leave everything," he called over his shoulder as he set the plates in the sink. He pulled a can of formula from a cabinet, popped it open and filled a baby bottle, splashing a small amount into the sink. "He demands a nightcap every evening. Twenty years from now, he'll insist he can't sleep through the night without a shot of brandy."

"I think formula and brandy are a bit different."

"Hard to say. He guzzles the formula, gets drowsy and passes out."

She heard another, louder, wail, this time streaming down the stairs rather than echoing through the intercom. The poor baby. If only he could talk, he might not sound so upset. He'd simply say, "I'm thirsty, Dad." Or would he call Levi "Da"? Did he know Levi wasn't his father? How much could an infant understand?

Corinne certainly didn't understand a lot of it, and she was no infant.

For some reason, she felt compelled to follow Levi up the stairs with the bottle. Maybe she'd peek into his bedroom to see how the fireplace looked—but no, she honestly *didn't* want to see how it looked. She didn't want to go anywhere near his bedroom as long as her mind wasn't working at full speed.

Levi didn't comment on her following him upstairs. He simply led the way into a small room that appeared even smaller because of the abundance of furniture crammed into it: a full-size futon sofa, a coffee table shoved to one side, a small TV set on a wheeled stand, a crib and a chest of drawers, the top of which was covered with a padded plastic sheet. A night-light protruded from a socket, shedding a circle of orange light on the wall behind it. Packages of disposable diapers were stacked along the wall under a broad, curtainless window. The room was, as Levi would say, filled with night.

He flicked a light switch near the door, turning on a lamp on an end table beside the futon. From the depths of the crib came D.J.'s plaintive whimper. "All right, D.J.—I'm here," Levi announced, crossing to the crib and reaching in.

The baby's cries increased in volume, signaling some sort of triumph as Levi lifted him up. His little face was ruddy, his hair sweaty, as Levi perched him on his shoulder. "Ba-ba-ba," he whined.

"Yeah, I've got your bottle."

"Ba-lee-lee-ba." Instead of relaxing into Levi's chest in relief that sustenance was imminent, D.J. twisted in Levi's arms as if trying to wriggle free. "Ba-ba-baaa!" he babbled, the final syllable stretching into a sob.

"Easy does it, tiger." Levi carried him toward the chest of drawers. "You keep squirming like that and I'll drop you."

"Ba-ba-ba!" The baby's voice rose resentfully.

"You want a dry diaper or don't you?"

"Ba-ba! Lee-ba!"

"He wants his bottle," Corinne said helpfully. She couldn't say for sure that he did, but she'd rather watch Levi give him a bottle than change his diaper.

"Ba-ba!" D.J. insisted, his voice vibrating with exasperation.

"All right, all right. The bottle it is." Levi grabbed a cloth diaper and the bottle and swung D.J. around in his arms.

The baby again tried to wriggle free. He stretched his hands and kicked his feet, screaming, "Ba-ba! Ba-ba!" with great indignation, as if to say, *You idiot—why don't you understand what I'm telling you?*

Levi wasn't an idiot, but he clearly shared D.J.'s mounting frustration. "Here's your bottle," he said, nudging the nipple toward D.J.'s mouth. D.J. pushed it away and let out a wail.

Corinne stood by helplessly. She felt bad for D.J. and worse for Levi. He was trying so hard to soothe the frantic baby, but nothing he did seemed to work. D.J. fought him with near desperation, shoving at him, grappling for something just beyond Levi, something in Corinne's vicinity.

Corinne. He was reaching for *her*.

No, of course he wasn't. Why would he want her? It only looked as if he was aiming at her because she stood near his head, and he was flailing his hands above his head.

"Ba-baaa! Ba-baaa!" He writhed within Levi's strong embrace, stretching, striving. "Ba-baaa!"

"Let me hold him," she said impulsively. Maybe it would help. It probably wouldn't hurt. And she couldn't bear to stand idly by while Levi struggled to keep D.J. from hurting himself.

Levi spun toward her, a puzzled frown marking his brow.

She moved closer to him, her arms outstretched. "Let me hold him for a minute. Maybe he'll calm down." She didn't know why she believed such a thing would happen. She couldn't remember ever holding a baby in her life, let alone consoling an overwrought one. But D.J. did seem to be targeting her, fighting Levi's hold and launching himself toward Corinne.

Lacking a better alternative, Levi shrugged and motioned with his chin toward a pile of folded cloth diapers on top of the bureau. "Grab one of those, first. You'll want to protect your blouse."

Deciding she'd rather not know what she had to protect it from, she shook open one of the diapers and draped it over her shoulder. Then she lifted D.J. into her hands.

He was heavier than she'd expected, more solid. She wasn't sure what she'd thought he would feel like—soft and squishy, or bony and angular. But he was firm and warm. She could feel the power inside him, a strength just waiting for his body to grow into it.

He immediately stopped crying. His eyes, damp with tears, peered up at her, curious, quizzical.

She adjusted her arms around him, cradling him. The cloth diaper on her shoulder was no longer protecting her from anything he might deposit onto her blouse from either extremity, but it didn't matter. He didn't squirm and fight. He just nestled himself into her embrace and gazed at her, his breathing still a little ragged but his body calm.

His eyes were as dark as Levi's. She could see her reflection in them.

She felt a touch at her elbow, Levi guiding her over to the sofa. She was grateful for his help; she couldn't see where she was going because she couldn't move her eyes from D.J.'s intense gaze.

Still with his hand on her arm, Levi lowered her to sit. She took comfort in the warmth of his palm against her skin, the way it steadied and reassured her. Once she was seated, Levi reached around her to slide the diaper from her shoulder. "Lift him a little," he suggested, and when she raised D.J., Levi spread the square of cloth across her lap, smoothing it over her thighs.

Too many sensations flooded her: awe at the reality of this baby in her arms, mild panic that she might hurt him, joy that her arms seemed to make him happy—and awareness of Levi's hands on her legs, her arms, her shoulder. Levi, hovering over her, watching her, smiling in surprise and encouragement. His fingers gliding along her thighs, his face just inches from hers.

"I'll get the bottle," he said, straightening up.

Good. She didn't want him standing so close to her anymore, close enough that she could feel his breath against her cheek. As long as he was a safe distance away, she could concentrate on the baby.

D.J. moved his arms in lopsided circles and took a swipe at her chin. When she lifted her head out of slapping range, he grabbed her breast and squeezed it.

"Hey!" she snapped, as if he were a fresh guy taking liberties. But he was only a baby. He didn't know that pawing a woman's breast was out of line.

"He's looking for milk," Levi murmured, handing her the bottle.

Corinne felt her cheeks grow hot at the realization that Levi had seen the baby grope her breast. Then she acknowledged he was right; babies regarded breasts as nothing more than a source of milk. She held the bottle upside down above D.J.'s face, and a drop of pale-white formula dribbled out and landed on his chin. He emitted an outraged squeal.

"Here, like this." Levi covered her hand with his and angled the bottle toward D.J.'s mouth. Gently, he steered her hand, nudging the nipple against D.J.'s puckered lips. D.J. twisted his face away and squealed again, but Levi moved the nipple back to D.J.'s lips, pressing until the baby reluctantly took it. He gave it a hard suck, then subsided and guzzled the formula.

"I'm sorry," she whispered to him, even though his eyelids began to droop. "I wish I had that other kind of milk to give you, but I don't." How tragic that he'd lost his mother. How sad that he had to get his nourishment from a plastic bottle with a weirdly shaped latex nipple on it, rather than from the breasts of the woman who'd given him life. Watching him suckle, she felt tears gathering in her eyes.

The futon cushion sank against her hip as Levi lowered himself to sit beside her. "Are you okay?" he asked.

She sniffled and forced a smile. "I was just thinking about how much he must miss his mother."

"Yeah." Levi lowered his gaze to D.J. The baby seemed half in a trance, blissfully devouring the bottle's contents. "The first few days, he really fought me over the bottle."

"The first few days?"

"After his mother died."

She wanted to ask when D.J.'s mother had died, who she'd been, how Levi had been connected to her. Here Corinne was, feeding a baby about whom she knew nothing other than that this architect she was supposed to be working with had custody of him. Probably Tara, the baby-sitter from across the street, knew more about D.J.'s mother than Corinne did.

But he was sitting so close to her, his shoulder brushing hers, his gaze merging with hers somewhere just above the baby's face—and she almost *didn't* want to know about the other woman in his life, even if she was dead. Corinne didn't want to think he had a life as complicated as her parents', where people were always falling in and out of love, raising one another's children and stepchildren, moving from house to house and family to family but never quite sure where home was supposed to be.

"He's my nephew," Levi abruptly volunteered. "His mother was my sister."

"Oh." She preferred that to other possibilities,

even though it meant he'd lost his sister. "How did she die?"

"A brain aneurysm."

"That's awful. She must have been young."

"Much too young," Levi said quietly.

She reflected on that for a moment, more tears filling her eyes. She wasn't usually a weepy person. She'd learned to stop crying every time her mother announced another wedding or divorce or move. No use grieving over the transience of life.

But this was truly heartrending. A man had lost his sister. A baby had lost his mother.

Levi had told her a little, and now she wanted to know more. "What about D.J.'s father? Where is he?"

"Who the hell knows?" Levi sounded less bitter than bewildered. "My sister never even told me his name."

"So you—you just got custody of D.J.?"

"It was what my sister wanted." His voice was just a shade above a whisper, as if he hadn't quite accustomed himself to the entire situation. It must have happened fairly recently. Earlier that evening, he'd said that a month ago he hadn't known what a walker was.

Why would his sister have asked Levi to raise her son? He had all those brothers and sisters—why choose a bachelor uncle? Why not the self-sufficient grandparents? Had D.J.'s mother wanted to protect him from growing up in a dark house?

They were questions she had no business asking. Instead, she stared at the child in her arms. He had nearly drained the bottle. His complexion had faded to a serene pink, and his hair curled as the sweat dried from it. Corinne twirled her pinkie gently through a ringlet near the crown of his head. His hand shot up, and he captured her pinkie in his fist. His fingers were tiny yet shockingly strong.

What a fascinating creature he was. Actually, for all she knew, he might be quite ordinary. She had no experience with infants, no grounds for comparison. But she found it amazing that this little boy could go from frenetic to tranquil in less than three minutes, and that he could be so small and yet so fierce.

She also found it amazing that the instant she'd taken him in her arms he'd stopped crying. She, Corinne Lanier, who hadn't even known whether she was holding him correctly...once she'd embraced him he'd relaxed and his beautiful, dark eyes had captured her.

He'd gone for her breast. Maybe he thought she was his mother.

No, of course not. Even babies must be able to recognize their own mothers.

D.J. emptied the bottle with a final, weary slurp and his eyes fluttered, not quite shut but not quite open. He had long, thick eyelashes. When she glanced at Levi, she noticed that he had long, thick eyelashes, too.

"He looks as if he's ready to fall back to sleep," she murmured.

"Would you mind holding him for just a minute longer?" Levi asked. "If I pick him up now, it might wake him up, and then it'll take me forever to quiet him down again."

"Okay." Her arms arched protectively around D.J., she leaned back into the futon's cushioning. Levi plucked the empty bottle from her hand, stood and carried it to the bureau across the room. From there, he gazed at her for a long moment, then returned and resumed his seat beside her.

Neither of them spoke. The only sound in the room was the rhythmic sighs of D.J.'s breath as he sank slowly into slumber. His mouth puckered and pulsed, as if he were dreaming about his bottle. The warmth of Levi's nearness spread through her.

She would never in a million years have imagined herself in such a situation, in the haphazardly organized nursery of a strange baby, holding that baby and sitting next to a tall, enigmatic, unforgivably handsome man as the night slipped away.

She would never in a million years have guessed that she could feel so peaceful.

DARK WAS WHEN he missed his mother the most. He used to smell her in his sleep and know that she was in the room with him, also sleeping but close enough to keep him safe. He would open his eyes into the darkness and hear her breathing. She would leave a tiny light on near the door, and it would make the bars of his crib slash across him in black shadows. He would see his bear, soft and brown next to him, and his mother would be lying in her bed. He would see the lumps of her body under the blanket, and her hair in a meshy pile around her face.

Now when he opened his eyes he didn't see her anymore. The man left a little light on, just as his mother had, but when he looked through the bars of this crib, she wasn't there. He didn't know where she was. Her smell wasn't in the air. Her breathing wasn't whispering around him.

So he would cry.

The man always came after a while. He'd change D.J.'s diaper and give him a bottle. The nipple didn't feel right to him; it was hard and shaped funny, and the milk inside it didn't taste like his mother's milk. But drinking it calmed him, and it seemed to please the man.

Tonight, he'd brought the woman with him. Her hands were so soft, and her arms curved around him, thinner than the man's and not quite as secure, but they felt lighter on him. She held him on her knees and stared into his eyes and he drank from the bottle. Her face was so pretty above him. She looked worried and gentle and the milk had tasted better than usual, just because she was holding him.

If he couldn't have his mother, he would take her. D.J. wanted a woman. He wanted someone as soft as his bear, someone dressed in even softer clothing, someone whose skin wouldn't scratch if she rubbed her cheek against him, someone whose fingertips sparkled. Someone with a high voice. He wished she would sing to him the way his mother used to.

She didn't sing. She only held him and fed him and gazed into his face until he was too tired to gaze back. When she held him his gums didn't hurt. He didn't feel hungry. He could let himself relax, let the dark settle in and protect him. He could sleep, knowing that when he woke up again, everything would be okay.

CHAPTER FIVE

NEITHER OF THEM spoke during the drive to the Arlington Inn.

Once Tara had returned to Levi's house to keep an eye on D.J., he and Corinne got into his car and headed toward downtown Arlington. They traveled through his drowsing neighborhood, street lamps spilling light through the night-black tree leaves, windows shedding amber rectangles onto shadowy front yards. Occasionally they passed another car, but Arlington at ten-thirty on a weeknight was far from lively.

Next to him, Corinne sat quietly, her gaze distant. She wasn't thinking about him, but he was sure as hell thinking about her.

Something had happened when she'd taken D.J. in her arms—and Levi would bet his next commission that was what she was thinking about: the way D.J. had nestled into her embrace and grown serene, the way all his tension and anger had melted away once he felt her arms around him. He'd clearly wanted her to hold him; the instant Levi had passed D.J. over to Corinne, he'd been transformed.

He'd wanted Corinne.

It was a yearning Levi could definitely relate to.

That was the thought that obsessed him while Corinne silently pursued her own thoughts. As he

cruised down Hauser Boulevard, eerily traffic-free at
this hour, Levi admitted that there was a whole lot
more to her than her long legs, her expressive eyes
and her obvious intelligence. Something inside her,
something D.J. had detected right away but Levi
could only sense, had altered the atmosphere in his
home, reshaped the molecules in the air.

Was it just that she was a woman? Was it that D.J.
was looking for a breast to nourish him and any
woman with breasts would have sufficed? Or was it
something particular about Corinne that D.J. responded to?

If the kid hadn't been in his life right now, Levi
would have made a play for Corinne. Why not? Even
though they had to rework a contract, he could still
think about her in terms other than professional. She
was smart and attractive; he was single; no harm in
trying.

But that would have been all it was—a try, a play.
No big deal.

In any case, D.J. *was* in Levi's life, and thanks to
D.J., Levi viewed Corinne in an entirely different
light. When he'd sat next to her on the futon, with
D.J. in her lap and the whisper-soft pressure of her
arm against his, something had happened. He didn't
know what. He just knew it was *something*.

The inn loomed ahead, its colonial facade quaint
enough to illustrate a postcard. He steered onto the
circular drive and coasted up to the front door, then
shut off the engine. He had to speak, to get her attention, to release some of the tension building inside
him. He couldn't just let her climb out of the car when
everything felt so unresolved between them, unreal-

ized but *there,* just waiting for them to acknowledge it.

He didn't know what to say, other than her name. "Corinne."

She turned to him. Her eyes had an almost other-worldly gleam to them, as if she were still lost in a meditation that didn't include him. Yet when she spoke, she made it clear that her focus was immediate and practical. "What are we going to do about Gerald's house?"

At the moment, that project seemed irrelevant to Levi. But he knew it was important. It represented accomplishment to him and income to the firm. It was a job and he wanted it done.

Yet sitting beside Corinne, her hair shiny and inviting, her lips pursed as she awaited his answer, he just couldn't bring himself to care about the Mosley house. "Let's meet tomorrow," he said, warning himself that if they did, he'd have to keep his mind on the blueprints and the contract and not on any mystical powers Corinne might possess when it came to soothing cranky babies.

"Can we do that?"

"If you stay in Arlington we can."

"I mean, what about D.J.?"

He chuckled grimly. "Barring a miracle, he'll be at the meeting, too."

She didn't smile.

He couldn't believe the prospect of seeing D.J. tomorrow annoyed her, not after tonight. Not after she'd cuddled him. Not after her touch had stopped his tears. But on the chance that it did, he braced himself for her objection.

All she said was, "What time?"

"Should we try for nine-thirty again?"

"Nine-thirty didn't work today."

No, but other things had. And if Levi's brain ever clarified itself, he might even figure out what those things were. "Let's try for nine-thirty anyway."

"All right." Twisting away from him, she reached for the door handle.

He had to let her go—and he had to restrain himself from doing something stupid, like telling her how beautiful she looked in the slanting light from the beveled-glass fixture above the inn's front door, and how beautiful she'd looked less than an hour ago, when she'd had D.J. cradled in her arms, and maybe mentioning that she had the most tantalizing mouth he'd seen in a long time.

If he were young and carefree, with nothing to lose, he'd kiss those lips. But he'd aged a lot in the past month, and he couldn't take the risks he used to.

Still, she was getting out of his car. And he wished she wasn't.

He extended one hand and brushed his fingertips against her cheek.

Her gasp was tiny, but he heard it. Or maybe he felt it, a small stirring of air. A faint, anxious smile flickered across her lips, and she shoved open the door.

What was he—crazy? Not for caressing her cheek but for thinking it was such a big deal.

It *was* a big deal. With a total lack of manners— and an urge to protect them both from what would happen if he got out of the car with her—he remained in his seat as she swung her legs out of the car and straightened up. She closed the door without slamming it, walked slowly and carefully to the inn's entry and vanished inside. The door shut behind her, abandoning him to his car and his drive home.

Only when she was gone did he realize he'd been holding his breath.

SHE HAD STRANGE dreams all night, dreams of holding a baby to her breast—dreams of Levi Holt kissing her breasts. Steamy, X-rated, embarrassing dreams of Levi touching her, suckling her, sliding his hands over her body as she lay beneath him on that futon in the makeshift nursery. These erotic dreams were intertwined with dreams of D.J. reaching for her, clinging to her, babbling at her in gibberish that somehow distilled into words in her mind: "I love you." And Levi whispering, "I love you," as her silk blouse dissolved beneath his questing hands.

She *never* had dreams like that. Not X-rated dreams, not romantic dreams, not maternal dreams. She rarely had any dreams at all.

When she woke up, she felt more tired than she had the night before. Her left cheek tingled where Levi had touched it, as if his fingers had branded her.

A shower revived her slightly. Two cups of coffee and a toasted bagel in the inn's dining room revived her a bit more. When she felt coherent enough to hold up her end of a conversation, she returned to her room and telephoned Gerald on her cell phone.

"Corey!" he said cheerfully. He thrived on a minimum of sleep, often working late into the night and arising without fail at 6:00 a.m. every day. "Are you still in Arlington?"

"Yes."

"So, what's going on? How much is this disaster going to cost me?"

"I don't know yet." She sighed. "Levi Holt and I still haven't had a fruitful meeting."

Gerald laughed. "Fruitful? What's that—some new business jargon?"

"You know what I mean," she retorted, not willing to share his mirthful mood. "Levi and I met, but we haven't gotten anywhere on the contract yet."

"You've been there a full day now. What have you done?"

We talked about our childhoods. We drank wine. We fed the baby. "We discussed his theory of architecture," she said, so it wouldn't sound as if she'd completely wasted her time in Arlington. "I brought my laptop with me, Gerald—I'm getting other work done, too. It's just this baby thing with Levi. It's hard to have a sustained meeting."

"So, you haven't had a fruitful meeting and you haven't had a sustained meeting."

"I'm hoping to have a fruitful, sustained meeting with him today," she said, although she wasn't sure that was really what she was hoping for.

Of course it was what she was hoping for! She didn't want the meeting to disintegrate into another console-the-crying-child session, nor did she want it to wander off into another philosophical discourse on the significance of natural light inside a building. She didn't want to find herself distracted by Levi's towering height, his penetrating eyes, his sensuous mouth and the friction of his lightly callused fingertips against her cheek. She didn't want to hold his nephew and feel her heart crack open in sympathy over everything that poor little baby had lost—and everything Levi had lost, too.

"And you're going to save me money?" Gerald pressed her.

"I'm going to try to keep you from losing money," she corrected him. "Getting rid of the bad design features you agreed to is going to cost something. I'll try to make sure it doesn't cost you too much."

"Do your best," Gerald requested. "It's what I'm paying you for."

That wasn't true. He was paying her because she had a damned good business head on her shoulders and he needed someone with her talent and training in his life. She bristled at his attempt to pull rank on her, to act bossy. "I'll do what I can," she snapped. "But remember—you were the one who signed the contract without thinking about it first. You were the one who said yes to all those stupid steps going up and down from the living room to the family room, and from the living room to the library, and from the kitchen to the family room, and—"

"I know, I know," Gerald said placatingly.

She was still seething, but she decided unloading on him would serve no purpose. "I should be back in the city by tonight," she said. "I'll let you know if I've accomplished anything."

"I'm sure you will. You're wonderful, babe. I'll talk to you this evening."

"Fine. Bye." She pressed the disconnect button and folded her cell phone shut before either of them could say anything more. She was simmering with anger, practically boiling over.

It took her a few minutes to figure out why she was so furious. Not because Gerald had pulled his boss-man routine on her—he did that on occasion, and she knew better than to take him seriously when he did.

No, she was angry because she hadn't made any progress with Levi yesterday, because she'd let herself become sidetracked instead of remaining focused on her task. Because she felt an odd affinity for his bereft nephew. Because Levi had those mesmerizing eyes.

Because she didn't want to return to the city tonight.

The realization stunned her. She sank onto the edge of her unmade bed and shook her head. Why didn't she want to go home? Her Manhattan apartment was a lot more comfortable than this hotel room—and the bagels in Manhattan were much tastier than that ring of dough she'd just been served in the hotel's dining room. She had work awaiting her back home, tasks she couldn't accomplish on her laptop while she was sixty miles away from her office.

Gerald was in the city. His imperious attitude notwithstanding, he was less her boss than her partner, her ally, her best friend. They were each other's social lives; they worked so many hours a day they had no time to meet other people, and that had never bothered her before.

It bothered her now, when she contemplated the possibility that Levi could be a friend. Maybe he could even be a social life.

Nonsense. He was her adversary, and with a baby in his care, he had no time for a social life, either— certainly not one involving a woman from out of town. By the time they finished their fruitful, sustained meeting this morning, they'd probably be growling at each other through gritted teeth.

Sighing, she shoved away from the bed, retrieved her leather pumps from a corner of the closet and wedged her feet into them. She was wearing another suit, a plain brown silk blend that was a year newer than yesterday's gray suit but just as dispassionate, and simple jewelry that conveyed solemn determination. She poked through her tote to make sure it contained everything she might need and slid her hotel room key into a pocket of her blazer. Then she left, determined to keep her meeting with Levi fruitful and sustained, determined not to think about how holding D.J. last night had filled her with an inexplicable warmth, something deep and radiant and totally baffling.

Determined, as well, not to think about how Levi's hand had felt against her cheek.

She arrived at the barnlike headquarters of Arlington Architectural Associates at 9:25, entered and strode directly through the downstairs area, smiling and nodding at the slender young woman who abandoned her drafting table and started toward Corinne as if to ask her what she wanted. She figured that if she walked purposefully enough, she wouldn't have to chat with any of the downstairs employees, explain her reason for being there and listen while they warned her that Levi was having kind of a rough morning. She already knew D.J. would be in his office, probably screaming his tonsils out. That wasn't going to stop her from doing her job.

She had to do it—not just because Gerald expected her to but because the only way she could shake off her unsettling feelings about Levi and the baby was to finish her business with him and go home.

The young woman—in beige capri pants today, with a turquoise T-shirt and her hair adorned by a matching turquoise ribbon that looked like the bow on a gift-wrapped birthday present—backed off, evidently impressed by Corinne's I-know-where-I'm-going attitude. Corinne climbed the stairs to the hay-loft level, turned left and halted in front of Levi's door. She didn't hear any screams. Maybe D.J. was asleep.

She knocked.

"Come on in," called a man whose voice she didn't recognize. Had she approached the wrong office?

Lacking a better option, she opened the door and let out her breath. This was Levi's office. She recognized the teak desk, the corkboard, the drafting table and the stroller in the corner. She didn't recognize the room's sole occupant, however, a man who looked quite at home, half sitting and half leaning against Levi's desk, his legs stretched out and his arms folded across his chest.

"Dennis Murphy," he identified himself. A good-looking man, with a shock of tawny hair and the sort of smile that was virtually impossible not to return, he shoved away from the desk and extended his right hand to her. "You want Levi, right?"

"Yes." She shook his hand. "I'm Corinne Lanier. I have a nine-thirty meeting scheduled with him."

"He's changing the kid's diaper. He should be back any minute."

"Okay." She was still smiling at Dennis Murphy, although she couldn't think of a good reason for the smile. "Do our meetings with him overlap?" she asked, concerned that Levi would make her cool her heels in some other part of the building while he attended to whatever business he had with this fellow.

"No," he said laconically.

Was Murphy going to participate in *her* meeting

with Levi? Was he a part of the construction team? Clad in a well-cut suit, a silk tie and buffed leather loafers, he certainly wasn't dressed to break ground, or whatever the step after breaking ground was.

Maybe he was one of Levi's partners, another architect who believed in opening a building to natural light. Or maybe—

"I'm Levi's lawyer," Murphy told her.

His *lawyer?* Did Levi intend to play hardball this morning? Had he called in his hired gun to intimidate her? After last night, she couldn't believe it! She'd thought they had some sort of friendship going, or at least an understanding, a mutual respect, a willingness to handle their disagreement in a civil manner.

Bringing a lawyer into the picture was *not* civil.

Rage zapped like an electrical charge along her spine, drawing her taller, squaring her shoulders. Glaring at the lawyer, she gave herself a mental pep talk. She would not let Levi and his legal hit man intimidate her. She would not let them steamroll her. She'd get the damned fireplace out of the master bedroom and the damned wine cellar out of the pantry, and Levi could tell his lawyer to stuff his briefs.

The lawyer had once again propped himself comfortably against Levi's desk and was regarding her curiously, his arms folded and his gaze assessing. "Are you involved with one of Levi's projects?" he asked.

She didn't want to talk to him. Without Gerald's lawyer by her side, she knew she was outgunned. But she was stuck with this meeting, and if she didn't answer he'd think he'd cowed her. "Yes," she said crisply.

"Which one?"

"How many does he have?" Good—instead of giving the lawyer information, she could get information from him.

He grinned. "He's always got a few things going, each in a different stage of development. And the collaborative projects with the other architects—it's hard to come up with a specific number. Of course, his schedule is so screwed up these days—" Footsteps on the walkway outside the door alerted them to Levi's return. "He hasn't played poker in weeks. It's criminal."

"Poker?" Was he involved in some sort of illegal gambling? Why would his lawyer call it criminal?

Levi entered the office with D.J. perched on his shoulder. D.J. was awake, facing the direction Levi came from and chirping happily. Seeing Corinne in his office, Levi smiled. "Hi! You've met Murphy?"

"Your lawyer," she muttered.

"Tell him he should play poker," Murphy urged her.

"Poker."

"We play every Tuesday night," Murphy explained. "He hasn't come since he got D.J."

"I can't get a sitter on a school night," Levi defended himself.

"So bring the baby. Evan's kids can play with him. Or Fil can take care of him."

"I'm not going to dump D.J. on Fil."

"Fil?" Corinne interjected, annoyed at being ignored but relieved that Murphy seemed more concerned about Levi's absence from some poker game than about his contract with Gerald.

"Evan's fiancée," Murphy told her.

"She's got her hands full with his kids." Levi

hoisted D.J. a little higher on his shoulder. "Maybe everyone should come to *my* house for poker. Let Evan find a sitter."

"He's got Fil," Murphy pointed out, shoving away from the desk once more. "I'm expected downtown in fifteen minutes. I'll vet the insurance stuff and fax you my notes, okay?"

"I appreciate it."

Murphy sent Corinne another smile, which she decided looked friendly rather than threatening. Then he turned back to Levi. "And I've got three words for you."

"Three words?"

"The Daddy School."

Levi frowned. "What?"

"Ask Evan. Ask Jamie McCoy. You did his house. He'll tell you all about the Daddy School. His wife runs it with my sister-in-law. You need it, Levi."

"What's the Daddy School?"

"If I stick around to answer that question, I'll have to charge my standard hourly fee—and I know you don't want to pay me any more than you already do." Murphy gave Levi a wicked grin, slapped his shoulder and bounded out of the room.

Levi pivoted to watch him leave. Once his back was to Corinne, Darren could see her. He let out a yelp. His eyes wide and round, he jerked in Levi's arms and clawed at his shoulder. He wanted Corinne to hold him.

She knew this without having to guess: he wanted her the way he'd wanted her last night. But last night had been, if not a mistake, a lengthy detour from her destination. She had to get her business done today. She had to resolve all the questions surrounding Gerald's house, nail down a new contract and go home to New York.

If she took D.J. in her arms, that wouldn't happen. The strange magic she'd experienced last night would take over. She'd feel unaccountably close to the baby—and to Levi. She'd be haunted by more thoughts of them both.

She fell back a step. D.J. let out another yelp and swung a hand in her direction.

Levi apparently was unaware of their nonverbal communication. He closed the office door and turned back to Corinne, tightening his hold on the squirmy baby. "Daddy School?" he echoed.

"Don't ask me. I have no idea what your lawyer was talking about." As long as he hadn't been talking about Gerald's contract, she didn't care.

D.J. was fighting Levi. He bent over and lowered the baby to the floor. It took D.J. a minute of trial and error to arrange himself in a crawling position. Once he was propped on his hands and knees, he progressed a few inches before flopping onto his belly.

"He's crawling," Corinne said, astonished by the feat.

Levi glanced at D.J., then lifted his gaze to her. "Well, yeah."

Perhaps it was perfectly normal for D.J. to be crawling. She wouldn't have known that because she'd never seen him do it before.

And at that moment she couldn't really think about the little boy propelling himself slowly across the carpet. She could think only of Levi, his dark, powerful eyes, his mussed hair, his loosened necktie and his strong, sinewy forearms, exposed where he'd rolled his sleeves up to his elbows. His left hand gripped the cloth diaper that had been draped over his shoulder when he'd been holding D.J. His right hand hung empty at his side, and Corinne found herself distracted by the tapered shape of his fingers—fingers that had touched her cheek last night.

He gazed back at her and she felt the full, piercing force of his eyes. Could he see through her? Could he see the dreams she'd had last night? Did he have any idea how disconcerted she was by him?

She wished he would look away, get down to business and start rhapsodizing about the kitchen's wall of glass so she could feel exasperated by him instead of this…whatever it was, this unruly emotion, this churning combination of fear and desire and—

He took a step toward her. Another step. She glanced down to make sure D.J. wasn't in his path, but D.J. was contentedly seated near his stroller, plucking at the carpet nub with his stubby little hands. She would have welcomed a howl of teething pain from him right now, but he seemed uninterested in coming to her rescue.

"Levi," she murmured as Levi took yet another step closer to her, so close one more step would have him trampling her feet.

"We need to get this out of the way," he said.

She was stunned to think he was as unsettled by her as she was by him—flattered but surprised. She wondered whether last night he'd had dreams like hers.

Of course, it was possible that what he wanted to get out of the way was a shouting match at close range. Maybe he thought that if they both cursed at each other for a few minutes, they'd be better able to renegotiate the house.

No. He wasn't going to curse at her. He was going to slide his hand around to the back of her neck, bow his head to hers and kiss her.

His mouth was so warm, so strong. His whole body felt warm and strong. His fingers flexed in her hair and his lips pressed against hers, first lightly and then firmly, then lightly again, tempting, teasing.

And then he leaned back.

"Okay," he whispered.

Okay? No, not okay. Her heart was thumping, her thighs clenching, her hands itching because she hadn't had a chance to touch him, to comb her fingers through his hair the way he'd combed his through hers. Her lips tingled the way her cheek had tingled where he'd caressed it last night—and all she could think of was pulling him back to her, kissing him again, deepening the kiss, making it real.

Either that, or slapping him. Not because she was mid-Victorian, but honestly—hadn't he ever heard of sexual harassment? They were in his office, supposedly working. They were professionals. He had no right to kiss her, no right at all.

Except that she'd kissed him back, kissed him eagerly. And wanted more.

No, nothing was *okay* about any of this.

He turned from her and strolled casually to his desk, as if it were a morning like any other and this was a meeting like any other. Watching him, she felt flummoxed, and incensed that he'd managed to flummox her. She prided herself on her competence and control. She knew how to get things done.

Being kissed senseless was not a good way to get

things done. She would have been better off if his lawyer had remained and Levi had kept his mouth to himself.

"Levi," she said, this time sternly, doing her best to conceal the quaver in her voice.

He lifted a folder—she recognized it as the folder she'd given him yesterday, with all Gerald's concerns about the house explained in writing—and turned back to her. Damn him for having such hypnotic eyes, she thought. Damn that irredeemably sexy mouth, which was quirking into a tentative smile. "Let's just get this thing figured out," he said, as if the problems with the design were trivial, "and then we can deal with the other thing."

The other *thing?* Was he referring to their attraction, the implacable pull that made her long to kiss him again, even when she resented everything about him? Maybe he thought that was trivial, too.

"Get rid of the wall of glass," she demanded. She didn't trust herself to say anything more personal than that.

He laughed. Damn his laugh, too.

"The wall of glass is staying. Let's talk about things that you actually have a prayer of convincing me to change. The bathrooms, for instance. You want more bathrooms on the second floor? Done."

"Good. I also want to get rid of the wall of glass."

He was still smiling, but his gaze was lethally serious. "If the wall of glass goes, I'm tearing up the contract."

"This is Gerald Mosley's country house. It isn't some sort of psychological exercise where you get to resolve your anger over the house you grew up in."

His smile disappeared completely, and his gaze

grew, if possible, even more deadly. "I'm not a hack, Corinne. If your pal is looking for a hack, let him look elsewhere. This—" he jabbed his finger at the folder "—isn't a psychodrama I'm acting out. It's an organic design, a work of art, an expression of my vision as an architect. If Gerald Mosley doesn't like it, take your business somewhere else."

She was tempted. Really, who needed this hassle? Another architect would come up with a saner design, something livable and sensible and easily cleanable, a building Gerald could reside in comfortably, a place he could call home. What he wanted was a house, after all, not an expression of a vision or a work of art.

She should tell that to Levi. She shouldn't be swayed by the way his eyes burned with a passion for his design, or by the knowledge that he felt stronger about his concept—a mere series of sketches and drawings held together by a signed contract and a deposit check—than she had ever felt about any house she'd lived in. Those houses had all been sane and sensible, but they'd never felt like home.

Even so, the wall of glass was a foolish indulgence. The fireplace in the master bedroom made the room nearly unusable. All those nooks were just going to be dust magnets. The solarium was going to look like a dump if it had muddy shoes and old coats in it. Far better to make the connector to the garage a regular, unglamorous mudroom. And if Levi didn't agree—

No *if* about it. He didn't agree, and he'd already told her he wasn't going to budge on certain issues.

He'd kissed her, and he was refusing to negotiate in good faith with her. She truly ought to slap him.

"Ba-ba-baaa!" D.J. abruptly crowed. Corinne spun

around, to see the baby making his plodding way across the floor to her. His crawling motions were laborious and clumsy, but he kept at it, hand in front of hand, knee sliding past knee—with an occasional push from one or the other foot. "Ba-baaa! Bee-baa!"

He aimed straight for her. She could step out of his path, but then he'd have to figure out how to adjust his direction, and it would take him an extra few belabored movements to reach her. She had no doubt in her mind that he viewed her as his destination.

He and she had a special rapport, a connection as dangerous in its own way as Levi's kiss had been. The only difference was that D.J. was a baby. He didn't know any better. He lacked the self-discipline to control his behavior. If a bond existed between him and Corinne, he would act on it.

Levi *should* know better. He *should* have self-discipline.

And damn it, he should listen to her about the house. Surely he must have heard the expression "The customer is always right."

D.J. had reached her foot. He planted one tiny hand on her shoe and screeched in a way that could have signified pain or ecstasy.

And Corinne discovered she was as much a sucker with him as with Levi. Just as she'd stupidly kissed Levi back, now she stupidly bent over and scooped D.J. into her arms. He wanted her. He needed her.

And in some unfathomable way, she wanted and needed him, too.

CHAPTER SIX

SHE WAS GONE.

She'd been there awhile. He'd settled on the floor near her foot, touching the smooth black surface of her shoe and then her ankle, which didn't feel like skin. Something stretched over it. Her leg looked just like a leg, but that film coated it.

He pulled at the film, trying to figure out what it was, and then all of a sudden she bent over and hoisted him off the floor and into her lap. He was used to getting picked up like that, scooped away from wherever he was and lifted through the air. Being moved around that way made him feel powerless. He wished he could get himself where he needed to be.

But this time he didn't mind, because of where he ended up. Her lap was one of the best places in the world. He felt safe there.

She and the man talked. He didn't understand their words, but he knew they weren't happy. There was a tightness to their voices.

He concentrated on the rippling lines in the wood on the desk, and the smooth cloth of her sleeve where her arm was wrapped around him, and the steady rhythm of her breathing. As long as she held him, he could believe she would never go away. But he'd believed that about his mother, and she went away. He still hoped she would come back, but it had been a *long, long time, so long he had to close his eyes to picture her now, and sometimes the picture was just a jumble. Her hair—he would remember the way it flicked into his face and he'd grab it and tug and she'd howl. And her dark eyes. Her smell, and the warm milk coming out of her breasts.*

What if this woman left, like his mother?

He would still have the man. D.J. knew the man wouldn't leave. He just knew it.

Eventually his mouth started to hurt inside and he cried a little, and the man lifted him off the woman's lap and put him on his shoulder. After that D.J. must have fallen asleep, because the next thing he remembered was lying in his stroller and knowing she was gone.

Knowing, deep inside, that she might never come back.

HER APARTMENT LOOKED the same, but it felt different. A little stuffy, a little stagnant—which made sense, she supposed, since she'd been away for two days and the air conditioner had remained off. A little quiet—which *didn't* make sense, because usually she could hear the cluttery din of traffic noise rising up from East Sixty-Third Street, twenty stories below. She supposed that if she strained her ears, she'd hear the traffic noise that evening, too. But the silence in her apartment had nothing to do with whether cars were leaning on their horns in the street beneath her window. It had to do with solitude.

Maybe she ought to get a cat. A new Muffy to keep her company, to be her family.

Oh, God, she thought with a sour laugh. She wheeled her suitcase down the hall to her bedroom, shaking her head at her own inanity. She was *not* going to turn into an obsessive spinster, one of those weird cat ladies she occasionally read about in the newspapers, a lonely woman who lived with thirty cats and when she died all the neighbors said, ''She kept to herself. If she had any family, I never knew about it.''

Forget the cat. If she wanted noise in her apartment, she'd put on a CD. And then she'd call Gerald, and they'd talk shop and tease each other, and she'd feel like her old self again.

Her apartment seemed dark, too.

Well, of course it seemed dark, she rationalized as she unzipped her suitcase and spread it open on her bed. It seemed dark because it was six-thirty and the sun was setting. Twilight always fell a little earlier in Manhattan; the tall buildings blocked the sun as it slid westward, and long before it dropped below the horizon, shadows stretched across the city. Her apartment was dark because of the surrounding buildings. It had nothing to do with the size of her windows.

Levi had refused to budge on that damned wall of glass in the kitchen.

But she wasn't going to think about him. She wasn't going to think about his intransigence on certain items—like the damned wall of glass, and the damned fireplace in the master bedroom—and she wasn't going to think about his kiss. She wasn't going to think about how shocked she'd been, not by the kiss itself, since it had actually been rather tame, but by the fact that he'd kissed her at all. And by the fact that, as tame as the kiss had been, she still hadn't recovered from the sweet pressure of his lips on hers, the way they'd touched and clung and then withdrawn before she'd had a chance to—

To what? Kiss him back? Pull him closer, open her mouth, lure his tongue in? Press her body against his, feel the lean strength of him, lose herself in the darkness of his eyes?

Or slap him?

A sarcastic snort escaped her. Yeah, sure, Levi had really scandalized her, offended her, shattered her prim sense of decorum.

Corinne wasn't a prude. She didn't make a habit of kissing men, particularly those she'd known barely twenty-four hours, but one kiss wasn't going to send her fleeing to the nearest nunnery.

Certainly not one kiss from someone like Levi Holt.

Who'd refused to compromise on the wall of glass and the fireplace, damn it.

Her phone rang, jolting her. She dropped the nylons she'd just removed from her suitcase and reached across the bed for her phone. Maybe it was Levi. Maybe—

"Stop it," she said aloud. The sound of her voice grounded her, and by the time she lifted the receiver she'd shoved Levi into a far corner of her mind. "Hello?"

"Hey, Corey. So you're home?"

"Hi, Gerald." She nudged the suitcase out of her way and settled on the bed. "Yes, I'm home."

"How'd you make out?"

We didn't make out, she wanted to say—it was just one kiss. But of course that wasn't what he was asking, and even if it was, she'd never give him that answer.

"You're going to have another full bath upstairs," she reported. "The solarium has been simplified into a very functional mudroom, the kitchen, living room, dining room and family room are all going to be on the same level and those nooks in the entry are going to be redone so they're dustable."

"Dustable?"

"Capable of being dusted. I did pretty well, Gerald. The wine cellar is going to be a self-contained unit, so you can try it out in the pantry and if you decide you need extra space, the whole unit can be moved without too much difficulty."

"Uh-huh." His tone implied that he knew she wasn't done.

"Holt wouldn't budge on the glass wall in the kitchen."

"But you said it would suck all the heat out of the house."

"It probably will, but he was really stubborn about it. He said that if you insisted on getting rid of that wall he would tear up the blueprint and charge you a kill fee."

"A kill fee?"

She sighed. Gerald was a genius when it came to high technology, but he was hopeless on the most basic business concepts. "That's the fee you'd have to pay to back out of the deal. It's in the contract, and it's not something you'd want to pay, because after paying it you'd wind up with nothing."

"Nothing at all?"

"A torn-up blueprint."

"Okay." He considered that prospect for a moment. "How about the other stuff?"

"The only other big item was the fireplace in the master bedroom. He was stubborn about that, too."

"Stubborn, as in I'd have to pay a kill fee?"

"Pretty much so."

"What am I going to do with my bedroom furniture?"

"Put it in one of the other bedrooms and order custom-made pieces for this room."

"I don't get it," Gerald muttered. "The glass wall in the kitchen, okay, it's this spectacular thing for people to ooh and aah over. But the fireplace—what's the big deal about that?"

"I know this will strike you as a bizarre concept, but Levi says it will make the master bedroom romantic."

"Romantic? Why should I care about that?"

Corinne couldn't help laughing. The question was so *Gerald*. Not only was he hopeless in the context of business matters, but he was clueless on the subject of romance. That was one of the things Corinne liked best about him. *Deceptive* and *seductive* were not part of his vocabulary. He thought scoring was something baseball teams did. It would not occur to him to lure a woman upstairs to his bedroom, lay a fire and then lay the woman.

Corinne was utterly safe with him.

And she liked safety; she really did. Risks were fun in the corporate world, but in matters of the heart… She'd seen what had happened to her parents when they'd taken romantic risks. Divorces. Remarriages. More divorces. Splintered families, fractured hearts, bitter recriminations—and for Corinne, moves from house to house, from parent to parent. What was the point? Where was the payoff for that kind of pain?

"Anyway, the bottom line is that the new price on delivery is thirty thousand more. The bathroom was a big-ticket item. The other stuff, the expense of modifying the designs, was for the most part offset by the simplification of the specs. The solarium would have cost a bit more than the mudroom, so while Levi is charging you to alter the design, he's deducting the difference in price and it's pretty much a wash."

Gerald said nothing.

"I did the best I could," she added.

"Let me ask you this," Gerald posed. "The way it is now, is it a house *you* could live in?"

She frowned. What was he *really* asking? Her objective opinion on the house's livability, or something more?

Good grief, she didn't even want to think about what that "something more" could be. A month ago—even a day ago—she'd have had no trouble thinking about it, but now...

Now, she'd kissed Levi Holt. A simple kiss, a meaningless kiss, a kiss that had led to several long hours of hard negotiations interrupted only by breaks for coffee and D.J.'s assorted antics. If she hadn't been distracted by the baby she might have gotten the fireplace out of the bedroom, or wheedled the new price down a few thousand dollars. But D.J. had been pawing at her leg, pinching her stockings and trying, incredibly, to pull himself to his feet. She'd been afraid he would hurt himself or tear her stockings.

Or maybe she hadn't been afraid of anything. Maybe she'd just wanted to hold him one more time.

So she'd taken him onto her lap, where he'd snuggled up against her and sat calmly. She'd felt strategically stronger with him in her arms—two against one, Levi's nephew turning his back on his substitute father and choosing to side with Corinne. Yet somehow, once she'd had D.J. in her arms, her arguments against the wall of glass had lost their potency.

Perhaps D.J. had been a double agent, cuddling up to her in order to sap her of her power.

What did it matter? Neither he nor his uncle was relevant to her life anymore. She'd finished dealing with Levi and left Arlington. The Holt boys were history.

"Corey?"

She realized she hadn't answered Gerald's question. "Sure, I could live in it," she said, choosing not to mull over the question's subtext.

"Good. So, have you had supper yet? I could pick up some Chinese and come over."

She considered his offer. If he came over, they'd eat General Gao's chicken and mu-shu pork and talk about the client Gerald was counseling to upgrade the technology behind his online venture before he attempted an IPO—initial public offering. They'd talk until midnight, and then Gerald would pat her shoulder or maybe—if he was in a particularly affectionate mood—kiss her cheek, and he'd leave.

It would be a way to ensure that she wouldn't spend the evening seated on her bed, gazing toward her window at the apartment building across the street and thinking about letting in the night. She wouldn't be thinking about an expanse of woods and a screened-in porch and the soothing rhythm of a baby's respiration whispering through an intercom speaker.

She certainly wouldn't be thinking, hours later, about any kiss Gerald had given her.

"I'm pretty tired," she demurred. "I'll see you at the office tomorrow, okay?"

"Sure thing." He wasn't even savvy enough to recognize that he'd been rejected. And honestly, Corinne wasn't rejecting him. She loved him. He was Gerald.

But tonight—tonight she wanted to think about the world outside her window, a universe dark yet full of life. She wanted to think about a baby who'd tucked himself into her arms as if he belonged there, and about a man who'd kissed her lips as if he belonged there, too.

She wanted to think about things she'd never thought about before.

"WHAT I'M SAYING," Levi bellowed, "is that the courtyard is adding a lot to the overall price and it's not contributing enough to the design. It's going to keep us out of the running." He had to yell because D.J. was howling. The kid had awakened from his nap in a royal snit, and neither a bottle nor an application of ointment to his gums had soothed him. Since Levi, Bill and Phyllis were meeting downstairs in the main room, the entire building, from the carpeted floor to the raftered thirty-foot-high ceiling, echoed with D.J.'s wails.

Phyllis glared at the squalling baby on Levi's shoulder before arguing, "The courtyard is essential to the design. We can't submit this proposal without it."

"I agree. But I think you've got to make the courtyard do more than it's doing the way it is now. Maybe plant some trees in it, turn it into a garden."

"That will increase the price even more."

"Yeah, but the courtyard will be making a clearer

statement,'' Levi rationalized, then muttered, ''can it, D.J., would you?''

''Maybe you should stuff a sock in his mouth,'' Bill grumbled. Levi heard him, because at that very moment D.J. chose to shut up. The violence in Bill's suggestion should have offended Levi, but he couldn't blame his partners. They resented his bringing D.J. to work. Hell, *he* resented it, too.

''The nanny starts on Monday,'' he assured Bill and Phyllis.

Phyllis used her hand to brush back her straight gray hair. In her late fifties, she'd become an architect at a time when most women had felt constrained to choose between motherhood and a career. She'd opted for a career, and she'd enjoyed great success with her soaring urban designs, like the office-residential tower they were discussing right now, which she intended to submit to a Boston developer currently accepting bids. But Levi couldn't help wondering whether his sudden surrogate fatherhood irritated her in some personal way.

Well, of course it irritated her. It irritated everyone. She and Bill and all the associates were working at one hundred percent strength, and Levi was giving only fifty percent. The other fifty percent was consumed by D.J.

At least he'd reached an agreement on the Mosley project. Sure, it was a project he'd landed before D.J. had entered his life, but it had almost gotten away from him, and he'd reeled it back in. He'd made some compromises, but he'd kept the kitchen the way he'd visualized it, the way the house demanded, the way Mosley and anyone else who ever entered that house would appreciate it. His project wouldn't bring in as big a commission as Phyllis's Boston project, but it represented a nice payday for the partnership, and even with D.J. mixed into the negotiations, Levi had managed to get the thing done.

One small, perplexed part of him suspected that D.J.'s interference might have actually *helped*, that the baby's presence had been instrumental in persuading Corinne to compromise.

He couldn't figure out what it was between them. An acceptance, an affinity, almost a collusion. When Corinne was around, D.J. acted differently. He was less agitated, more attentive. They connected on some nonverbal level. Just as her nearness seemed to calm D.J., his nearness seemed to soften her. Once she'd lifted him into her lap yesterday morning, her arguments had seemed blunted, and she'd ultimately capitulated on the design features most important to Levi.

On the other hand, maybe D.J. had had nothing to do with it. Maybe Levi's kiss had convinced her.

Hell, that kiss had sure done something to him.

She'd left town after their meeting, and he missed her. It was ridiculous; she was just a client's representative. Levi's only significance to her was as an architect she disagreed with on a few items.

But he'd kissed her. Just once, just a light, friendly, PG-rated kiss, but it had been like a taste of a rich gourmet treat, so delicious it had made him ravenous. He wanted more.

He had to ignore the want. She was back home in New York and he had a baby to take care of—and a couple of partners who were not very happy with him at the moment. D.J. wasn't terribly happy, either. He whimpered and shoved at Levi, performing isometric exercises against his shoulder and arm and occasionally head-butting him for good measure. Two of the associates had wandered off to a corner of the room to huddle, as far from D.J.'s high-decibel bleating as they could get. Levi wished he could join them there.

"All right," Phyllis said, studying her design on the computer monitor. "We could plant a few trees in the courtyard."

"Make it a garden—*oof!*" He grunted as D.J. gave him a sharp kick to his diaphragm. "A garden spot. A bit of outside trapped within the building. Don't just plant the trees—incorporate them. Make them the reason for the courtyard's existence."

"It's a good idea," Bill agreed, then smiled faintly at Levi. "Why don't you go someplace and mellow the kid out. He's really being disruptive."

"I'm sorry," Levi mumbled, suppressing a touch of envy over the fact that, while Phyllis had forgone children for her career, Bill was able to enjoy both children and a career because he had a wife at home to handle the parenting chores. She'd been a math teacher until Bill's first child was born, and she'd declared she would return to teaching when the children were older, but in the meantime, Bill never had to worry about who was going to watch his babies while he was at work.

Phyllis gave Levi's free arm a squeeze. Everyone at Arlington Architectural Associates knew why he had a disruptive baby perched on his shoulder. They sympathized. Bill had donated the crib D.J. now slept in—his youngest was two years old and had graduated to a junior bed—and the entire staff had chipped in and bought a collection of toys for the baby. "We thought it would be more sensible than flowers,'' Phyllis had explained.

But for all their condolences and compassion, they were sick of listening to D.J. screech and squawk. Levi was sick of it, too.

"Monday," he repeated. "The nanny starts Monday."

"And we're all counting the minutes," Bill teased. "Go take him for a drive. That might knock him out."

"I have some other ideas," Levi said, gesturing with his free hand toward the computer monitor. "You might consider widening the entry a little. That would make it look more welcoming—*ow!*" D.J. had given him another sharp kick in the solar plexus. The kid had the makings of an Olympics-caliber judo expert, or perhaps a bouncer in a bar.

"Get out of here," Bill ordered him.

Nodding and rubbing his lower ribs, Levi spun around and strode toward the door.

He was less gentle than he might have been while strapping D.J. into his car seat, but D.J. didn't seem to mind. Levi had learned over the past month that D.J. preferred rough-and-tumble to gentle. He liked being tossed around, being hoisted into his car seat, being treated with a level of physical force Levi wouldn't have considered appropriate for a baby. Maybe it was because D.J. was a boy, or because he had outgrown his newborn fragility. He liked to roll around on the floor, crawl, ricochet off the walls in his walker—and he liked when his uncle Levi manhandled him. For the first time in thirty minutes, D.J. stopped crying.

Levi resisted the temptation to race back inside and

finish discussing the office building entry with Phyllis. Bill was right; a spin around town would probably lull D.J. to sleep, and if Levi paced the drive correctly, he could get back to the office in time to work for another hour before the kid woke up and started screaming again.

Lacking a better idea, he headed west, figuring he'd check out the site of the Mosley house. After Corinne had left his office yesterday, he'd sent word to his construction engineer that he should go ahead and start digging the foundation. He might as well see how things were progressing there.

The west side of Arlington was deceptively rural. It looked pastoral because the houses were set far apart on sprawling acreage, but no one actually farmed all that acreage. What farms existed in the Arlington area—small vegetable farms and apple orchards—flanked the eastern end of town.

But the west side was where the interesting architectural specimens were. West siders were, for the most part, wealthy weekenders and urban expatriates. They'd buy parcels of land, tear down whatever structures currently stood on that land and then hire architects like Levi to build their mini Xanadus for them.

His first commission had been on a house on the west side. A newspaper reporter who'd become a syndicated columnist had bought a small, run-down ranch house and had asked Arlington Architectural Associates for some ideas on how to expand it. Bill and Phyllis had given the assignment to their new associate—Levi, fresh out of architecture school, the ink still damp on his diploma. He'd developed a whimsical design of extensions spreading out from the core of the house. There had been lots of windows, lots of glass, a screened porch. No dark rooms, no low ceilings, no imprisoning gloom. Nothing that could even remotely resemble the house Levi had grown up in.

"You don't know how lucky you are," Levi murmured to D.J., who was making pleasant cooing sounds in his car seat behind Levi's right shoulder. "You've had some lousy breaks, but I'll never let you grow up in a house like that. I swear it, buddy. You have my solemn vow."

"Da!"

"That's right. Da." Around a bend in the road, Levi spotted a man approaching the mailbox at the mouth of his driveway. "There's my very first client, D.J. Would you like to meet him?"

"Da!"

"Yes, he's someone's dad." Just by reading Jamie McCoy's *Guy Stuff* column in the *Arlington Gazette,* Levi would have known this. Jamie based his weekly essays on his own life, and over the past couple of years they'd often dealt with his experiences with his daughter. Until a month ago, Levi had found such columns amusing but not particularly relevant.

They still weren't particularly relevant, but he could now read them with a small degree of personal expertise, and he could laugh and groan and nod over Jamie's descriptions of paternal frustration.

He slowed the car as Jamie reached his mailbox. Jamie glanced at Levi, apparently recognized him and broke into a grin. "Levi Holt!"

Levi stopped and rolled down his window. "Hey, Jamie. How's the house?"

"We may need a new extension on it. No joke— my wife wants another child."

"She can have this one if she'd like," Levi muttered, jerking his head toward D.J.

Jamie leaned down and peered through the window. "Hey, there, big guy! How's it going?" He turned his gaze back to Levi. "I guess you've been doing a lot of living since I last saw you."

Levi shook his head. "Not that kind of living. He's my sister's son. She passed away unexpectedly and named me his legal guardian."

"Oh. Wow." Jamie frowned. "That sucks."

Levi remembered why he'd always liked Jamie McCoy. Not only was the man more open-minded and easier to work with than certain other clients, who sent headstrong, beautiful women to Arlington to fight their battles for them, but he was frank and unpretentious. He said what he was thinking and didn't lapse into platitudes.

"Daddy! Daddy!" A child's shrill voice drifted down the gravel driveway, followed by the child it belonged to—a cheerful girl in denim shorts and a gray T-shirt reading Dartmouth Athletic Department, a miniature version of the T-shirt Jamie was wearing with his denim shorts. The girl had on bright-pink sneakers rather than ratty white ones like her father's, and all manner of sparkly hairclips adorned her mop of curls. "Daddy, I saw a cappapillar!"

"Caterpillar," Jamie corrected her. "Wanna see something even cooler?" He lifted her up so she could peek through the car window. "It's a baby!"

"Ba! Baaa!" D.J. was clearly excited by the sight of a child, even if she was more than twice his age. "Ba-baa!"

"Baby!" the little girl cheered. "Why is he saying ba-baa?"

"He can't talk yet," her father told her.

"That's stupid." The girl wriggled out of his embrace and romped back up the driveway, apparently preferring caterpillars to humans.

"She's going to make an inspiring big sister," Jamie said, then snorted. "Obnoxious twerp. I've got to work on her manners." He peeked back into the car. "I don't think you're stupid," he reassured D.J., who squealed with laughter.

Levi observed Jamie's obvious ease with his daughter and D.J. When Levi had first met him, he'd been a bachelor, defiantly boyish and carefree. How had he journeyed from that blissfully adolescent condition through the state Levi was in—responsibility seasoned with equal measures of panic, resentment and overprotectiveness—to an emotional level of relaxed equanimity?

"How old is your daughter?" he asked.

"Just graduating from the Terrible Twos."

"Is she terrible?"

"She's the stuff of nightmares," Jamie boasted, then laughed. "Her current passions are graham crackers, Hootie and the Blowfish and Lego. And caterpillars," he added. "Last week's passions were raisins, dinosaurs and Disney sing-along videos. Next week's passions will probably be kumquats, skydiving and Armani."

"But you're weathering it okay?" Levi needed reassurance, even though he could not imagine a time D.J. would ever be interested in Armani. Caterpillars and skydiving, yes, but not high fashion.

"Oh, Sammy and I are doing great. She's the best thing that ever happened to me. I don't know—maybe she's tied with Allison for the best thing. Allison's my wife."

Levi supposed having a wife would make weathering a child's first few years a hell of a lot easier.

"I didn't know the first thing about babies," Jamie remarked, his gaze wandering back and forth between Levi and D.J. "Thank God for Allison. She teaches classes in fathering."

"She does?" Levi sat straighter. What was it his lawyer had said yesterday? Something about classes...

"The Daddy School," Jamie told him. "She and her best friend founded it. She's a neonatal nurse, her friend runs a preschool, and they put together a dynamite program. Plus it's free, although they accept donations."

"The Daddy School," Levi repeated, nodding. "That was what Murphy was talking about."

"Murphy? Dennis Murphy? That's right—I seem to remember he was on retainer with your architecture firm. He's my lawyer, too, on the rare occasions I need one. His sister-in-law is my wife's best friend—the preschool teacher who does Daddy School with Allison."

"Small world."

"Hey, welcome to Arlington." Jamie glanced at D.J. one last time, then straightened up. "Allison teaches Daddy School classes Monday evenings at the YMCA. Seven-thirty. Give it a try. She's good."

"You're completely unbiased," Levi joked.

"Absolutely."

"Daddy!" His daughter's voice pierced the afternoon air.

Jamie sighed, although he clearly wasn't upset

when he muttered, "The princess requires her knight in shining armor. Listen, I'm serious about tacking on another room. I'll be in touch, okay?"

"Sure." Levi didn't let his eagerness show, but he felt it inside. Another commission—even if it was only a one-room addition—would make him feel he was contributing to the firm. Despite being saddled with D.J., so saddled he'd had to leave work to calm the child down, Levi could pull his own weight. He could get the job done. "Give me a call and I'll put something together for you."

"Great. Take it easy—and good luck with the kid. Trust me, Levi, fatherhood is a cinch once you get the hang of it. Okay, well, not a cinch. But kids are kids. They're exactly like us, only smaller."

Levi laughed.

"Seven-thirty Monday at the Y," Jamie called over his shoulder. "You'll thank me for recommending it."

Maybe Levi would thank him. He probably did need some lessons in how to be a daddy. He'd been winging it, grabbing scraps of advice from colleagues and neighbors and figuring out the rest on his own. A few classes might accelerate his learning curve.

It wouldn't hurt. And what else did he have to do on a Monday night? Sit on his back porch, staring out at the woods behind his house and thinking about the woman who'd once shared that back porch with him, and that view?

She was gone, and he had his own life to live—a life dominated by a needy little boy. Definitely, a few classes would help.

CHAPTER SEVEN

GLANCING UP, Corinne saw Gerald looming in her office doorway, his bespectacled blue eyes zeroing in on her and his grin cutting a toothy crescent into his face.

As usual, he was dressed in a sloppy T-shirt, baggy khakis and battered skateboarding shoes; as usual, his hair was a melee of reddish-brown waves that appeared not to have been subjected to the civilizing influence of a comb in the past several days.

As usual, the sight of him made Corinne smile.

"That guy from Bell Tech is a jerk," Gerald announced, failing to look as peeved as he sounded. "How much is he paying us?"

"Enough that you'd better not call him a jerk to his face."

"We don't need the money," Gerald pointed out.

Maybe he didn't need it. He was much richer than Corinne. When he'd sold his company, the profit she'd earned from her shares had left her wealthier than she'd ever dreamed, but she wasn't in Gerald's league financially. If she retired on what she had, she could get by with careful stinting and constant monitoring—but she didn't want to stint and monitor every penny. She liked living comfortably, worry-free.

Besides, she enjoyed working. She was too young

to retire. So was Gerald. Consulting kept them busy and challenged.

It also gave them something to complain about. "He's a pompous ass," Gerald grumbled. "He interrupts me all the time and doesn't listen to anything I say."

"His VP of marketing listens to everything we say," Corinne assured him.

He entered her office and slumped into a chair. His pants were too long, and she noticed that the hems were frayed from being dragged along the floor. Gerald was an inch shorter than Corinne, but his height didn't seem to bother him. A good barber, a good tailor and a pair of contact lenses could transform him into the sort of man most women would stop to admire.

The thing was, he didn't care—either about his appearance or about most women. On the rare occasions he dated, he always whined to Corinne afterward about the women he'd been with: "All they want to talk about is TV shows. I don't watch TV. I don't know what I'm supposed to say when they remark, 'This is such a *Sex and the City* moment!'" Or, "We saw this movie about a meteor that was going to destroy the earth, but the science was so bogus! It made no sense. I tried to explain why it couldn't happen, but she didn't want to hear it. She got all upset with me for suggesting the science wasn't right."

"You have the social skills of a turnip," Corinne would chide him. "Maybe you should spend more time watching TV and less time picking apart the scientific fantasies in movies."

"Maybe I should stick with you," Gerald would

respond. "You're the only woman in the world who puts up with me. You're smart, you're funny and—"

"I'm beautiful," she would coach him.

"Yeah, that, too." He'd reward her with his bright, toothy smile and she'd laugh and give him a hug.

She wasn't interested in hugging him today. She wasn't interested in shooting the breeze with him, either. She wanted to finish reviewing the files on her desk. As soon as she was done, she intended to lock up her office and leave town.

As if sensing her impatience, Gerald surveyed the small room and spotted her overnight bag in the corner behind her desk. "What's that? You're running away from home?"

"Just getting out of the city for the weekend," she said, wondering why she hesitated to tell Gerald the truth. Not that her answer was a lie, but it certainly hadn't been complete. She didn't know how to explain to him what she hadn't yet been able to explain to herself.

She wasn't "just getting out of the city for the weekend." She was going to Arlington, Connecticut. She would catch one of the commuter-line trains— they left Grand Central Station every half hour or so. She'd booked a room at the Arlington Inn for Friday and Saturday night and reserved a car at the auto rental outlet adjacent to the train station.

Addressing the logistics of her two-day jaunt had been simple enough. Addressing the impulse behind it wasn't so simple. Predicting what would happen once she reached her destination was impossible.

She hadn't told Levi she was coming. She wasn't even sure she wanted to see him. Thinking about him was like riding a roller coaster, her opinion soaring and plummeting and twisting around itself. But seeing D.J....

She felt a need to be with him, a compulsion, an implacable urge to wrap her arms around his sturdy little body, to inhale his baby powder scent and nuzzle his wispy hair with her chin, to give him a bottle and feel him grow heavy in her embrace as he dozed. She wanted to hold him, stroke his velvety cheek, sing him a lullaby. She wanted to connect with him the way she had one strange evening a week ago.

She couldn't begin to figure out why she felt such a strong need to see D.J. Her yearning to hold him was irrational. She wasn't into babies. No biological clock ticked deafeningly in her soul.

Maybe she was turning into an eccentric, a weird spinster obsessing over someone else's baby. Today she might be focused on D.J., and tomorrow she'd be adopting thirty cats. In another month she might stop showering and start talking to herself.

The image gave her a quiet chuckle. Just because she wanted to visit Levi's nephew didn't mean she was in any danger of cracking up. She didn't even want to spend a lot of time in the baby's company. Just an hour or two, long enough to peer into his chocolate-brown eyes—eyes that resembled his uncle's in an uncanny way—and let his warmth embrace her—a warmth that was utterly unlike the warmth she felt in Levi's presence.

She reminded herself over and over that Levi wasn't the one she was traveling to Arlington to see. She wasn't even sure she liked the man. He hadn't played fair with her when she'd been in Arlington last week. He'd been tricky and slippery. He'd kissed her just enough to scramble her brain, and then he'd rammed his own version of Gerald's dream house into the contract.

That stupid wall of glass. It was Levi's conceit, and he'd kissed her so she'd be too muddled to fight him on it.

She wasn't sure why the glass bothered her so much, other than for the practical reasons that all the heat would seep out through the glass in the winter and in through the glass in the summer. But Gerald would probably adjust to it easily enough. He'd think it was awesome, and he'd be oblivious to the effect it had on the temperature of the house's interior. Nor would he be concerned when he saw the heating bills, or the air-conditioning bills. Details like those usually blew right past him.

He'd told her he was satisfied with the job she'd done in altering the design as much as she did and in holding Levi to a relatively small increase in the price. It was going to be his house, after all. Not hers.

Unless he asked her to marry him. It wasn't a particularly far-fetched notion. They were best friends, after all. They spent more time with each other than with anyone else. If Gerald ever proposed to her, she would smile, but she wouldn't laugh.

She'd also probably say no, given the way she felt now.

Damn. She didn't know *how* she felt, other than out of sorts, restless, as if something were missing inside her, leaving behind an empty, echoing hollow. When she thought about it, she believed that space carried D.J.'s shape. He would fit into it so neatly, so perfectly.

Just for a while, a couple of hours, a day or two. Just until she stopped aching.

It occurred to her that Gerald was staring at her quizzically. Had he been talking to her? She'd missed every word.

"So, where will you be?" he asked.

"I don't know," she fibbed. If she shared her feelings with him, he would probably recommend a few sessions with a shrink. "I'll have my cell phone with me, if you need to contact me."

"When are you leaving?"

"As soon as I finish reviewing these files." She twisted her wrist to see her watch. "Three o'clock the latest."

"You're acting mysterious, Corey."

"There's no mystery. I just need a little time by myself."

"Are you having a midlife crisis?"

Although she laughed, she was touched by his concern. "I haven't even turned thirty yet. I don't think you can have a midlife crisis until you're at least forty."

"Yeah, but you're so organized and prompt. You always get things done ahead of time."

She laughed again.

Gerald didn't join her. "Seriously, Corey—I depend on you to be the stable one around here. Don't flip out on me, okay?"

"I wouldn't dream of flipping out on you," she said in her most reassuring voice. She only wished she could reassure herself. Chasing up to Arlington to hold the six-month-old nephew of a man she didn't trust, a man whose kiss had dazed her, a man who viewed houses as philosophical statements rather than places to live in safety and comfort...

Maybe she *was* flipping out. But the only way she

could imagine flipping back in again was to return to the site of her madness, confront it, figure it out and fix it. That was what Corinne did best: fix problems. Straighten out messes. Put things to rights.

One weekend in Arlington ought to fix everything. At least, she hoped it would.

LEVI HATED wearing a hard hat, especially in the summer. The heat made him feel as though his brain were baking inside the unventilated plastic. But rules were rules. Everyone wore hard hats at active construction sites.

And unlike the crew, he'd only had to don his hat a couple of minutes ago. They'd been working all day, finishing work on the footings so the foundation could be laid on Monday. He'd gotten to spend most of the day in the comfort of his office, his head blessedly free of plastic protection. He'd only decided to loop past the site a few minutes ago, to see how things were progressing.

He could take the time to visit building sites now. Martina Lopes, D.J.'s nanny, had liberated him. D.J. no longer set the agenda and decreed, in his raucous preverbal way, how Levi could allocate his time.

He wasn't sure why he didn't feel freer. He *was* freer. But even though D.J. no longer occupied Levi's office during business hours, sleeping and eating and howling and otherwise interfering with Levi's ability to function as a professional, the baby remained a constant presence, an incessant clamor in Levi's mind.

He'd spent the week catching up on all the work he'd neglected from the time he'd brought D.J. home from California to that past Monday, when Martina had appeared on his front porch at 8:00 a.m. and sent him off with assurances that she and D.J. were going to be fine and Levi had nothing to worry about. Besides catching up, he'd devoted a fair amount of time to collaborating with Phyllis on her proposal for the tower in Boston. He'd felt good getting back to his old workaholic routines, and even better escaping the oppressive presence of D.J. for eight or nine hours a day.

But while he could escape D.J., he couldn't escape thoughts of him. Every time Levi glanced at his watch, a part of his mind calculated how much more time he'd be able to work before he would have to go home and relieve Martina—and another part calculated how long he'd been away from D.J. and how soon they'd be together again.

It was insane. He'd never expected to become a father; he sure hadn't wished for it. He'd been so damned grateful when Martina finally started working for him. Ridding himself of the responsibility of twenty-four/seven parenting had been like shedding the residue of a construction site, the layer of dirt and plaster dust. He'd felt as if he'd scrubbed himself clean and his skin could breathe again.

But something was missing when he was at work, away from D.J. He knew it, he felt it and it irked him.

The project foreman strode over to where Levi was lounging against the front bumper of his car. "Hey, Levi," Rick Bailey shouted above the racket of construction equipment, the engines of the trucks and tractors rumbling as they crawled over the site. "What's up?"

"Just thought I'd see how things were looking." Together they gazed across the scruffy grass at the concrete footings drying in the hole excavated for the foundation. Levi had worked with Rick on projects before, and trusted him to do the job right. He hoped his appearance at the site didn't make Rick think Levi was checking up on him.

"Things are looking good," Rick assured him as he dug into the hip pocket of his jeans. He pulled out a handkerchief and mopped the sweat from his face.

"Great."

Rick eyed him expectantly. Maybe Levi ought to say something more. But what? *I'm dying to go home and make sure D.J. is okay, but I'm afraid of turning into some fanatical, doting daddy, so I thought I'd waste some time here.* No, he didn't think so.

What was it Jamie's wife had said at the Daddy School class he'd attended Monday night? Allison Winslow, the neonatal nurse at Arlington Memorial Hospital, had talked about how babies sucked a piece of your soul into themselves and you never got it back. Most of her talk had focused on all the other things babies sucked into themselves: milk and formula, pureed bananas, rug lint and, if parents weren't vigilant, all manner of small items that could lodge in a tiny throat and choke the child. Levi had listened, jotted some notes about age appropriateness for certain foods and promised himself he'd do another inspection of his house to make sure there were no buttons or thumb tacks or other tempting objects within D.J.'s reach.

But the one comment of hers that had resonated with him was how babies also devoured a piece of a parent's soul, and once they did, the parent could never get it back.

He'd never imagined taking care of a child would

be like that. He certainly hadn't sucked pieces of his parents' souls from them. They'd raised their children to be dutiful little soldiers—do as you're told, don't question authority, don't expose yourself to contradictory ideas, challenging opinions or anything that disagrees with the truth as we've taught it to you—but their parenting had been curiously soulless. The predominant theme had been blind obedience.

Levi had rebelled. So had Ruth. That was why he'd wound up an architect in Connecticut and she'd become a weaver in northern California.

Levi wondered if she'd felt the profound attachment to D.J. that he felt, the sense that D.J. owned a critical chunk of her and would always own it, that one small but significant sliver of her identity had been absorbed by him. If she were alive, Levi could ask her. But then, if she were alive, he wouldn't have D.J. Right about now, he'd be packing for his annual trip to California, looking forward to meeting his nephew for the first time.

Instead, his sister was dead and he was feeling as if D.J. had been a part of his life forever. As if D.J. owned him. As if when D.J. wasn't nearby, wailing or wreaking havoc, pooping or shrieking nonsense syllables, something was missing from Levi's existence.

During this first week with Martina taking care of D.J., Levi had suffered phantom pains, as if one of his limbs had been amputated. Even when he arrived home every evening and sent Martina on her way, the pain never completely disappeared.

As soon as she left and Levi took over, D.J. would invariably lapse into rambunctious behavior. Levi would give D.J. teething toys to chew on, prepare some boiled mashed carrots or peas for the kid—in the Daddy School, Allison Winslow had explained how easy it was to make fresh baby food, and he was giving it a try—change D.J.'s diapers, bathe him and try to quiet him down for the night. Through it all D.J. would gurgle and babble and kick and pull at him. He'd splash water out of the tub, pee the instant Levi fastened a fresh diaper onto him, spit up fluids tinted orange from the mashed carrots he'd eaten. And Levi would wonder how he could possibly miss such a monster.

Rick was relating a joke one of the guys had told him over lunch, something involving a variety of religious leaders in a bar, and Levi tried to pay attention, laughing when he sensed Rick had reached the punch line. But his mind was elsewhere. At least the part of his mind possessed by D.J. was.

The sound of a car steering along the dirt path from the road caught his attention. Rick must have heard it, too, because he spun around and squinted at the approaching vehicle. "This seems to be the hot spot today," he muttered. "We were just getting ready to pack it in, and now we've got more company."

"If you're finished, go," Levi urged him. "Tell the guys to have a good weekend." He returned his gaze to the car. As the low-riding sun slid light across the windshield, the driver turned into nothing but a shadow. But the car kept coming, veering slightly so the glare vanished from the windshield, and then he recognized the driver.

What was Corinne Lanier doing here? Had she come back to continue their debate about the house's design? Had she finally realized that while she'd won a few battles, he'd won the war last week, and he was going to build a magnificent house over her petty objections?

And why, even though he suspected she had returned to Arlington only to hassle him, did a weight seem to lift off his back as she drew near, a cloud seem to glide from directly above him to the horizon and beyond? Why did those phantom pains hurt a little less?

"Do you know who that is?" Rick asked, shielding his eyes with his hand in an effort to identify the woman behind the wheel.

"She works for the guy who's buying this house."

"Oh, great." Rick pulled a face. "Don't tell me she's going to be here all the time, micromanaging the job."

"She won't." Levi could offer no basis for that conclusion, but he sensed in his gut that she hadn't come to Arlington to interfere with the work crew. If she was going to get in anyone's way, it would be his, not Rick's. "Don't worry about her. I can handle her." Right. He could really handle a woman with her brains, her determination, her big hazel eyes and her long legs.

He remembered that brief kiss they'd exchanged in his office last week. Actually, they hadn't exactly exchanged it. He'd taken it, and she'd given it—without much resistance, he recalled. Maybe she'd come here to take the kiss back.

He'd gladly give it and more.

Thinking about kissing her made his phantom pains fade even more. As long as he could become fixated with her merely by watching her through the sheen of light on the car's windshield, as long as he could be affected by his memory of the shy pressure of her lips beneath his, the silken texture of her hand when he'd touched it and the deceptively delicate quality of her voice, he could believe he was more than just D.J.'s replacement father. He could believe he was actually a normal, healthy man, someone who responded to a woman, someone whose entire life didn't revolve around a six-month-old boy.

She shut off the engine. As the door opened and she swung her legs out of the car, Rick frowned. "You sure you can handle her?"

Levi slid a glance at him. "Watch me," he said, hoping he wouldn't make a fool of himself with Rick as his witness. He smiled, pushed away from his own car and strode toward her.

She stood, and he saw right away that her own smile was uneasy, almost apprehensive.

"Hello, Corinne," he greeted her smoothly, hand outstretched. "I guess you can't stay away, can you."

Something flickered in her expression, a spark of light illuminating her eyes for a fraction of a second. "I don't know," she answered. "Maybe I can't."

She sounded so uncertain, so bewildered, he couldn't take any pride in the knowledge that he was handling her. "As you can see, some heavy work is going on here. If you want to look around, you're going to have to wear a hard hat."

She peered at his helmet, and for a brief moment her smile looked genuine. "Do you have one in burgundy?" she asked, gesturing toward her tailored skirt.

His gaze followed her hand, but instead of noticing the color of her skirt, he noticed the legs that extended below the above-the-knee hem. God, she had great legs, the calf muscles strongly curved, the ankles narrow, the knees oval knobs of bone that struck him as absurdly sexy. He'd like to touch her knees, caress them. Kiss them.

If he kept thinking that way, he wouldn't be able to handle her at all. "Sorry," he said. "The hats only come in bright colors for added visibility. Glow-in-the-dark yellow, glow-in-the-dark orange, glow-in-the-dark blue."

"Well, then, I guess I won't look around. What's that—the foundation?" she asked, pointing to the low walls of concrete embedded in the ground.

"The footings. The foundation goes on top of them."

"I see." Her nod told him she didn't really see, but she'd prefer not to receive a detailed lecture on the subject.

Rick was still observing them. Levi motioned toward him. "That's Rick Bailey, the site foreman. Best in the business. He'll make sure everything's built the way it's supposed to be."

She eyed the burly man. Rick's shoulders were small mountains, his chest thick, his waistline showing only a hint of incipient middle-age paunchiness beneath his snug-fitting T-shirt and battered blue jeans. "I'm glad. I mean, Gerald will be glad."

Rick nodded and touched his hard hat in a friendly salute, then sauntered back to the center of the action, his thick-soled work boots leaving patterned treads in the soft earth.

"So, what's going on?" Levi asked, then realized that wasn't the most diplomatic way to find out whether she'd come here to see the construction site or him. "I mean, what brings you to Arlington?"

She considered her answer long enough to convince him it wasn't a simple one. "I don't know," she finally admitted. "I've been thinking about the house, and wanting to get out of the city, and...I don't know."

Interesting. Peculiar but definitely interesting. "Do you have plans for dinner?"

She sighed, such a deep, wistful breath he wanted to give her a reassuring hug. Although damned if he knew what she needed to be reassured about.

Squaring her shoulders, she smiled pensively. "No, I don't have plans for dinner."

She was free tonight and she'd smiled at him. He saw all sorts of potential in the moment. "Maybe I can rustle up a baby-sitter and we could go somewhere," he suggested. With more warning, he would have planned something classy—dinner at Reynaud, for instance. But Arlington's most elegant restaurant required reservations secured way in advance. No way would he be able to get a table for two there tonight.

In fact, he'd be lucky to get a baby-sitter. While Tara might be available on short notice on a weeknight, having her sit on a Friday night probably required advance reservations, too.

"Don't get a baby-sitter," she said. "I'd like to see D.J."

"You would?" The moment lost a bit of its potential. "I was thinking of dining out." It occurred to him that he hadn't eaten at a restaurant since D.J. had entered his life. He used to like going to restaurants.

"Surely there are restaurants babies are allowed to go to," she said with a smile.

"McDonald's," he suggested.

"For example."

"Not exactly gourmet cuisine."

"No, but D.J. would fit right in."

Levi assessed the situation, his lips pressed together to prevent him from blurting out that an outing to McDonald's accompanied by D.J. was not the way he'd choose to spend an evening with Corinne. If the glow in her eyes was anything to go by, dinner with D.J. at Mickey-D's was exactly the way she'd choose to spend the evening.

Once again he recalled what his friends had told him, about how certain women were turned on by men who were attached to babies. He'd never have pegged Corinne for that kind of woman. She was single and pretty obviously childless, and she didn't coo and gush over the kid the way some women might. The night she'd had dinner at his house, she'd held D.J., but she hadn't talked baby talk or recited "This Little Piggy" while playing with his toes. She hadn't pinched his cheek and called him precious.

Instead, she'd acted as though D.J. were a fascinating inconvenience. She'd looked perplexed but curious as she'd held him, neither welcoming nor objecting to what had obviously been a new experience. Her expression had closely mirrored his emotions when he'd first taken custody of D.J., that vaguely panicked, vaguely awed sense of "How did I get into this, and what am I supposed to do next?"

"McDonald's," he finally muttered.

"I'd have to change my clothes, of course. I came here straight from the office—" She cut herself off, her cheeks flushing slightly.

He contemplated not just her blush but the words that had triggered it. She'd traveled straight to Ar-

lington from her office with no clear objective, at least
not anything she was willing to admit to.

Her tremulous smile was almost enough to make
him not care why she was here. Maybe she'd come
for the sake of Mosley's country house. Maybe she
wanted to fight him over the kitchen's glass wall
some more, or the fireplace, or she just wanted to
micromanage the construction, as Rick had feared.
But Levi didn't want to believe that. He wanted to
believe she'd come to spend time with him.

Maybe…damn it, maybe she'd come because she
wanted to go to McDonald's with D.J. It made no
sense that she'd travel all the way from Manhattan to
Arlington just to munch on burgers and fries in an
inexpensive family eatery. She could have done that
just as easily in her own neighborhood.

But not with D.J.

And not with Levi.

Something was going on with her, something beyond the house and the choice of a restaurant. Whatever it was, Levi was too intrigued to let it go.

"There are two McDonald's restaurants in Arlington," he told her. "Also a Burger King, a Wendy's,
a Taco Bell, two Pizza Huts and a dive called Moise's
Fish House, which has the best clam chowder in Connecticut. You're overdressed for all of them."

"I've got a room at the Arlington Inn," she said.
"I'll check in and change, and maybe you and D.J.
can meet me there. Would D.J. be allowed into that—
what was it, Moses? The chowder place."

"Moise's Fish House." He opened her car door for
her. "Go check in and change. D.J. and I will pick
you up in forty-five minutes."

"Thank you," she said, her voice sparkling with

earnestness, as if she thought he were doing her a
huge favor. Introducing her to the chowder at Moise's
was a huge favor, but subjecting her to another evening with D.J....

The way she smiled, the way her eyes locked with
his for a long, searching moment before she settled
into the driver's seat, made him think that being subjected to another evening with D.J. was her dream
come true.

CHAPTER EIGHT

HE LOVED going in the car. The seat was comfortable—nicely padded but not too soft—and when the man opened a window, great gusts of air blew into D.J.'s face. But what he loved best were the vibrations, the rumble of motion, the blur beyond the windows, the knowledge that he was going somewhere, having an adventure, moving.

He loved it. He wished he could sit next to the man, so he could see the world rushing toward them through the front window.

The man's name was Levi.

Levi. His special man, like a daddy.

The new lady who stayed with D.J. was okay. She was much smaller than Levi, but her hands were almost as large as his. They held D.J. with a firm purpose that made him feel both secure and sad. He preferred the way the other woman had held him.

But she was gone. She left Levi's office that day and never came back. Instead he had the big-handed woman. She was nice. But she wasn't the woman he liked best.

The car was slowing down. He felt the pressure of the straps against his belly and shoulders as his body took an extra second to stop. Levi opened his window and talked to a man in a funny coat and hat who leaned down so they could look at each other. Levi

said something to the man. Then Levi stuffed some-
thing into the man's hand, and the man straightened
up and walked away.

Levi didn't talk anymore. The car seemed so silent
when it wasn't moving. No wind to listen to, no growl
of the engine, no hum of the tires against the road.

D.J. grew bored waiting for something to happen.
Shouldn't they get out and be somewhere new? He
kicked his feet and made some noise, thinking that
would remind Levi things were supposed to happen
when he stopped the car and turned off the engine.
But he only glanced over his shoulder at D.J., gave
him a funny little smile and reached between the front
seats to squeeze D.J.'s foot.

Suddenly the other door opened and there she was.
The woman. The one he liked.

He smelled her and saw her in the same instant,
and it was like his eyes and his body being filled with
her all at once. The evening sunlight fell on her hair
and made it shimmer. Her shirt was the same color
green as in his box of crayons.

The woman smiled at him, and her smile went into
him the way her smell did, filling him up from the
inside. She reached back and surrounded his hand
with hers. Her warmth seeped through him, just the
way her smell did and her smile. He laughed because
he was so happy.

She laughed, too. Maybe she was as happy as he
was.

MOISE'S FISH HOUSE was the sort of eatery a person
could feel comfortable bringing a baby into. The floor
was a checkerboard of black and white tiles, the walls
were washed with faded lemon-yellow paint and dec-

orated with trite seaside scenes in cheap frames and
the tables were draped in blue-checked vinyl. The
waiter who led Corinne and Levi to a table dragged
over a high chair for D.J. before Levi even had to
request one.

Levi strapped D.J. into the wooden seat while Corinne settled into one of the ladder back chairs beside
him. His pudgy baby cheeks dimpled as he grinned
at her, and his little feet pumped under the table. She
was probably projecting her mood on him, but he
seemed as excited to see her as she was to see him.

No, she wasn't excited to see him. Pleased, perhaps. Satisfied. She'd felt excited when she'd seen
Levi at the construction site—but that was very different from what she felt seeing D.J.

What was it with these two males? What strange
power did they exert over her? The instant she'd
caught sight of Levi, she'd understood the reason she
had driven from the car rental outlet directly to the
lot where Gerald's house was being built: because
she'd wanted to be with him, and she'd thought he
might be there, and while she couldn't have justified
visiting his office, she could justify a stop at the construction site. "I was just curious to see how things
were coming along," she could have said if anyone
had asked.

She'd traveled to Arlington unsure why she was
making the trip, but the moment Levi had loomed into
view, a living contradiction in his neat blue shirt, silk
tie, impeccably tailored trousers and that hard hat, the
reason she'd made the trip had become clear to her,
even if she wasn't quite ready to admit it.

It was Levi she'd wanted to see all along. Levi.

She'd wanted to see D.J., too, of course—and she'd

realized that as soon as she'd opened the car door and was greeted by his adorable face, his flying hands and feet, his lively eyes.

They looked so much like Levi's eyes.

Gazing at D.J. caused something warm and solid to nestle in the cage of her ribs. When she directed her attention to Levi, seated across the table from her, the warmth in her chest shape-shifted, developing a spininess that pricked and tweaked.

He was an amazingly sexy man. Even with his kid at his side, even in a casual polo shirt and jeans, his hair mussed from the wind that tangled through it during their drive, he was far sexier than any man had a right to be.

"Whatever else you get," he said, passing her one of the laminated menus, "you've got to order the clam chowder. It's incredible."

She skimmed the unpretentious menu. "Well, I guess I could get a cup—"

"A bowl. A cup won't be enough. Everything else is good, too."

"Lee-lee-lee," D.J. chimed in, drumming his hand on the high-chair tray. Corinne handed him her teaspoon, and he let out a delighted giggle. Then he banged the spoon on the tray.

"Why did you do that?" Levi asked.

Afraid she'd committed a dreadful mistake, she shot him a look. He appeared not angry but bemused.

She felt just as bemused. "I don't know," she admitted. She hadn't really thought about it, hadn't consciously imagined D.J. turning a teaspoon into a drumstick. It had just seemed so natural to give it to him, almost instinctive.

She turned back to D.J. He'd stopped using the

spoon to hit the tray and was sucking on it, rubbing the curved metal over his gums. How would she have known it would soothe his teething pain? How would she know anything about him?

Why was he gazing at her so intently? Why was *Levi* gazing at her so intently? Why did she feel as if Manhattan were light-years away, as if the only world that mattered was the world of the Holt men in Arlington, Connecticut?

"There's this thing called the Daddy School," Levi abruptly said.

"The Daddy School?"

The waiter arrived at their table, barrel-chested beneath his white butcher's apron, and the sight of him helped to bring her back to reality. She ordered a swordfish steak and a cup of clam chowder, which Levi immediately amended, requesting a bowl of the soup for her and one for himself, along with a grilled salmon and a banana for D.J. "I'd order some wine, but they don't have a liquor license here," he said, sounding apologetic.

She didn't need wine. Her mind already felt fuzzy enough.

"So, what's the Daddy School?" she asked.

"I have this client," Levi explained. "He's a newspaper columnist. James McCoy—maybe you've heard of him."

"The guy who writes—what is it called? *Guy Stuff*, right? That hilarious column about how idiotic men are?"

Levi grinned. "It's a hilarious column about how *superior* men are," he corrected her. "Anyway, Jamie lives in Arlington. His wife, Allison, is a nurse at Arlington Memorial Hospital. She and her best friend run a program for fathers, helping them to become better fathers.''

"Why are you telling me this?"

"I went to my first class on Monday," he said. "I'm trying to learn how to do this better."

She considered arguing that he was already doing an excellent job as a father. D.J. looked healthy and clean. His skin was clear, his wispy hair untangled, his eyes bright and alert. For a child who had endured a terrible loss, he didn't seem to be suffering. "Do you really need lessons in how to be a father?"

The sound Levi made was something midway between a laugh and a snort. "Are you kidding?"

"D.J.'s doing wonderfully."

"Sure—now that he has you to give him a spoon to play with."

A scowl tightened her brow as she tried to figure out what Levi was getting at. "You mean, he wasn't happy and healthy until I gave him that spoon?"

"He's healthy," Levi conceded. "Maybe he's happy, maybe even happy a lot of the time. But not like this. Look at him. He can't take his eyes off you."

Actually, D.J. didn't seem to have any trouble taking his eyes off her in order to focus on the spoon, the tray, his fingers and everything else within his range of vision. But whenever he did peer at Corinne, something changed in his face. His smile grew deeper, fiercer. She'd thought she was ascribing her own unfathomable emotions to him—but maybe his emotions matched hers. Maybe he was as content in her company as she was in his.

She didn't want to think about her own feelings, not when they left her so confused. So she turned the conversation back to Levi. "It seems to me you're doing a lot of things right for him. You even figured out a way to work while he's in your office. That's an amazing feat for anyone—to work with a baby in the room."

"I wasn't exactly at it full-out when he was in my office," Levi reminded her. "Anyway, he's got a nanny now. He stays home with her during the day. Things are returning to normal." Levi reached for a piece of bread from the plastic basket the waiter had left on the table, then hesitated. "That's not true. Things aren't normal. They'll never be normal again."

"Yes, they will," Corinne argued, because he seemed to need assurance. "You just have to come up with a different definition of *normal.*"

Levi glanced at D.J., then helped himself to a thick slice of bread. He smeared some butter on it and took a bite. "This is the first time I've taken him to a restaurant."

"He's doing fine, so far."

"Yeah." Levi looked at him again, his eyes softening. "So far."

Perhaps she was getting used to a new definition of *normal,* too. Sitting with him and D.J. at this unpretentious seafood restaurant felt normal to her. The rare times she dined out, she and Gerald usually would go to someplace dark and quiet and very New Yorkish, with carpets muffling the waiters' footsteps, diners muting their voices and nary a high chair in sight. But spreading an unfolded paper napkin across her knees and smiling as the waiter delivered two enormous bowls of chowder to their table seemed perfectly normal to her.

"Look at this!" she exclaimed as she stared warily at the bowl. "You could float an aircraft carrier in it."

"Once you taste it, you'll be glad I ordered the big size for you," Levi predicted.

She tasted it—and was glad. "Ooh! It's delicious."

"They use huge clams," he pointed out. "And other things no one else puts in chowder. Leeks, all sorts of herbs, and milk instead of cream so it doesn't get all sludgy."

"And the potatoes aren't mushy."

"Mmm." Levi was too busy devouring a spoonful to speak.

"Ba-baa! Lee-lee!" D.J. clinked his spoon on the tray, evidently delighted that they were enjoying their soup.

She consumed nearly half the bowl without a pause. It was too good to stop eating, too good to talk through. But after a while she realized that scooping chowder into her mouth without speaking to Levi was rude. "So, this Daddy School," she said. "Is it in a classroom?"

"A community room at the Y," he said. "It meets once a week."

"And it's specifically for men raising babies alone?"

"No—some of the students are married. My lawyer is. He's the one who first mentioned it to me. I think you were at my office when he did, weren't you?"

She remembered with a nod. That last morning, when they'd hammered out a new contract, she'd been afraid he was going to try to intimidate her by having his attorney present.

Instead, he'd intimidated her with a kiss.

Remembering that kiss caused the warmth inside her to grow, and her cheeks tingled as heat spread upward into a blush. The kiss Levi had given her had been tame, dry and close lipped—and perhaps manipulative. Yet it had left a permanent impression on her, a palpable nick in her soul.

Ridiculous that she could have responded so strongly to it then, that she could respond so strongly to a memory of it now. Maybe she ought to be leery of Levi. She didn't like the idea that she could be so moved by a staid little kiss.

She desired Levi. It struck her with the same astonishing impact as her first taste of the chowder had: she wanted him. No use denying it. No use pretending he hadn't gotten to her.

She wasn't particularly adept at relationships. She didn't trust them. She'd witnessed far too many bad ones in her formative years, growing up in her parents' various households. Perhaps if her father had taken Daddy School classes, he would have skipped a few of his marriages, aware that all those stepmothers he'd kept foisting on Corinne had undermined her confidence in love and marriage. And her mother, constantly moving her from home to home, from one family to the next…

Corinne assumed that some people managed to relate to the opposite sex successfully, but she'd never seen much evidence of it and no one had ever taught her how it was done. That was why she'd planned her life so carefully: the MBA, the career, the smart investments, the ability to go it alone. The determination not to believe in something that likely would never exist for her.

Well, she wasn't going to fall in love with Levi—

or with his cute little nephew, who had taken to gnawing on the spoon again. What she felt when she recalled Levi's kiss, when she fell under the power of his riveting brown eyes, was physical attraction, pure and simple. Love had nothing to do with it.

"Actually," he was saying, "Murphy started taking Daddy School lessons when he was divorced and suddenly found himself with custody of his twins. They're a bit older—around nine years old now, I think. But he found the classes useful, even after he remarried."

"So it isn't just about how to change diapers?"

"I figured out diapers on my own," Levi boasted, then paused as the waiter arrived with their entrees— and a banana on a plate for D.J. Ignoring his salmon, Levi peeled the banana and used his knife to cut it into thin disks. "Diapers are real easy, and any man who claims he can't do them is lying because he doesn't want to deal with the messy part of it. Other things are a little more complicated. Like food. I wouldn't have known D.J. could handle so many solid foods if I hadn't learned it in class." He set the plate in front of D.J., who let out a joyous chirp.

"Why did you wind up with D.J.?" she asked.

"My sister wanted it that way."

"Why?" She smiled hesitantly. "Did she know you were going to take to it so well? Were you always a nurturing sort of guy?"

"I'm not a nurturing sort of guy," Levi said, then sighed and turned to D.J., who had now taken to pounding on the plate with the spoon. Levi pried the spoon from D.J.'s clenched hand, and the baby shouted in protest. While his mouth was open, Levi poked a piece of banana between his lips. The sweetness of the fruit distracted him enough to make him forget about the spoon.

If that wasn't a nurturing thing to do, Corinne didn't understand the meaning of *nurturing*.

"Maybe your sister knew you better than you know yourself," she said.

Clearly unpersuaded, he wiped his fingers on his napkin and dug into his salmon.

"What was her name?" Corinne was shocked by her own nosiness—but she really cared. She wanted to learn everything about how Levi had wound up with D.J., how D.J. had wound up with Levi, how these two men had combined to captivate her.

"Ruth."

"Tell me about her."

He studied her, his eyes dark and penetrating. His gaze seemed to grip her, to hold her tight. "What do you want to know?" he finally asked.

"Anything you want to tell me."

He accepted her answer with a nod. "She was my baby sister. Six years younger than me. She and I were kind of the family oddballs. The black sheep." He speared a chunk of fish and ate it, then responded to D.J.'s panicked wail by lifting another piece of banana to the baby's mouth. Corinne took the opportunity to taste her swordfish. It wasn't quite as miraculous as the chowder, but it came close.

"My parents felt the world was a dangerous and corrupting place," Levi continued once D.J. had settled down and pinched his tiny fingers around the banana piece. "They wanted to isolate us from it. We were all home-schooled. We had no television set and very few toys and books. I used to bike to the library sometimes. I was afraid to bring the books home—I figured my parents would take them away, and probably take away my bike, as well. So I stayed there and read for hours. I never told anyone what I was doing—but when Ruth was about eight, she followed me on her bike. I was afraid she'd rat on me, but she didn't. She found a book and started reading, too.''

Corinne had little difficulty picturing Levi nurturing his young sister's mind. Whether or not he realized it, he was a remarkably nurturing man.

''Ruth and I were both artistic. My parents viewed art as frivolous. They didn't want us wasting our time with drawing and coloring pictures, so that was another activity we had to sneak. We'd sketch on scrap paper. We'd scribble on toilet paper. Since Ruth was the youngest, all her clothes were hand-me-downs, and once she outgrew them they'd be too worn-out to pass along to anyone else, so she'd cut them up and sew them into outfits for her dolls. She loved fabrics. My mother did lots of sewing, and she taught Ruth how to quilt. When she wanted to learn weaving, my parents thought maybe that meant she was going to settle down and be a good girl, mastering the domestic arts, so they sent her to a friend of theirs who had a loom. She taught Ruth—but the stuff Ruth wanted to weave was bright, with pictures and images in it.'' He ate a bit, reminiscing. ''When she was seventeen, she ran away from home.''

''Where were you then?''

''By then, I'd finished college.'' He sighed. ''Going to college had been almost impossible. I found out about how to apply to college from the librarian. I wasn't able to take all the college placement tests, but I applied to a bunch of colleges with her help, and I got accepted to Indiana University on a scholarship. My parents refused to let me go. I threatened to report them to Social Services if they stood in my way.'' Another deep sigh. ''By that time I was as tall as I am now. And full of anger. I think I must have scared them, because they told me they'd pray for my soul and they let me go.''

Corinne was stunned. His story sounded like something out of Dickens, not the sort of thing that was supposed to happen to people of her generation, here in the United States. She'd gone to college with the blessings of her parents—and all her stepparents. She'd already decided she would never get married, never depend on a husband to support her, and she'd known she wouldn't be able to support herself adequately without a college degree. Her parents, the whole army of them, were fully behind her. Two of her stepfathers contributed some money toward her tuition so she wouldn't have to sign too many loans.

But to get a college education without any support—worse, to do it with parents who had actively fought against it—must have been so much harder. Levi had to have been incredibly strong and motivated to have achieved so much in spite of his parents. Mixed in with her attraction to him was enormous respect for what he'd accomplished.

''So when you decided to devote yourself to designing houses with lots of light,'' she said as comprehension dawned, ''it had to do with more than just the darkness of the house you grew up in.''

''It had to do with the darkness of my home,'' he said. ''I grew up in darkness, in so many ways. All my siblings did, but Ruth was the only one besides me who was desperate to get out into the light.''

''And she did?''

"She lived with me for a while. I was in architecture school then, at the Rhode Island School of Design. She was just a kid. She sat in on some weaving courses at the school, and I tried to get her to enroll. But she wasn't looking for a father or a mentor, and I guess that was what I was trying to be. She'd spent seventeen years listening to my father tell her what to do, and there I was, trying to get her to do what I thought she should do. She left and headed for California." He smiled vaguely. "At least she didn't hate me for it, the way she hated my father."

"Did things work out for her in California?"

He nodded. "She struggled a lot, and once I became an associate at Arlington Architectural, I used to send her money to help her out. But she found a community of artisans and craftspeople there, and she was very happy. She wove beautiful stuff—blankets, wall hangings, articles of clothing she used to call wearable art. I have a wall hanging of hers I could show you, in my—" he caught himself and smiled sheepishly "—in my bedroom. If you'd like to see it."

Corinne smiled, not yet prepared to agree to visit his bedroom. The room's fireplace probably wouldn't do anything for her—she still thought a bedroom fireplace was a silly whimsy—but his sister's wall hanging would touch her, she was sure.

"How old was she when D.J. was born?"

"She'd just turned twenty-six. And five months later she was dead. It was such a fluky thing. She'd been in good health, strong and full of life…" A wave of sadness seemed to overtake him, and he said nothing for a long moment, just poked at his salmon with the tines of his fork. At last, he broke off a chunk and ate it. "She'd been sharing a house with a few other artisans in Mendocino," he said. "That's north of San Francisco, on the coast. Have you ever been there?"

Corinne shook her head.

"It's beautiful country. I'd fly out and visit her every June, and the scenery was breathtaking. Anyway—" he ate a bit more "—these people she was living with told me that after D.J. was born, she'd written a will naming me as his guardian."

"She really must have trusted you."

"I don't know why, but she did." He glanced at D.J., who looked attentive even though he couldn't possibly understand what Levi was saying.

"And you have no idea who his father is?"

He lifted another circle of banana from the plate in front of D.J. "All she told me was that he was from the Los Angeles area. He worked for a film company. He'd been passing through and they'd had a fling. Oh, and he was handsome. She told me that."

Corinne watched Levi nudge the soft piece of banana between D.J.'s lips. D.J. had banana smeared on his cheeks and chin, and he gleefully gummed the piece Levi was feeding him. He clasped his hands around Levi's; they, too, looked glazed and sticky with banana.

Levi's sister had been wise to trust Levi. Corinne would also have trusted him, with her whole heart.

That thought shook her. She lowered her gaze to her plate. As tasty as the swordfish was, the chowder had filled her up so much she couldn't come close to finishing her meal. When the waiter came to check on them, she leaned back and informed him she was done.

"You want me to wrap this for you?" the waiter asked.

If she were in New York, she would have said yes. She could have brought the leftovers home and heated them for dinner some other night. But in Arlington, what was she going to do with the extra food? She didn't have a refrigerator in her room at the Arlington Inn.

"Wrap it," Levi instructed the waiter. He must have read Corinne's questioning look, because he added, "I can keep it in my refrigerator for you."

And then what? Was she supposed to go to his house Sunday to pick her doggie bag up before she left town?

She didn't want to wait to go to his house until she was about to leave town. She wanted to go back there now—to spend more time with him and D.J., to see the artistry of his sister's wall hanging, to experience his house through the eyes of someone who now understood why certain architectural concepts were so essential to him. To hold D.J. in her arms, maybe give him a bottle the way she had a week ago, even try her hand at changing his diaper, since Levi claimed it was easy. To cradle him and cuddle him and let him know how lucky he was that his mother had named Levi his guardian.

She had no particular interest in security, domestic stability, daddies and babies, home and hearth. She had as full a life as she could manage back in New York—a demanding job, a productive investment portfolio, a professional colleague who doubled as her closest companion. She didn't need anything Levi Holt could possibly offer.

Except, perhaps, some space in his refrigerator for

a couple of nights. And a little bit of the magical warmth she felt when she was with him.

"All right," she said, nodding to the waiter to take her half-full plate and wrap its contents for her. Then she smiled at Levi. "Thank you."

The smile he returned said that she was more than welcome.

CHAPTER NINE

D.J. WAS A MESS. His hands were sticky from the banana, and everything he'd touched with them—his cheeks, his T-shirt, his shorts, his left knee, his hair—was sticky, too. But he'd gotten through an entire meal at a restaurant without pitching a fit or soiling his diaper. Levi supposed he couldn't complain about a bit of smeared fruit.

Maybe he was selfish. Maybe he was undeserving of the honor and responsibility of being D.J.'s surrogate father—because he really wished he'd been able to leave the kid home. The meal might have been more pleasant, more sophisticated, more relaxing, if D.J. hadn't accompanied them. He would have had time alone with Corinne, time to find out why she'd returned to Arlington. Time to see if the attraction he felt toward her was reciprocated. Time to see if six weeks as a full-time daddy had diminished his ability to think and act like a full-time man.

Last Tuesday, unable to scare up a baby-sitter, he'd brought D.J. with him to his friend Evan's house for their regular Tuesday-night poker game. It had been the first poker game he'd attended since coming home from California with D.J.—and all his poker buddies had insisted that women loved daddies who included babies in their activities. They'd implied that if he wanted to impress a woman, he ought to do just what

he'd done tonight: spend an evening with that woman
and let D.J. chaperon them.

He wouldn't have guessed Corinne was the kind of
woman who got turned on by little babies, though.
Unlike the women he met in the supermarket when
he and D.J. went shopping, she didn't make goo-goo
noises, didn't turn misty-eyed and pinch D.J.'s
chubby little cheek and coo to him about what a good
boy he was. Not once had she ever gushed, "He's so
cute!"

In fact, although D.J. had been seated at their table
at Moise's, just inches from her right hand, she'd all
but ignored him while she'd somehow gotten Levi to
tell her more than he'd ever told any other woman
about his childhood, his parents and his sister Ruth.

Carrying D.J. carefully so as to prevent the kid's
banana-smeared parts from touching him, he led Corinne from the garage through the mudroom and into
the kitchen. He settled D.J. in his walker, and D.J.
scooted off like an Indy 500 contender, ricocheting
around the room and screeching gleefully. En route
to the sink to scrub the stickiness from his hands, he
nodded toward the refrigerator. "Just make some
space on a shelf," he invited her.

She carried her leftovers to the fridge and found a
spot for them inside. As she closed the door, D.J.
zoomed past her and she flattened herself against the
broom closet to keep from getting run over. "This
child will never be allowed to drive, if I have any say
in the matter," Levi vowed.

Corinne laughed. "You'll hand him the keys to
your Porsche the minute he's old enough."

"Are you kidding? By the time he's old enough,

my Porsche will be an antique. A classic. I won't let him get within a hundred yards of it.''

D.J. reinforced Levi's dim view of his driving skills by hot-rodding across the room. ''If he's pushing the thing too fast, maybe it's because he's getting too big for it,'' Corinne suggested.

''Too big?'' Levi frowned. D.J. fit perfectly in the seat. And despite his recklessness in the walker, Levi didn't want him to outgrow it too soon. Zipping around in it was one of his favorite activities.

''I mean, too old,'' she clarified. ''If he wants to go that fast, maybe it's because he's ready to go faster.'' She watched D.J. career past the table. ''What do you think about a tricycle?''

What Levi thought was that Corinne was woefully ignorant when it came to babies. He checked himself before guffawing. She looked so earnest and concerned as she evaluated D.J.'s journey about the room, a journey as wild and directionless as a balloon with a leak. How could he laugh at her? ''Babies don't get tricycles until they can walk,'' he explained. ''He can't even stand up yet.''

''Well—but he's standing in the walker, isn't he?'' She gestured toward his feet, which he stretched and pumped against the floor.

''He's using his feet to push himself. But no, he can't stand yet. Most babies don't start walking until they're closing in on their first birthday.''

''Really?'' She gave him a wide-eyed look, as if awed by his knowledge.

He liked being viewed as an expert, especially since he knew how far he was from actually being one. ''I asked the Daddy School teacher after class on Monday,'' he confessed. ''There are books on the subject, guidelines that spell out what an average baby can be expected to do at each age. By six months most babies can sit up. By eight months most of them can crawl. By twelve months most of them can walk. By fifteen months they can say a couple of words. I bought one of the books and it was pretty informative. I even read a little of it to D.J. I thought he ought to have an idea of what to look forward to."

"I take it you didn't read him the chapter that says by sixteen years he can drive."

"He'll never drive," Levi declared, and his gaze merged with hers. Her eyes were bright with sparks of laughter. Beautiful eyes, he thought. Mesmerizing eyes. Eyes that danced with life and energy.

Had she come back to his house because of D.J. or because of him? Or because she wanted to store her leftovers in his refrigerator?

Did it matter? She'd come back, just as he'd hoped she would. She was here. With him.

There were things he could do, ways he could make a woman feel welcome in his home. Ways he could let this particular woman know that he was keenly aware of how long her legs looked in the snug-fitting beige jeans she had on, and that he'd noticed the shadows of her collarbones below the curved neckline of her short-sleeved sweater, and that watching her fall in love with the clam chowder at Moise's had made him imagine the way she'd look in the thrall of other, equally sensuous pleasures. But to give voice to the general theme of his thoughts seemed totally inappropriate with D.J. zigzagging around the kitchen, chortling and hooting.

The kid needed a bath. He needed a clean diaper

and a bottle and his crib. Everything else would have to wait until D.J. was taken care of.

"I've really got to get him washed up and settled down," he said apologetically. Regardless of his poker buddies' predictions, he doubted Corinne would want to bide her time and twiddle her thumbs while he dumped D.J. in his boat-shaped baby tub and scrubbed the kid clean. Maybe he could offer her some scintillating reading material to keep her occupied while he fulfilled his paternal duties. The best book he'd read lately was *Your Baby's Many Milestones*.

"What can I do to help?" she asked.

He studied her face, trying to discern whether she really wanted to be of assistance or was simply offering out of courtesy. She moved her hands along her arms as though she would have rolled up her sleeves if only her sweater hadn't had short sleeves to begin with.

"You can watch me give him a bath," he said.

"I'd love that."

One more glance at her face convinced him she meant it. "All right, then." He swooped down on D.J. as the kid was making a kamikaze pass and hauled him out of the walker. D.J. let out an indignant howl and reached for his walker, but Levi proceeded out of the kitchen, holding him tightly so he couldn't squirm loose.

He trooped up the stairs with D.J., Corinne close behind. In the bathroom, Levi put D.J. on the mat, and D.J. pushed himself up on his hands and knees, practicing his crawl position. Ignoring him—Corinne could catch him if he miraculously managed to propel himself through the door—Levi adjusted the bathtub faucets to a warm spray and slid the little rowboat-shaped tub under the spout.

"He can't go in the big tub?" Corinne asked, instinctively blocking the doorway, even though D.J. didn't seem likely to crawl off the mat.

Levi shot her a quick look over his shoulder. "Too slippery. He could fall backward and crack his head. Or drown." He appreciated her asking, and appreciated even more that she hadn't looked at the baby tub and said, "Isn't it cute!"

Corinne clearly wasn't the sort of woman who cared about cute. He'd dated a woman a year ago whose entire apartment was filled with cute things—little rosy-cheeked statuettes, butterfly-shaped magnets on her refrigerator, Beanie Babies dolls arranged along several shelves in her guest room. If not for this passion for cute things, Levi might have pursued a serious relationship with her. But "cute" had never cut it with him, and after a few dates he'd communicated to her that they didn't share the same taste. Specifically, he'd told her he didn't think much of her Beanie Babies collection, and she'd told him to leave, which had been exactly what he'd wanted to do.

He wondered if Corinne collected anything. Beanie Babies? Baseball cards? Pottery? Boyfriends?

He really, really hoped she didn't collect boyfriends. Given how attractive she was, he couldn't believe she didn't have dozens of ardent men waiting for her back in New York City, praying that she might acknowledge their existence with a smile or a nod. But he hoped she wasn't doing more than smiling and nodding.

In any case, she wasn't in New York City now. She had deliberately chosen to spend her weekend in

Arlington—and not because of Mosley's house. She hadn't said a word about the project over dinner. She hadn't asked when the foundation would be poured, why the blueprint hadn't changed in spite of the alterations he'd made to the design, or whether by some miracle he'd changed his mind about the wall of glass in the kitchen. She'd stopped at the house site and seen Levi, and the house had gone forgotten.

She'd come to Arlington for him. Him and D.J. If she had a truckload of men waiting for her back in New York, they obviously didn't matter to her, at least not this weekend.

The baby tub was half-full and Levi shut off the water. "Okay, buddy," he said, rolling D.J. onto his back on the shag-soft mat. "Time for your bath."

"Lee-lee!" D.J. screeched, his voice echoing off the concave fiberglass of the tub stall. He kicked his feet in circles as if pedaling a bicycle, and for a moment Levi wondered whether Corinne might have been onto something when she'd recommended getting him a tricycle.

No, not yet. Not until D.J. grasped the concepts of safety and moderation, two big ideas that seemed irrelevant to him at the moment.

He peeled off D.J.'s shorts and shirt, trying to ignore the fact that Corinne was watching him from the bathroom doorway. The room was spacious, but it felt almost too small with all three of them inside it. He felt Corinne's nearness too keenly. The humidity of the bathwater seemed to magnify her scent. Although he wasn't looking at it, he knew the mirror above the sink held her reflection. So even if he turned away from her, he'd still see her.

He worked off the tapes of D.J.'s diaper, hoping he

wouldn't find anything gross enough to sour Corinne's mood. Luck was with him; the absorbent layers held about three pounds of pee but nothing more substantial. Levi rolled the diaper into a compact ball—he was proud of his efficiency, able to do this with one hand—and lifted D.J. into the tub. D.J. let out a jubilant squeal. He loved baths. They gave him the opportunity to splash water all over Levi.

He noticed a movement in his peripheral vision and lifted his gaze in time to see Corinne pushing away from the door, approaching him. She reached the mat and knelt next to him, her eyes on D.J. "He won't slip in this?" she asked, running her hand along the smooth plastic edge.

"No. It's contoured so he can't." Levi spoke calmly and authoritatively, while his body stirred to a new level of alertness. He tried to place her fragrance—honey and mint, cool and warm at the same time. Her hair glittered with coppery highlights beneath the overhead fixture, and the skin of her throat was so smooth and taut it took a surprising amount of willpower not to let go of D.J., pivot on his knees and kiss her there, in the arching hollow of her neck.

Before Levi could get too distracted, D.J. wrenched his body in an attempt to face her. The motion caused a small tidal wave of water to wash up to Levi's elbow as he tightened his grip on the kid's slippery arm.

"Lee-lee-lee!" D.J. squawked, attempting to launch himself at Corinne again.

"I'm causing problems here, aren't I?" she said apologetically, reaching for the bathtub edge to push herself away.

"No." If he'd had a free hand he would have grabbed her and held her next to him. He could think of no reason that kneeling next to her on a bath mat in this close, muggy bathroom should fill him with such a stark longing, but he didn't want her to leave. "I think—cut it out, D.J.," he scolded sharply as the baby made another attempt to escape, shoving his strong little legs against the sides of the plastic boat. "I think he wants you where he can see you. Maybe if we switch sides…"

She shuffled around to his other side on her knees. He felt her press one hand to his back for balance, and a hot spark of desire skimmed down his spine. He almost laughed at the realization that he could be thinking about sex while engaged in the least sexy activity he could imagine.

Well, no, giving D.J. a bath wasn't the least sexy activity he could imagine. Changing his diaper would win that prize.

Once she'd settled back on her heels, positioned to Levi's right, D.J. could see her. A huge grin broke across his face, and he kicked his legs, churning the water. "Ba-ba-baa!" Leaning forward, he extended his hands toward her.

"I think he wants you to give him his bath," Levi observed, privately amused. He himself wouldn't mind having Corinne give him a bath, either. The two of them in a shower together…

He squelched that thought. "I don't know how," she murmured.

"Take the washcloth—" he indicated it with a jerk of his chin "—and that bottle of baby soap. Put a little soap on the cloth and go to it."

She shot Levi a measuring look. She didn't appear anxious or insecure. If anything, she seemed to be accepting this chore as an interesting challenge. Turning back to D.J., she smiled. "Okay, D.J., let's give this a try," she said, her voice soft and soothing. She squirted some soap onto the wet cloth, then shuffled closer to Levi, until her hip was pressed to his and her shoulder bumped his. He gave her a little more room, but not much; he wanted to keep his hands on D.J. so the kid wouldn't fidget and hurt himself or drench her with splattered water.

Carefully, gently, she rubbed the cloth over D.J.'s round belly. Up under the crease of his neck. Over his shoulders, down his plump arms. She concentrated on each star-shaped hand, getting the palm and the back and then scrubbing between his tiny fingers. The first few times Levi had bathed D.J. he'd forgotten to clean between his fingers, and after pulling D.J. from the tub and drying him off he'd felt the stickiness of the kid's hands. He had no idea why D.J.'s hands were so sticky—from food, probably—but he'd learned to pay special attention to them during bath time.

Corinne obviously had a good instinct for this kind of thing. She slid the washcloth through the water to D.J.'s feet and gave his toes the same individual attention. He giggled and kicked but let her wash them.

"There you go, D.J.," she said, running the cloth up and down his back. "You must be clean. You're shining!"

"I'll get his hair," Levi suggested. Shampooing was trickier than bathing his body. The label on the shampoo bottle promised that it wouldn't sting a child's eyes, but Levi didn't want to test that guarantee and discover it wasn't true. "If you'll just hold his hand, he'll think you're still washing him."

She leaned forward to take D.J.'s hand. Levi felt

the curve of her breast against his elbow and inched his arm away. D.J. gripped her fingers and made assorted chirps and sputtering sounds. She stroked her thumb across his knuckles—which, on his pudgy hands, resembled dimples at the bases of his fingers. Levi tore his gaze from the sight of her thumb and concentrated on cleaning the banana residue from D.J.'s hair.

Once his hair was rinsed, Levi reached behind him and pulled D.J.'s towel from the rack. "Okay, buddy—all done," he announced, lifting him out and placing him in the towel. "Do you want to dry him?" he asked Corinne.

A silly question as he considered it. What was the big deal about drying a baby? All it entailed was wrapping the towel around him and patting him down. But Corinne eagerly took on the task, dabbing droplets of water from D.J.'s face, swabbing him with the soft green terry cloth, drying his toes as conscientiously as she'd washed them.

"Clean diapers are in the other room," Levi said as he stood. "Would you like to carry him?"

Apparently she would. Wrapping him more snugly in the towel, she lifted him into her arms and peered up. Levi cupped his hands under her elbows and helped her to her feet. For one moment, as she stood facing him, his hands curved around her arms, the only thing that separated them, that kept him from leaning toward her and touching his lips to hers, was D.J.

Once again, Levi suppressed his desire. Releasing her, he turned and stalked into D.J.'s makeshift nursery, silently chastising himself for resenting the kid. It wasn't D.J.'s fault that Levi couldn't kiss Corinne.

To be sure, he ought to be grateful to D.J. If not for him, Corinne might not have had dinner with Levi.

He couldn't prove that, but he sensed it in his gut. D.J. was important to her, not because he was cute but for some other reason, something Levi couldn't begin to comprehend. He could only sense it from the way she gazed into D.J.'s face, from the arch of her arms around the baby, the tilt of her head, the strange peace that settled over D.J. when she held him.

Would Levi feel that peaceful if Corinne held him, if she arched her beautiful arms around him and gazed into his face? Or would he feel wild and greedy?

It wasn't like him to think so hard about a woman, to wonder so much. Before D.J., he used to approach women, and either they would encourage him or not. Either something would connect or it wouldn't. But the ambivalent emotions—the need and the wariness, the ache of wanting and the hesitation about acting on that want—they were new to him. He didn't understand them. He might as well blame them on D.J.

In D.J.'s room, he indicated to Corinne that she should put the baby down on the waterproof pad on top of the dresser. "Don't let go of him or he'll roll off," he warned as he crossed the room to grab a diaper. "Here—you want to try doing this?"

"Sure." She flashed him a smile that was one part confidence and three parts astonishment, as if she couldn't believe she was actually going to attempt such a feat. Then she turned to D.J. and unfolded the towel.

"Work fast," Levi cautioned her. "He can hose you down if he feels the urge."

She laughed and slid the diaper under D.J.'s bottom. "Should I put powder on him?"

"Not necessary. Just get the thing taped shut before he geysers."

She did a pretty good job of it, fastening the tapes evenly around D.J.'s waist. "There!" She beamed, obviously quite proud of herself.

He pulled open a drawer and removed a sleeper for D.J. "You're doing so great you may as well keep going. You should probably move over to the futon to put this on him, because he's going to squirm a lot."

"Okay." The ratio of confidence to astonishment changed. She looked pretty sure of herself as she carried D.J. to the futon and laid him down on the cushions.

Levi watched for a minute, then realized he wasn't needed there. She could handle getting D.J. into his pajamas without any assistance. "I'll go downstairs and fix a bottle for him," he said.

She nodded, but she was too busy guiding D.J.'s legs into the pajama bottoms to look at him.

He felt almost relieved to get away from her, away from them both for a while. At the foot of the stairs, he paused and took a deep breath. Closing his eyes, he pictured her smile, her graceful fingers smoothing the tapes on D.J.'s diaper. He pictured the way D.J. stared at her, his eyes brimming with trust and devotion. Why? Why was D.J. so taken with Corinne?

Shaking his head, he strode to the kitchen, filled a bottle with formula, warmed it in the microwave for a few seconds and then returned to the stairs. Halfway up, he heard the lullaby:

"Hush, little baby, don't say a word.
Mama's gonna buy you a mockingbird..."

He slowed his steps, muffling them so his approach wouldn't interrupt her.

"And if that mockingbird won't sing,
Mama's gonna buy you a diamond ring..."

She had a beautiful voice, as clear and delicate as fine crystal.

"And if that diamond ring is brass,
Mama's gonna buy you a looking glass.
And if that looking glass gets broke,
Mama's gonna buy you a billy goat..."

He'd reached the top of the stairs. Halting, he hovered outside the door so she wouldn't see him and stop singing.

"And if that billy goat won't pull,
Mama's gonna buy you a cart and bull.
And if that cart and bull turn over,
Mama's gonna buy you a dog named Rover..."

He tried to remember where he'd heard the lullaby before. On the radio, probably. A rock-and-roll version of it. His mother had never sung it to him. She'd have criticized it as too materialistic—and she'd have been right, he thought with a wry grin. But then, she'd never sung any other lullabies to him or his siblings, either. Lullabies were frivolous. They were luxuries, unnecessary.

"And if that dog named Rover won't bark,
Mama's gonna buy you a horse and cart.
And if that horse and cart fall down,
You'll still be the sweetest little baby in town."

He remained in the hallway as the last note faded into silence. It seemed to seep into him, thick and warm as oil, softening him inside, causing a confusion of feelings to melt together in his gut. Grief that D.J. had no mother to sing him lullabies. Gratitude that D.J. had Corinne to sing to him tonight. Fear that Corinne could become important to D.J. and then she'd leave. Fear that she could become important to Levi.

He didn't have time to deal with his bewilderment. What emotions he could manage ought to be devoted to D.J. alone. A healthy attraction to Corinne was fine, and if that attraction was mutual, even better. But he couldn't let himself get emotional about her.

Too late. His emotions were already involved. He'd been reacting to far more than her nearness when she'd been giving D.J. his bath, far more than the pressure of her shoulder, her hip, the soft swell of her breast. What he'd really been responding to he couldn't name, but it had to do with that powerful connection between her and D.J., the intensity he sensed in her when she held his little boy.

Until he could figure it out, he wasn't going to be able to resist it.

He roused himself with a sigh and entered the room. Corinne was standing near the window, D.J. cradled in her left arm, his head resting against the crook of her elbow. She held him so he could gaze out at the night sky. The room's light fell gently over her back and caught in the strands of D.J.'s hair.

She turned to acknowledge Levi's entrance, and D.J. reached up and pinched at her shirt. Was he looking for milk or trying to get her to turn back to the window so he could see outside?

Turn, Levi almost ordered her. *Let him see the sky.* "Here's his bottle," he said, his voice emerging a bit rough.

"Am I supposed to feed him, too?" she asked with a grin.

Had she thought he was imposing on her? "Only if you want to," he assured her.

She exchanged a glance with him. Her smile was enigmatic, her eyes alive with silver-and-green light. Then she extended her hand toward the bottle. "I want to."

They settled on the futon as they had the last time she'd given D.J. a bottle. Her expression grew tender as she watched the baby drink, and she looked much more natural feeding him tonight than she'd looked a week and a half ago. D.J. kept his gaze on her as long as he could, but after about half the bottle was gone he seemed intoxicated, his eyes closing, one hand fisting against the bottle and the other clutching Corinne's thumb.

Levi sat beside her, close enough to feel the heat of her. She might have been D.J.'s mother, the way she was feeding him. Of course she wasn't; Ruth was D.J.'s mother and always would be. But the affection illuminating Corinne's face, her protective posture, her patience and serenity…

Damn. She was supposed to be a hard hitter from New York, but she was transforming into someone

else: a woman who could reach a motherless baby the
way no other woman could, the way Levi himself
could only dream of.

Why was she here? For Levi or for D.J.?

He just didn't know.

EVEN AS HE DRANK, *her lullaby echoed inside him.
Hush, little baby...*

*His mother used to sing it to him. This woman sang
it differently, but it was the same song. His mother
went away and took the song with her, and he was
afraid he'd never hear it again.*

*But this woman had brought it back. She'd given it
back to him.*

Hush, little baby...

*The woman had let him watch the stars while she
sang. He'd seen tiny spots of silver in the black sky,
and the white smile of the moon.*

*The woman had come back, and she'd brought the
song with her. And now she was feeding him. It was
almost like having his mother again. Almost.*

*If he couldn't have his mother, he wanted this
woman. He wanted her to sing and feed him and hold
him like this. He wanted her voice and her arms
around him and the love he felt coming from her.*

He wanted her to stay forever.

CHAPTER TEN

THE DEEPER D.J. sank into sleep, the more he seemed to weigh. Corinne's hands began to grow numb as he snuggled heavily into her arms, his breathing slow and constant, a small milky bubble trembling on his lip. Levi reached around her to dab away that droplet with a tissue, then took the empty bottle from her and stood. He helped her to her feet the way he had in the bathroom, his hands strong and warm beneath her elbows, his fingers curving around her upper arms.

She carried D.J. to his crib and lowered him onto the mattress. The sheet was a cotton knit, softer than the linens on her bed, and it featured a pattern of puffy white clouds scattered across a pale-blue background. She lifted the matching blanket and spread it over him and his teddy bear. He poked his thumb into his mouth and sighed.

Neither she nor Levi spoke. He hovered close behind her, standing guard over both her and the baby as if they were all in this together, a solid, single unit sharing one goal: to ensure a good life for one special child.

The emotion that pulled at Corinne's heart baffled her. She'd only just met D.J. ten days ago, and she'd viewed him then as a pest, a complication in her dealings with Levi. That first day she'd gone to Arlington Architectural Associates, her only goal had been to

develop a saner design for Gerald's dream house. And
D.J., fussing and wailing on Levi's shoulder, had been
a distraction, a problem, an obstacle to be overcome.

Now that day seemed eons in the past.

If she could step out of her body and view this
moment from a distance, she would hardly know herself. She was no longer the same person she'd been
just days ago, the competent, poised manager who
fixed everything, who saved Gerald from his own
foolish impulses and packaged his genius in profitable
ways. She had become someone else: a woman who'd
figured out how to change a diaper and wrestle a
squirming baby into his pajamas. A woman who sang
lullabies. A woman who felt she belonged right where
she was, between a tall, quiet man and a sleeping
infant, a woman who wanted to lean back into the
strong chest of the man who'd introduced this child
into her life and trusted her with him.

D.J. sighed again, took a hearty suck on his thumb
and smiled. He was dreaming something happy, surrounded in his bed by blue sky and clouds while the
stars of a night sky filled the window above him.

Levi touched her shoulder, and the warmth that
filled her chest at the sight of D.J. slumbering spread
upward to the place where his hand rested on her. He
flexed his fingers against her, and she realized he was
signaling her that it was time to leave the baby.

Reluctantly she turned from the crib and let Levi
lead her out of the room. By the door, he turned on
the night-light and switched off the lamp.

They took a few steps down the hall and stopped.
The only light in the hall was a distorted rectangle of
amber from D.J.'s night-light spilling through the
open doorway onto the carpet. Corinne turned to Levi.

Once her eyes had adjusted to the dark, she peered up into his face.

He was watching her, looking as bewildered as she felt. He must have recognized that something had changed between them, something had changed inside her. A new dynamic had skewed the atmosphere; a strange magic had folded its cloak around them. When Corinne Lanier started singing lullabies, the world was clearly rotating at a different speed.

They stared at each other for a long minute, neither speaking, Corinne not knowing what she would say if she did open her mouth. Would she demand that Levi explain what was going on between her and D.J., between her and himself? Would she ask him to tell her why every cell in her body quivered with expectation, every nerve bristled in anticipation, why she was braced for the earth's crazy spin to send them into a new orbit? If she asked such questions, how could he possibly answer?

By kissing her.

This kiss wasn't like the one he'd given her at his office. It wasn't swift and strategic, designed with a specific goal in mind. Rather, it was slow and tender and exploratory. His lips touched hers, brushed, caressed. Then he paused and leaned back, giving her the chance to say no.

She couldn't say no. She didn't want to. She tilted her head toward him and he touched his mouth to hers again, this time less hesitant, more assertive.

The earth might be spinning out of control, but Levi's kiss seemed to anchor her. It was the most rational element in an irrational universe, an act that made sense of everything.

She kissed him back. She lifted her hand to his

chest as he cupped his hand to her cheek, and let his breath merge with hers as his mouth opened against her. She closed her eyes and absorbed his sigh, leaned toward him and met the thrust of his tongue.

He was a phenomenal kisser. She should have guessed he would be; he was handsome and patient and sensitive, so it seemed reasonable that he would know how to use his mouth to maximum effect. He teased, withdrew, skimmed his tongue against her teeth, nibbled teasingly on her lower lip. His hand moved past her ear and dove into her hair, simultaneously stroking her scalp and angling her head so he could deepen the kiss.

She tried to keep up with him. He was more adept than her; he had either more experience or better instincts. Probably both. Corinne didn't have time to meet men, and she wasn't going to kiss men she barely knew—not the way she was kissing Levi. The only man she was close enough to kiss this way was Gerald, and he was…well, Gerald.

She couldn't imagine kissing him like this. She couldn't imagine pressing into him, clutching at his shirt, yearning for the feel of flesh and muscle on the other side of the fabric. She couldn't imagine Gerald bringing his arm around her waist and pulling her so close she felt the swell of his arousal against her belly. She loved Gerald, but she didn't want him. Not like this.

She wanted Levi. She wanted him with a crazy, pulsing hunger, an almost desperate yearning. He could make everything become comprehensible to her. He could make things fall into place, make her feel whole. His kiss was like a lullaby echoing inside

her, opening her up, reassuring her that trusting him
was the right thing to do.

The kiss went on and on. She felt drunk with it,
even as it clarified her mind. It offered safety, yet
dared her to take risks. It riled her and soothed her.
It made her want and want and want.

His hands moved on her, one twining through her
hair and the other gliding down to her hip, holding
her as he rocked against her in an unmistakable
rhythm. A small gasp escaped her at the intimacy, and
he pulled back to gaze into her face. Even in the dark
she could see him, her own longing reflected in his
eyes.

Yes, she thought. This made sense. No need to
question it. She would simply accept it.

He bowed to kiss her again, this time on her cheek,
then the bridge of her nose, then her temple. Her head
fell back and he grazed her throat and the skin below
her ear. His hands moved forward to the tiny buttons
running down the front of her sweater. He easily
opened them and his mouth chased his fingers, kissing
her collarbones, her sternum, the hollow between her
breasts.

Heat billowed through her, her own arousal as
strong as his. She tugged at his shirt, but he kept
kissing her, skimming his mouth along the lacy edge
of her bra and then centering on one nipple, sucking
on it through the thin silk. She gasped again, arching
her back, wanting even more.

Straightening, he peeled the bra up out of his way
and filled his hands with her breasts. His mouth came
down on hers again, hard and greedy, and she clung
to him, savoring the taste of him, the pressure of his

large hands against her skin, the friction of his thumbs chafing her.

If she could manage to string a few words together, she would say—what? That this was crazy, that the old Corinne was gone and he was actually kissing a stranger, a lullaby singer. That a hallway outside a makeshift nursery was not an appropriate place to do what they were doing. That the silence and the darkness made every sensation more acute, more erotic.

Or she would speak the truth: *I want more, Levi. I want you.*

She said it with her kisses, her fingers, her sighs. She pulled at his shirt, groping it clumsily until, after some struggle, she freed it from the waistband of his jeans. Her reward was to slide her hands under it, to stroke his hot, smooth back, to feel the subtle ripple of muscle beneath her fingertips. He stopped caressing her breasts long enough to yank his shirt over his head and toss it aside, freeing her to run her hands all over his torso, up to his knotted shoulders, down his arms, forward to his sleek chest, his abdomen, the wings of his hipbones riding just above the edge of his jeans. Her touch caused him to moan, so softly she barely heard him, but that low vibration of sound gratified her enormously.

He wanted her—as much as she wanted him.

Fingers worked at belt buckles, waistband fastenings, zippers. He had her pants open first, and he slid his hand down inside her panties and stroked between her thighs to where the want burned most fiercely. She swayed, and he urged her against the wall, pushing at her pants until they fell past her knees and dropped to the floor. He kissed her, kept one hand on her breast and rubbed the fingers of his other hand against her, again and again. She would have cried out if his mouth hadn't been covering hers.

She tried to strip off his jeans, but her hands refused to obey. Her fingers clenched from the tension building inside her.

After an unbearable moment he released her breast and dug into his pocket. He shoved her panties down and she wriggled one foot free of them, then reached for him just as he unrolled a sheath over himself. She helped him, her hand chasing his along his erection, and then he cupped her hips and surged deep into her.

The wall held her up. So did Levi, lifting her legs around his hips, easing back and then surging again, filling her, possessing her. Her body shook, drawing tight inside. All her energy gathered around him, around the place where they moved together, where they found each other and themselves.

Her climax was quick and intense, causing her toes to curl, her breasts to ache and her fingers to pinch his back. Her soul throbbed in its own secret pulse, embracing him as he gave one final thrust and groaned against her mouth.

A long time passed before he loosened his hold on her. She sank against the wall, her legs oddly nerveless as they slid down past his crumpled jeans. Her feet found the floor, but she clung to his shoulders, certain that if she tried to stand without assistance she'd collapse.

He dipped his head and kissed her mouth, a sweet, gentle kiss. "I have a bed," he whispered.

She smiled. "Now you tell me."

He smiled, too. His face was so close to hers she felt the curve of his lips against her cheek. Slowly, cautiously, he disengaged from her, waiting to make sure her legs could support her before he released her completely. He pulled up his jeans but didn't bother to close them. Then he gathered their scattered articles of clothing with one hand, folded his other hand around hers and led her down the shadowy hall to the room at its end.

The first thing she noticed was the fireplace. Constructed of unrefined blocks of granite, some rounded and some squared, it resembled the stone edifices of the house's exterior. She recalled Levi's theory of architecture—that the outside should be brought indoors—and figured he must have designed this fireplace to echo the outside of the house.

The fireplace's mantel was a stretch of wood, lacquered but rough-hewn. Three kerosene lamps stood on it, one with a ceramic base, one of clear glass and one of stained glass. After tossing their clothing onto a chair, he crossed to the mantel and lit the gas lamps. The room glowed.

"I guess you don't build fires in late June," she murmured.

"I'll build one if you want one."

"Please don't." The last thing she needed was a roaring fire. She still felt overheated by what had happened in the hall. *Standing up,* she thought, dazed at the realization. *Against a wall.* What had she been thinking?

She hadn't been thinking at all. And she didn't regret the mindlessness of it. The old Corinne might have been shocked, but to the new Corinne, making love with Levi the way she had seemed as natural as singing D.J. a lullaby.

Levi lifted one of the gas lamps and carried it to a night table. Following him with her gaze, she noted the simple, modern bureau standing on one wall, the doors leading to a closet and a bathroom, the velvety gray carpet, the floor-to-ceiling windows overlooking the woods behind his house, and the wall hanging, a textured weave of natural hues—brown and tan and gray—in an abstract pattern of geometric shapes. His sister had made it. It was beautiful.

Finally she turned to the bed. It was extra long— he needed that length to accommodate his height— and invitingly wide. With Levi standing beside it, the flickering flame of the lamp washing across his bare chest, the bed looked even more inviting. With his jeans gaping at the unfastened fly, revealing a wedge of dark hair, the bed looked better yet.

He must have figured out what she was thinking, because a slow, irresistibly sexy grin tugged at his mouth. "I'll be right back," he promised, sauntering across the room and disappearing into the bathroom.

Alone, she could have turned on a light and given the room a more diligent inspection. She could have studied how he'd managed to fit all the necessary furniture into his room even though one wall had been sacrificed to the fireplace. She could have taken mental notes to share with Gerald once she was back in New York.

She didn't want to think about Gerald or New York, or her job as the person who made everything work out. She was sure something somewhere needed to be fixed, but she didn't want to be the one to fix it. She just wanted to wait for Levi to come back.

He did, carrying a box of condoms, which he dropped onto the night table next to the gas lamp. Then he kicked off his jeans and pulled Corinne down onto the bed beside him. Rolling onto his back, he brought her with him until she was balanced on top of him, straddling his waist. Her hair fell forward in a fringe around her cheeks, but he tucked it back behind her ears and gazed up at her, smiling, as if he couldn't imagine a more satisfying sight.

"Levi," she murmured, a tiny scrap of the old Corinne niggling at her.

"Yes."

She wished he wouldn't keep combing his fingers through her hair. The backs of her ears had miraculously turned into erogenous zones. Or maybe it was just that when she was with Levi, every square millimeter of her body became an erogenous zone. The insides of her knees pressed against his sides, her insteps brushing his thighs, her palms flat against the pillow framing his head—every part of her tingled, eager and alert.

"I'm not usually like this," she finally said because he was waiting for her to complete her thought.

"Like what?"

"Like any of this." A nebulous answer, but it captured the enormity of her feelings.

He nodded, toyed with the blunt-cut ends of her hair for another moment, then rolled onto his side, once again bringing her with him. She landed on her side facing him, her head resting on the pillow where her hand had just been. "Tell me about it," he said.

At first she thought he was teasing her. But he looked earnest, his eyes dark and searing as he studied her face. "I'm a marketing specialist from Manhattan. I live a pretty tame life. I work late and eat takeout and fall asleep during the eleven o'clock news. I don't..." She sighed, unsure how to finish the sentence.

Levi finished it for her. "You don't have sex standing up."

A blush warmed her cheeks. "Well, that, too. I don't diaper babies. I've never diapered a baby before in my life."

"You did a damned good job of it for a rookie," he said solemnly.

He was definitely teasing her. Scowling, she gave him a gentle poke in the ribs.

He captured her hand with his own and held it between them, just below his chin. "When you came to Arlington today—did you come for D.J.?"

She opened her mouth to say no, then reconsidered. She honestly wasn't sure why she'd come, so she didn't answer.

"You didn't come to hassle me about Mosley's house, did you?"

"No."

"Did you come to seduce me?"

She blushed again. "No." Not that she was complaining about how things had worked out.

"Then you must have come for D.J."

"I think I came for you both."

"That's a relief." His smile undercut the sarcasm in his tone. "I'm not used to competing with a kid in diapers for a woman's attention."

"Well, you both got my attention."

He twirled a strand of her hair around his finger while he ruminated. "Do you have anybody back in New York?"

Not just *anybody*—he was asking if she had a boyfriend. And she didn't, not really. Gerald wasn't a boyfriend. He was her friend, her colleague, her closest buddy. And he was a man.

But not a boyfriend.

"I guess you do," Levi said quietly.

"No."

"It took you an awfully long time to answer."

"I don't date much," she told him, then chuckled. "That's an exaggeration. I don't date at all."

"Why not?"

She thought of all the easy explanations: she didn't have the time, she didn't have the energy. But Levi deserved the whole truth. "I don't have much faith in it."

"In what? Dating? Men?"

"Relationships."

"Really? Why?"

He looked genuinely interested. She'd never discussed her background with Gerald—but then, he'd never asked. Levi had asked, and his curiosity touched her in an unexpectedly personal way. "I've got, at last count, one father, two stepfathers, one mother and three stepmothers," she told him. "I've seen firsthand that most relationships don't last. You can date, you can make commitments, you can get married—but nothing comes with guarantees. Promises get trashed. Vows get tossed aside. Why knock yourself out trying to create something that's just going to fall apart?"

Again he mulled over his thoughts before speaking. "Okay," he said, propping his head up on his hand, as if the higher elevation would enable him to think more clearly. "First of all, dating and getting married are two different things. Why can't you just date without worrying about how it's going to end in the long run?"

"Because I don't have the time," she said, then

cringed inwardly. That was the easy answer, but it didn't ring true to her. "Because where else is dating going to lead to? Sex, a commitment or a breakup."

"Sex is good," he suggested, a hint of mischief illuminating his eyes. "Even if you're standing up."

She felt yet another blush burn her cheeks, but before she could recover his smile was gone, his gaze solemn. He obviously didn't want to talk about sex. He wanted her to explain what seemed patently obvious to her. "Even if sex is good," she said, "it's going to lead to either a commitment or a breakup. And most of the time, the commitment's going to end in a break-up, too. The whole thing seems pretty pointless to me."

"What makes you so sure a commitment is going to end in a breakup? I've seen relationships that have lasted a long time. My parents have been married for forty years."

"Are they happy?"

A wry smile twisted his mouth. "If you asked them, they'd say they were."

"And if you asked them whether they loved each other?"

"They'd say…" He sighed. "They'd say love isn't that important in the grand scheme of things."

"See?"

"They're just two people, Corinne. Your parents are two more people—or maybe, what was it, six? Seven?"

"Seven at last count." She rolled onto her back and watched the flicker of the gaslight's flame reflected on the ceiling above the bed. "My mother and father, Norman, Clark, Betsy, Cynthia and—I forget the wife between Betsy and Cynthia. She didn't last long."

"It sounds as if none of them did."

"She was the shortest. Maybe two years, tops. I didn't see her too often because she and my dad lived in Los Angeles. I spent a few weeks with them one summer, but she was hardly ever around. I was supposed to spend the whole summer, but I was so miserable I made my dad send me home. After that, he'd fly to Phoenix to visit me. Jeri—that was her name. Jeri Ann or Jeri Lynn."

Her peripheral vision caught him shaking his head. "That's so different from what I grew up with."

"You might have felt stifled by your parents' home, Levi, but at least you had some stability in your life. I never knew where I was going to be living from one year to the next. Or who I was going to be living with. My parents called it shared custody, but it amounted to me having so many different addresses I didn't know where I was supposed to be, most of the time. I had stepsisters and stepbrothers, but they came and went. I always thought, if I kept the house neat and made sure everything was where it was supposed to be, at least something in my life would be orderly. Something would be the same in the evening as it was in the morning. I never got too attached to any of the 'steps,' because I knew that sooner or later they would leave. Or else my mom and dad would leave them. Someone was always leaving." She twisted her head to look at him. "Do you realize how lucky you were to have your sister Ruth? I know she's gone now, but not because someone got tired of someone else and left."

Levi ran his fingers through her hair again. "Some

relationships are forever," he said. "It wouldn't matter if I got tired of D.J. That one's forever. I couldn't walk away from him, even if I wanted to."

"Some parents walk away from their kids."

"Bad parents." He sighed. "I don't mean to pass judgment on your parents, but—"

"But you just passed judgment on them." She grinned. "They aren't bad people. They're very human. They're just fickle, and searching for happiness."

"They're self-centered and undisciplined." A faint laugh escaped him. "Six weeks with D.J., and I'm acting like an expert. Sorry. You're right. I shouldn't pass judgment on them."

But he was right, too. Her parents *were* self-centered and undisciplined, and they'd taught their daughter not to place her faith in long-term love, because their own behavior had proved that it didn't work.

Gazing up at Levi, she found herself contemplating the strangest thought: maybe, sometimes, it *did* work. Maybe, if a man could make such a strong commitment to an orphaned baby, he could make a commitment to a woman. *That one's forever,* he'd said about his relationship with D.J. A man like him might be able to say that about a woman, too—and mean it.

That was a frightening idea. If she let herself believe such a thing was possible, such a man existed, she'd have to rethink everything she'd ever understood about life and men and love, and she wasn't prepared to do that. She'd found the stability missing from her childhood by creating it for herself. It was hers, and she didn't want anything to threaten it. Levi, with his concepts of forever, threatened it in a big way.

He ran his hand through her hair once more, this time trailing his fingers down to her shoulder. His fingertips were callused; even though he was an architect, who plied his trade at a drafting table in his quiet second-floor office, she supposed he sometimes got his hands dirty at construction sites. She'd seen him in his hard hat that afternoon, and she could easily envision him helping his foreman, carrying tools, wielding a shovel, swinging a board into place. He'd learned how to work hard as a child, and he wore that experience on his hands.

That was only one reason they felt so good moving across her body. That, and his ability to read her responses, and his willingness to touch her not just in those few areas that men seemed to be obsessed with, but all over—the underside of her chin, the concave stretch below her rib cage, the pale inner skin of her forearm.

But the most important reason it felt so good to be touched by him was that he was Levi. He was like no other man she'd ever met. And even though she knew she would come to her senses tomorrow, tonight she wanted to believe in a man who could talk about forever.

ONE THING he'd always loved about women was how different they were from him. Not different in the limiting ways his parents had taught him—females in charge of cooking and cleaning while males performed repairs, scaled ladders and painted clapboard siding—but different in their minds and their bodies.

Corinne's body was a wonder, even lovelier than

he'd guessed. Her skin was soft and supple, her breasts deliciously round, her waist taut, her hips generous, her belly button an incredibly sexy punctuation mark midway between her ribs and her crotch. And her legs—oh, God, they were amazing. He'd realized, once his crazed interlude with her in the hallway was done, that she wasn't the sort who indulged in that kind of raw passion on a regular basis. She was mature, poised, sophisticated—but she always had a shyness about her, a reticence he hadn't really understood until just now, when she'd told him about her upbringing.

She did hold back. He hadn't just imagined it. She was self-protective, reserved, wary. Yet when he'd made love to her in the hallway—totally unpremeditated and possible only because he'd optimistically slid a condom into his pocket before heading off to her hotel that evening—he'd stripped away all her defenses in a way that might have alarmed her if she wasn't so strong inside.

He'd stripped away her defenses because she'd allowed him to. What happened had been her doing as much as his. Not only hadn't she stopped him, but she'd encouraged him. She'd been as caught up in the craziness as he'd been.

Now that he'd made love to her once, he understood her body a little better. She liked being stroked as much as he liked stroking her. She liked keeping her eyes open, watching him. Apparently she liked the feel of his shoulders; she'd clung to them in the hall and she was touching them again now, tracing the bulges of muscle and bone as he ran his hand along the arch of her ribs, the flare of her hips.

He understood her mind a little better, too—but not

well enough. What she'd revealed about her parents illuminated some aspects of her, but not the strange bond between her and D.J.

It existed, as real as the bed beneath them, as real as the golden light that circled the kerosene lamp on the night table. When she and D.J. looked at each other, Levi could practically see a cord of emotion running between them. When she held D.J., her body seemed to radiate an aura.

Why? D.J. was just a baby. A good baby, a healthy baby, a baby as handsome as his mother had predicted he'd be. But also a whiny baby, a fussy baby, a messy, demanding, occasionally smelly baby—in other words, a normal baby.

What was going on between Corinne and D.J.? What was that cord, that aura, that bond?

She skimmed her hand forward, over the hump of his shoulder and down his chest, and he decided he didn't want to think about D.J. any more. Right now, the only bond that mattered was the one between her and himself.

She had astonishing hands. Soft and graceful, but what made them unique was the way his body felt beneath them. Her caresses short-circuited his nervous system, electrifying him. Every muscle in his body flexed at her touch; every nerve spiked. His blood sizzled, his skin hungered for her—and when she rose up and pressed a kiss to the center of his chest he felt that kiss everywhere, in his bones, his throat, his groin, his soul. He could have told himself his powerful reaction to her was because she was the first woman he'd been with since he'd brought D.J. home to Connecticut—but it wasn't as if he had never before gone without sex for an extended period. He'd endured plenty of stretches of celibacy in his life, and they hadn't affected him all that much.

But this... This was Corinne. Theirs was a transcendent connection. It was something that defied analysis, something that operated on a level he hadn't even known existed. It was need and completion and magic.

As their kisses grew deeper, their hands more eager, their bodies more desperate, he let his thoughts evaporate. Whatever was going on didn't have to be rationalized. It could just be accepted, one more act of fate and faith in his life.

Rolling Corinne onto her back, lowering himself into her welcoming arms, finding her and filling her and feeling her all around him, he gladly accepted what he simply couldn't explain.

CHAPTER ELEVEN

SOMEONE HAD DECORATED the YMCA room in the week since Levi was last there. Perky posters featuring illustrations of healthful activities hung on the walls: a colorful depiction of the food pyramid, a photograph of children playing soccer with the word *Exercise!* printed in vivid orange letters above them, a bright rendition of a toothbrush with a generous nurdle of toothpaste adorning the bristles.

D.J.'s bottom two teeth had broken through. His teething pain had obviously abated; he hardly ever fussed and whimpered these days. Levi wondered whether he was supposed to brush D.J.'s teeth. There wasn't much to brush, only two hard white bumps, like dots of puff paint adorning his gums.

He'd learned about puff paint from Evan's daughter, Gracie, at last week's poker game. She'd just graduated from preschool, and she viewed herself as an art expert, having mastered such techniques as glitter, markers, finger paint and puff paint.

Would D.J. someday reveal an artistic flair? He had a set of nontoxic crayons, which he mostly used as drumsticks—but then, he used everything as drumsticks. Banging on things was obviously one of his preferred activities.

Still, his mother had been artistic, and his uncle—well, architecture was kind of a hybrid, but it required an aesthetic sense and a certain amount of creativity. It was the perfect discipline for someone with the mind of an engineer and the soul of an artist. Levi wasn't sure what kind of mind D.J. had, but he certainly seemed to have a lot of soul.

Levi had left him and Tara in the den twenty minutes ago, Tara watching TV and D.J. propelling himself around the room in his walker—at a modest pace, since the den had carpeting, which slowed the walker to an almost reasonable speed. Levi hoped D.J. would tire himself out so he'd be ready for bed by the time Levi got home. A quick bath, a quick bottle and a valiant attempt at a lullaby—D.J. obviously didn't appreciate his singing voice as much as he'd appreciated Corinne's—and into the crib, hopefully for the night.

The folding metal chair Levi sat on was too small for him. He felt as if he could rest his chin on his sharply bent knees. Evan took Daddy School classes, too, but in a different program, one run by the director of Gracie's preschool. She led classes for fathers of older children. The classes Allison Winslow taught at the YMCA were for fathers of infants and men whose babies hadn't even been born yet.

One of Levi's classmates had just changed status. The young man strutted into the room bearing a fistful of pink bubble gum cigars. Allison, who arrived at the room with him, seemed just as delighted as the new father. "Bobby! You had a girl?"

"We sure did!" Bobby beamed and passed out the cigars, basking in the congratulations of his fellow students. Bobby didn't look old enough to be a father. The kid was easily ten years younger than Levi, and Levi himself didn't feel old enough to be a father.

Maybe he'd feel old enough if he had a woman by his side. A woman to whom D.J. meant as much as he did to Levi. A woman whose heart lay open to D.J., who could put D.J. to bed and tuck him in and then leave the room and open her heart to Levi.

He felt a sharp twinge of arousal and shifted his legs, nearly kicking the chair next to him. It was Monday night, and he wasn't going to see Corinne again until Friday.

He might not feel old enough to be a father, but he was definitely too old to be a weekend boyfriend. After enjoying a solid forty-eight hours with Corinne, Levi had found her departure Sunday afternoon torturous. The time they'd spent together had been almost mundane: a bit of puttering in the backyard, a drive to the Mosley site to check on the drying footings, a detour to the video store to rent *The Buddy Holly Story*—he had no idea why they'd chosen that flick, but they'd both enjoyed it. So had D.J., until he'd dropped off to sleep in the middle of "That'll Be The Day."

Once the movie had ended, they'd rewound the tape, carried D.J. up to his crib and headed down the hall to Levi's room.

He felt another tug in his groin. It amazed him that he could feel so utterly attuned to her, as if their bodies had been born knowing each other—and yet he still didn't actually *know* her. He knew how to make her sigh, how to make her moan. Without having to think about it, he could read her body with his own. He could tell when she was on the verge of coming, and hold back, slow down, stretch it out for her until she was gasping and pleading, her legs clasped hard around him and her hands fisted against his back. And then, when neither of them could wait another instant, he could let go, sending them both over the edge.

They were so compatible it was almost uncanny.

But that was in bed. Out of bed, he wasn't so sure.

It wasn't as if they didn't get along. They did, wonderfully. He liked talking to her, listening to her, looking at her. He loved hearing her sing to D.J. But knowing that she could sing a lullaby a hundred times better than he could, knowing that she could embrace his baby in all kinds of ways, wasn't the same thing as *knowing* her.

Why had she returned to Arlington last Friday? For Levi or for D.J.? She'd said she'd returned for both of them—but why would a beautiful single professional woman travel all the way to Arlington for a baby? Why would she sing to D.J. in a voice filled with such profound devotion?

Levi didn't understand it.

And the damnedest thing was, he didn't think she understood it, either.

"Okay, everyone, let's settle down," Allison urged the class as several of the fathers unwrapped their bubble gum cigars and the rest, like Levi, pocketed them. "Bobby, why don't you tell us what you've discovered about being a father, now that you're actually one."

The new dad in the spotlight grinned. A small diamond winked from his earlobe and a tattoo—it looked like Chinese ideogram—darkened one forearm. He was a flashy dude, but obviously a very proud papa at the moment. "We named her Chandra," he said. "She is so gorgeous you could die. I swear, I'm gonna tear out the eyeballs of any guy who looks at her the wrong way. You're all my witnesses to that. I swear it.''

Most of the men chuckled. Allison laughed out loud. Levi remembered his brief encounter with her daughter, when he'd driven to Jamie McCoy's house. Allison was Jamie's wife, and their daughter, who had just turned three, seemed perfectly capable of tearing out a person's eyeballs without any assistance from an overprotective father.

''What else? Is she keeping you up all night?''

''Me? No. My wife takes care of that.''

Again a few men chuckled. Allison didn't smile. ''How about at mealtimes? Can you and your wife sit down and have a calm dinner?''

''Calm? Hell, no.'' Bobby grinned, but his eyes darkened with frustration. ''Nothing's calm. *Calm* isn't in our vocabulary right now, if you know what I mean.''

''I do know what you mean. All the daddies in this room know what you mean. Those of you who are still awaiting your bundles of joy, I hope you're paying attention. Life isn't calm when you've got a baby in the house. In fact, it often doesn't calm down again until your baby leaves home, eighteen or twenty years from now.''

A murmur spread through the room. Levi rearranged his legs to keep them from getting stiff. He'd had a pretty calm dinner with Corinne on Friday night at Moise's Fish House. Give D.J. enough banana, and the kid could stay reasonably calm. Saturday night Levi had grilled chicken and they'd eaten on the porch. D.J. had spent most of the mealtime careering around the porch in his walker, which wasn't exactly calm, but they were able to tune him out enough to have an extended conversation. They'd talked about Corinne's first experiences with winter, as someone who'd grown up in Phoenix and never built a snowman in her life, and about the Boston office complex Levi and his partner Phyllis were bidding on.

"How about sex?" Allison asked Bobby.

A few of the men squirmed in their chairs, apparently embarrassed. Bobby scowled. "Hey, come on! She only just had a baby. The poor woman has to heal."

Allison smiled her approval. "Yes, she does. But here's something some of the other dads in the room will tell you. Your sex life is probably going to change because of the baby. This is something we need to talk about. It causes a lot of fathers problems."

More murmuring. More squirming. Levi drew in a deep breath and leveled his eyes on Allison. He'd enrolled in the Daddy School hoping for pointers about child care, not for sex education from a slim, curly-haired neonatal nurse.

Yet his sex life had changed with the arrival of D.J. At first it had become so removed from his consciousness he hadn't even had any urges, let alone acted on them. And then Corinne had entered his world.

Should he thank D.J.? Was he the only student in the class who could honestly say his baby had actually improved his sex life?

Anger pinched his brow and tightened his mouth. He didn't want to believe D.J. was that essential to his relationship with Corinne. Of course he was glad she liked the baby; of course he appreciated her tolerance of and patience with D.J. But deep in his heart, Levi wanted to believe he and not his orphaned nephew was the main attraction for her. He wanted to believe that there was more passion in her kisses than in her lullabies.

He told himself not to get all worked up about it. She would be back in Arlington Friday evening, and he would observe her with D.J., and he would have her in his bed. He would reassure himself that he wasn't in competition with D.J. for her affection. What was going on between her and the kid was a universe apart from what was going on between her and Levi. If she lived closer, he wouldn't have to wait until the weekend to put his concerns to rest, but the situation was what it was.

She lived in New York, and he was a weekend boyfriend.

"YOU'RE GOING BACK to Arlington again?" Gerald asked.

He'd slouched into her office ten minutes ago, pretending to be wrung out from their meeting with the people from Bell Tech. The session had gone quite well, but Gerald wasn't used to sitting around conference tables and discussing business processes in a civil, sedate manner. He liked to babble jargon and spew ideas, and he grew irritated with people who didn't understand what he was talking about—which was the vast majority of people he encountered. He didn't grow irritated with Corinne only because he depended on her to help him navigate through the real world—and because she never grew irritated with him.

He'd come to her office to rehash the meeting. For the past ten minutes, he'd complained about how poorly the meeting had gone, and she'd assured him that the meeting had in fact gone quite well. The Bell Tech people were enthusiastic about working with Gerald and they wanted to meet with him and Corinne again. She'd told them it would have to be early next week. She couldn't schedule a meeting for Friday.

Now Gerald was questioning her about that. Unwilling to hide the truth from him, she said. "Yes, I'm going back to Arlington."

"Why? What's wrong? Are the builders screwing up my house?"

"No. At least, I assume not. When I was there last weekend, everything seemed fine."

"So why are you going back?"

He stared at her across her desk, his hair mussed and his eyes keen through the lenses of his glasses. Gerald was so smart it was a point of pride with him that he should be able to comprehend everything. When he didn't—like now—it irked him, and he'd continue questioning her until he got an answer he could program into his operating system.

She wished she could give him an answer *she* could comprehend. "There's a baby up there."

"A baby?" He scowled and fell back in his chair. He swung one foot up and balanced it across the other knee. His shoe was untied, and the lace tapped quietly against the treaded rubber soul. "What baby?"

"Levi Holt's baby."

"The architect? Is this the baby who caused all the problems when you went to renegotiate the contract?"

"Yes."

"So, what does this baby have to do with you?"

"He... I know this will sound strange, Gerald, but he needs me."

"The baby needs you?" She nodded, and his scowl intensified. "How does Levi's wife feel about that?"

"He doesn't have a wife. All he has is this baby."

"Does not compute." Gerald shook his head. "I thought *I* was the weird one in this consulting firm, Corey. You can't be weird, too. One of us has to be sane."

Her laughter sounded sad. She didn't believe she was insane, any more than she believed Gerald was. Her connection to D.J. was odd, but she hoped that if she kept returning to Arlington it would eventually start making sense. And in the meantime, she'd be with Levi.

Levi.

She had to stifle a sigh. While her feelings for D.J. mystified her, her feelings for Levi were as clear as distilled water. He enthralled her. He astounded her. He made her feel cherished and desirable. He accepted her as she was. She didn't have to knock herself out to impress him.

And in bed—oh, God, in bed he was amazing. She'd never thought of herself as a particularly sensual woman, but he made her bold and daring, even aggressive. His touch awakened all sorts of brave impulses inside her, all kinds of erotic longings. Who needed a fireplace in the bedroom, with the conflagrations that erupted between her and Levi whenever they entered that room and exchanged a gaze?

Just thinking about him left a trail of heat tingling down her spine.

"Is this one of those biological clock thingies?" Gerald asked.

Corinne chuckled at Gerald's tactlessness. "Thingies?"

"You know what I mean. You're closing in on your thirtieth birthday and you want to have a kid."

"No. I don't particularly want a kid. It's just *this* kid." Her smile faded as she realized how bizarre she must sound to Gerald, who counted on her not to be weird. "Maybe he and I knew each other in a past life," she said. "Maybe we've got some sort of karmic connection."

Gerald shook his head again. He appeared gravely troubled. "You're sure it has nothing to do with my house?"

"Your house is going to be fine—other than that stupid wall of glass in the kitchen and the fireplace in the bedroom. Don't worry about it, Gerald. It's going to be everything you dreamed, and then some."

"I'm worried. When you tell me not to worry, I worry. At least I do when you've got that glazed look in your eyes."

"What glazed look?" She blinked vigorously. "Can we finish reviewing the Bell Tech meeting? Because I've got work to do."

"I know what work you've got to do. I'm your boss," Gerald said, a statement that would have alarmed her if his voice had had an ounce of conviction in it. However, he sounded not bossy but deeply concerned about her, and his concern touched her. In any case, he would never dare to boss her around. He might have been the genius behind their first venture, but without her marketing skills to back him up, he would probably still be traveling from ad agency to media outlet, trying to convince skeptical clients to buy his graphics software and wondering why companies weren't more interested in it.

He needed her. Corporate hierarchies were irrelevant.

Maybe she shouldn't have been so honest with him about her plan to return to Arlington. She shouldn't have mentioned that a sturdy little boy had stolen a piece of her heart. Or maybe she should have been *more* honest and told him a tall, dark-eyed man had stolen a different piece of her heart. Gerald was her best friend. She ought to tell him.

But she couldn't—because she didn't know what to say. The passion burning between her and Levi could be just a brief, brilliant blaze, a flare that would die down the instant its fuel supply was spent. In another month D.J. would be an entirely different person. Babies changed so fast.

And then where would she be? Still by Gerald's side, imagining herself by his side forever, two compatible loners teaming up and facing the world together. Even if what she felt for Levi was love—and for all she knew, it was—it wouldn't last. As best she could tell, love never did. It couldn't be trusted.

She'd enjoy the blaze's heat and dazzling light for as long as it lasted. Once it had extinguished itself, she and Gerald would still be together, friends, in no danger of getting burned.

THEY DROVE for a while, and when they stopped moving they were at a place he'd never seen before, a long walkway with a ditch next to it and a little shed hanging over their heads. "The train's going to come," Levi said. "You know what a train is, don't you?"

He knew, because the lady with the big hands read him a book about a train carrying toys over a hill.

The train that chugged to the platform where Levi stood holding D.J. was loud and clangy, all hot, sleek metal. It rolled to a halt with a screech.

Lots of people poured off the train, but he saw only one: the woman. She was back. She and Levi saw each other almost as soon as D.J. saw her, and they walked toward each other, smiling so much D.J. knew they were as happy as he was. D.J. had believed she would come back, and here she was.

She was carrying a bag, but she set it down on the platform and wrapped them both in her arms, a huge double hug, one arm around Levi and one around them both. She kissed Levi's cheek and then D.J.'s head and then Levi's cheek again, and his mouth. D.J. was so excited he squealed and twisted in Levi's arm, trying to grab her cheek.

She caught his hand and he wrapped his fingers around her thumb. Her hands were much smaller than Levi's, and it was easy for D.J. to get his fingers to circle all the way around. Her hands were smoother, too, no rough, hard places like on Levi's. She said something to Levi, and he passed D.J. to her so she could hold him. She wasn't as strong as Levi, or as high off the ground, and her shoulder wasn't as hard and wide. But she smelled so good, that warm woman smell he loved. He cuddled up to her, feeling the curve of her breast against his belly and pressing his mouth to her chin.

"Hello, D.J.," she said cheerfully. "Did you miss me?"

Of course he'd missed her. He wished he knew how to tell her.

The drive home was better than the drive to the train, because she was in the car. He could tell Levi was pleased that she was there. Whenever the car stopped, he would look over at her, his eyes soft and his head tilted. Everything was better when she was with them. Maybe if she realized this, she wouldn't leave anymore.

Dinner was good. They ate on the porch and Levi let him stay in his walker. He loved being in the walker on the porch, because the floor was cool and slick and the outside seemed to be all around him. They talked, soft grown-up voices murmuring, sometimes a touch between hands.

Then came his bath, which she gave him. She was so gentle, talking to him while she sloshed water all over him, telling him he was getting bigger and growing more hair and his teeth looked very nice and he had the stickiest fingers in the world. She dried him and dressed him and Levi gave her a bottle to feed D.J. Even though it wasn't her breast, he was so glad she was feeding him he didn't mind.

And then, the best part. She lifted him in her arms and sang the lullaby, the one that went, "Hush, little baby, don't say a word..."

The one he knew. The one his mother used to sing.

It was getting harder and harder for him to hold on to his mother. She had long hair; he remembered that. And she would sleep across the room from him, and he could see her shape in the darkness. She used to laugh a lot, and call him Darren—but he could no longer picture her face. It was fading like the world when the sun disappeared at the end of a day. Trees he'd seen clearly through his window slowly dimmed, grew darker and less distinct until he could no longer see them. That was how it was with his mother's face.

But the lullaby—he remembered that. His mother used to sing it. "Hush, little baby..."

Hearing it again almost made him cry—and it almost made him laugh. The music went into him like air, sweet and full of life, swelling inside him. He felt cleansed by the song, washed inside the way the bath had washed him outside.

She kissed his forehead and laid him in his crib. He hugged his bear close and felt his blanket settle over him like a quiet breeze. Then she joined Levi at the door and turned off the light. The lullaby was still in his head when he fell asleep.

CHAPTER TWELVE

RAIN HAD POUNDED down on Arlington Friday night, augmented by drumrolls of thunder and an occasional flicker of lightning. By Saturday morning, the storm had passed, leaving the northwest corner of Connecticut green and fresh.

D.J. was babbling in his crib at the other end of the hall. Levi could hear him; his needle was set on the kid's frequency. It had taken him weeks to develop that sensitivity. The first few nights after he'd brought D.J. home, he'd been so exhausted his sleep had been deep enough to block out the world. D.J. had had to holler at top volume to get his attention—which the kid wanted constantly, which had contributed to Levi's exhaustion, which had made D.J. have to holler even louder. It had been a self-perpetuating downward spiral.

But now they knew and trusted each other. If D.J. wasn't desperate for a diaper change or some food, he simply chattered to himself, or maybe to his teddy bear. Nonsense syllables, gobbledygook, the hushed sound of a happy child greeting the new day.

Corinne must have also been tuned in to D.J.'s frequency. She hadn't needed two months to grow accustomed to his sounds, just a few nights in Levi's house. Her eyes fluttered open the moment D.J.'s gibbering penetrated Levi's partially closed door, and she smiled. "He sounds cheerful."

"He is."

"I guess he slept through the storm."

Levi grinned and tightened his arm around her. He and Corinne hadn't slept through it. The first rumble of thunder had awakened them, and he'd gotten out of bed and crossed to the window for a closer look at the downpour. He loved rain.

Corinne apparently loved it, too. "We used to get storms like this in Phoenix," she'd told him, joining him at the window and watching the rain slash silver across the night. "The ground would be so dry it couldn't absorb all the water, and we'd get flash floods. Then, the next day, we'd be back to desert weather."

They'd stood together in front of the window, their bodies naked and warm from the bed, the rain so close yet safely sealed away from them. He'd moved behind her, his arms ringing her waist like a belt, and gently nipped her ear. She'd leaned into him and he'd skimmed his hands up to her breasts, and she'd turned to face him and they'd started kissing again, hard, greedy kisses, until they'd tumbled back onto the bed and made love. The rain had lashed the windows and he would have sworn that the instant she climaxed the sky filled with a searing white flash of lightning.

Falling in love hadn't been on his agenda, not while he was still adjusting to the whole fatherhood thing. But then, fatherhood hadn't been on his agenda, either. His parents would have lectured him not to question but simply to accept what fate had delivered unto him—and in this instance, they'd be right. He was simply going to accept it, all of it—the baby and the woman.

D.J.'s voice rose in pitch, not quite demanding but close. Corinne started to pull out of Levi's arms, but he refused to let her go. "He can wait a minute," he whispered, urging her onto her back and taking her mouth with a deep kiss.

She returned his kiss for a few heavenly seconds, then pulled away. "He needs us," she said.

Levi stifled a curse. He recalled the subject of Allison Winslow's Daddy School class on Monday night, her lecture about how a baby could interfere with his father's sex life. He supposed this was part of what he had to accept.

He didn't have to be overjoyed about it, though.

Reluctantly, he climbed out of bed, donned a pair of jeans and lent Corinne his bathrobe, which fell to her ankles but didn't drag on the floor. She rolled the sleeves up an extra cuff, tightened the sash around her waist and hurried out of the bedroom, as if D.J. were crying out for her.

Maybe he was. He immediately released a flurry of giggles when Corinne entered his room. "Hi, D.J.," she greeted him. No gushy patter, no baby talk, no calling him "cutie" or "doodlebug" or "jelly bean." Just "Hi, D.J.," as though he were an old pal she was used to seeing on a regular basis.

Levi hesitated in the doorway while she glided across the room to the crib. The sight of her and D.J. greeting each other so easily, with such familiarity, caused something to glint inside him, a diamond buried in his gut. As beautiful as that diamond was, its sharp edges poked at him, causing twinges of discomfort.

If he loved Corinne, he had to be delighted by her rapport with D.J. And he was. But...

Damn it, he was selfish. And shortsighted and stupid and stubborn—but he didn't want it to be so easy for her. He'd had to work hard to cultivate the parenting habit, to overcome his fear and resentment and accept his fate without question. He wanted it to be hard for her, too. He wanted her to turn to him for help, to lean on him, to let him facilitate her relationship with D.J. He wanted to be the number-one Holt in her life.

Objectively, he knew his feelings were ridiculous. She wasn't comparing the two of them, favoring one over the other. Or if she was, Levi was clearly her favorite. After a night with her, he knew that what existed between them was immeasurably powerful.

But what existed between her and D.J. wasn't exactly trifling. The way they interacted, D.J. chortling and burbling and reaching for her as she reached for him in a perfectly synchronized movement... It was as if they didn't even need him.

Annoyed with himself for his petty jealousy, he entered the room and pulled a clean diaper from an open package. "What do you say we have some breakfast and take a drive. There are some beautiful back roads outside of town, up into the hills. Everything always looks kind of magical after a rain."

She spun around and smiled, such a sweet, open smile he hated himself for having resented her closeness to D.J. "That sounds wonderful," she said.

Breakfast was far from peaceful—cream of wheat and a banana for D.J., toast, coffee and fruit for him and Corinne, everything eaten briskly because D.J. was obviously ready to assault the day. Corinne took a quick shower while Levi got D.J. dressed, and then he left the two of them together while he showered. As he stood under the hot spray, he tried not to think about what they were doing in his absence, how much thicker their bond was growing.

What kind of an idiot was he? He could just imagine what his poker pals would say if he tried to explain it to them: "I don't like the way things are going. Corinne gets along too well with D.J." Evan, who had fallen in love with his fiancée in large part because she'd adored his children, would tell him he was certifiably insane. Murphy would laugh in his face. Brett, who was a militant bachelor, would shrug and shake his head and insist he didn't get it. Tom Bland, a private investigator in town, would offer to open a file on Corinne, to make sure she wasn't the sort who might spirit D.J. away and flee the state. Tom tended to view every problem, no matter how minor, as deserving of its own investigation.

What Levi had with Corinne wasn't a problem. It was a terrific relationship with amazing potential. He ought to be over the moon with gratitude that he found a woman like her just when D.J. had invaded his life.

He reminded himself of that several more times while he dressed. He located Corinne and D.J. outside on the back deck, gazing out at the grass. Lingering raindrops glistened across the lawn like clear pearls. Corinne held D.J. high in her arms, one hip jutted out for balance. They could have been a mother and child.

Oh, Ruth, Levi whispered. *I hope what I'm doing is okay. I hope this thing between D.J. and Corinne is good.*

It felt good as they drove out of town and into the

hills, passing old barns, rambling corrals penning horses, countless apple orchards and dense woods. If the ground had been less damp from last night's storm—and if D.J. hadn't been with them—Levi might have suggested hiking one of the trails that cut through the state forests and climbed the modest hills. From the peaks of those hills they'd be able to see all the way into New York State.

But Levi wasn't in the mood to push D.J.'s stroller all the way up a trail on a hot early-July morning. So they only drove through the scenery, and he told Corinne that someday they could hike in the forests.

"How's the house coming?" she asked as they headed back toward town.

"Do you want to have a look?"

"Sure." She smiled. "I've never seen a house get built. In New York City, they build skyscrapers, but everything is steel beams. It's not like seeing an actual house grow up out of the ground."

"Did you ever play with building blocks as a kid?" he asked.

"I had Lego. How about you?"

"No Lego. We had some of those classic wooden building blocks. I loved building things with them— houses, towers, bridges, entire cities—but they fell apart too easily."

"Do you ever build models at work?"

"Sometimes. We do a lot of computer modeling, though. Mosley's house was modeled on the computer. You can get all sorts of views, inside and out, on the screen."

He cruised the main route that ran along the western edge of town. Estates, some charming and some ostentatious, sprawled across the acreage. A few of the houses were old—refurbished farmhouses and manors. His partner Bill had renovated some of them.

He steered onto a side road, and from there onto the narrow dirt lane that led past a stand of trees to the construction site. The foundation was in and the framing begun, tall beams and studs rising from the concrete base. The wood had been thoroughly washed in last night's storm, and it remained shaded in sections where the dampness clung.

No one was at the site. When a project was on schedule, Levi couldn't see any reason to pay a construction crew overtime to work on weekends, and since he'd adjusted the completion date on Mosley's contract when Corinne had negotiated the design changes, this project was on schedule.

To her, the site might look desolate. To him, it looked like a house gestating, soon to be born as a genuine home. He could visualize the walls rising around the skeleton of boards, fleshing them in, creating a living entity. He could picture the stone facades, the sloping roofs, the broad panes of glass letting the outside in.

Wanting to impart his vision to her, he shut off the engine, climbed out and unlatched the tiny trunk space beneath the hatchback, where he stored D.J.'s folding stroller. He snapped it open, then straightened up to find Corinne standing by her open door and leaning into the back seat to unstrap D.J.

Cripes. They were like a married couple, he thought—a happy little family, Daddy getting the stroller while Mommy got the baby. Life would be so much easier for him if there always was a mommy to get D.J. If Corinne was a permanent part of his life, he would never have to get both the stroller and the baby all by himself. What a concept.

A dangerous concept—especially because it seemed so obvious to him, so natural. This warm, sunny Saturday morning could be any day, the two of them working in a smooth choreography as they attended to D.J. He could visualize it as clearly as he visualized an entire house simply by viewing a bare-bones structure of two-by-fours.

Corinne smiled as she approached him with D.J. in her arms. She settled the kid into the stroller and he kicked his feet in a movement Levi knew reflected excitement. D.J. loved his stroller, for some reason. He displayed as much joy being strapped into it as he did being strapped into his car seat or settled in his walker. This was a boy who liked wheeled vehicles.

The stroller didn't move too smoothly on the rutted, spongy ground. Corinne struggled to steer it and Levi took over, navigating it around mounds of dirt and textured ruts left by the trucks and construction equipment. "Here's where the garage is going to go," he said as they ambled to one side of the foundation. Maybe he could get Corinne to see the house where only the potential for one existed. "The back patio is going to spread out from here, and then the pool will go in somewhere around here." He gestured toward an expanse of muddy dirt.

"Poo! Poo!"

"That's right, D.J.—a pool."

"Poo-poo-poo!"

Corinne laughed. "Something tells me he wants to go swimming."

"He's too young," Levi said automatically, then rethought his answer. He had no idea if D.J. was too young to go into a pool. If Ruth was alive, she'd probably be taking him into the ocean with her. She was wild that way, afraid of nothing. And maybe allowing a seven-month-old baby into the water wasn't such a dangerous thing. He'd have to look it up in his guidebook, or ask Allison Winslow at the next Daddy School class.

He wished he knew such details, the things other parents knew because they'd had months to prepare for the arrival of their children. He also wished the thought of donning a swimsuit and bringing D.J. to the pool at the YMCA didn't elicit an unwelcome dread inside him. He supposed the Y scheduled children's swimming hours, during which the pool would fill with mothers and their babies—in their diapers? Ugh—and he'd be the only full-grown male in the water. He'd feel awkward and out of place. When he swam, he wanted to *swim,* consuming laps until his lungs ached and his arms felt leaden. How could he do that with D.J.? He'd have to stay in the shallow end, the water washing over his ankles while D.J. giggled and splashed and peed.

He glanced at Corinne beside him, gazing out at the area where the pool would be installed. Her hands in the pockets of her jeans, her T-shirt draped loosely over her shoulders, her hair ruffled by a breeze, she frowned slightly, as if exerting herself to visualize what he saw so clearly it could have been a photograph in front of him.

She seemed a world away from the naked woman who had stood watching the storm with him last night—and yet the world she was in now appealed to him just as much. It was a world in which a mother and a father could take turns bringing their baby into the shallow end of the pool. A world in which two people shared responsibility for the baby, instead of one well-intentioned but overwhelmed man bearing that responsibility alone.

He'd thought he wouldn't want to visit that world with Corinne. He'd been worried about whether D.J. was a greater draw for her than Levi. But the prospect of teaching D.J. how to swim—just one of countless skills D.J. had to be taught—spun Levi 180 degrees around. Maybe it would be just as well if Corinne cared more for D.J. than for him. It would sure make his life easier. And regardless of whom she cared for more, he already knew sex with her was great.

He couldn't decide whether to curse or to laugh at the detour his mind had taken. He'd gone from wanting all Corinne's adoration for himself to recognizing how convenient it was that she adored D.J. He was actually even thinking of her in the context of something resembling marriage.

"I'm still not sure Gerald is going to want one of those free-form pools," she commented. "He's not exactly a free-form guy."

"He can work that out with the pool contractor," Levi said, relieved that this issue wouldn't require another renegotiation of Mosley's contract.

"I've seen those free-form pools, and they can look really pretty if you landscape them and put in a waterfall or a rock formation. But Gerald isn't into gardening, and waterfalls seem so right brained. I just don't think that's his kind of thing."

The sound of an approaching car caught Levi's attention. He turned to stare through the house frame, the timber filtering his vision like bars on a prison cell, casting vertical stripes across his view of the large SUV that rumbled up the dirt drive. It was an army-green Range Rover, the sort of vehicle a suburban warrior who'd never seen actual combat would drive.

"Who's that?" Corinne asked, squinting through the house frame. "One of your construction workers?"

He couldn't think of anyone on the crew who drove a green Range Rover. "It might be a trespasser," he muttered, moving protectively closer to her, his muscles tensing in alertness.

The SUV bounced to a halt next to his Porsche, the engine died and the driver's side door was pushed open. He tightened his grip on the handle of the stroller and kept his eyes on the door, waiting for the intruder to reveal himself.

The car door swung shut and Corinne let out a yelp. "Gerald!"

Levi's adrenaline level subsided as Corinne picked her way carefully through the muddy terrain, past the invisible patio and around the invisible garage to the front of the invisible house, where her left-brained boss stood. The few times Levi had met Gerald Mosley he'd been more impressed by the guy's open-mindedness than anything else. Mosley was a small man with a nondescript appearance. He had thick, tawny hair, eyeglasses and a face that seemed settled into a permanently quizzical expression. His attire was stylishly ill-fitting, better suited to a teenage mall rat than a grown-up multimillionaire.

Corinne greeted him with a bit more warmth than Levi would have expected a woman to greet the man she worked for. Following behind her, slowed by the stroller's lack of maneuverability over the ruts and furrows, he watched her give Mosley an exuberant hug, then step back, plant her hands on her hips and shake her head. "What are you doing here?" she asked.

Levi couldn't make out Mosley's muffled reply, because D.J. was shrieking with pleasure at the bumpy ride he was getting in his stroller.

"We just stopped by because I wanted to see how things were coming along," she said to Mosley as Levi drew nearer. He assumed Mosley must have answered her question by turning it back on her. "Levi was showing me where the swimming pool is going to go. If you decide on the free-form pool, Gerald, you're going to have to think seriously about how to landscape it."

"Why?" Mosley asked. "I was figuring you could take care of the landscaping." Then he turned to Levi, his expression a strange hybrid of a smile and a scowl.

Levi extended his hand to Mosley. "How are you doing?" he said blandly, giving nothing away. Although Mosley had, if anything, a greater right than Corinne to see how his dream house was progressing, Levi felt uneasy about his having come to Arlington without warning. He felt even uneasier about Mosley's suggestion that Corinne could take care of the house's landscaping.

And uneasier yet when Mosley said, "What do you think of my car, Corey?"

Corey?

"Did you rent it?" she asked.

Mosley shook his head, his smile a paradoxical blend of diffidence and bravado. "I bought it this morning."

"You bought it?" Her arms still akimbo, she glowered at the massive SUV. "What are you going to do with it?"

"Drive it. I'm going to need a car here in Arlington. I figured I might as well buy one."

"But you're not living in Arlington yet. Your house isn't going to be ready for months. Right, Levi?" she asked, acknowledging him with a glimpse before continuing to scold Mosley. "Where are you going to park that thing in New York?"

"I'll rent a space in my building's garage."

"That's going to take up more than one space," she predicted, eyeing Mosley's new transportation with vaguely defined contempt.

"Yeah, but it's a cool car. I like being way high above the road." Mosley's gaze sloped from the Range Rover to Levi's road-hugging sports car.

"Poo-poo-poo!" D.J. chimed in.

Mosley swung his eyes toward D.J. "That's the baby?" he asked.

Levi felt his defenses rise again, even though Mosley hadn't said anything particularly troubling or offensive. Before he could speak, Corinne said, "Yes. This is D.J."

"Poo-poo-poo!"

"He's saying poop," Mosley muttered, his upper lip curling.

"No, he's not. He's talking about the pool."

"How can you tell?"

"Trust me—I can." She hunkered down next to D.J., as if she could translate his baby talk better at his level. "D.J., this is my friend Gerald. Gerald, this is D.J."

Mosley stared at her as if she'd morphed into an

alien creature in front of his eyes. "Corey, we've got to talk."

She straightened up and smiled hesitantly. "Can't it wait until Monday?"

"No." Mosley's eyes jittered from the baby to Levi to Corinne and back to Levi, this time faintly apologetic. "I hope you don't mind, but I've got to talk to her."

"Go right ahead," Levi said with more generosity than he felt.

Gerald wrapped his fingers around Corinne's elbow and guided her away from Levi and D.J. They walked across what would someday be the front lawn to the southern side of the foundation, as far from Levi as they could be without seeming rude about it.

"Poo-poo!" D.J. commented emphatically.

"Poop is right," Levi muttered. He didn't know why seeing Corinne and Mosley together troubled him, but it did. The way they bent their heads together, and the way Mosley's hand remained on Corinne's arm, the way they both seemed to be talking at once, as though they knew each other well enough to know what was being said without having to listen to it.

Why wouldn't they know each other that well? They worked together. Mosley trusted Corinne enough to have her negotiate the details on his house. He wanted her to landscape his pool.

A curse escaped Levi, a less euphemistic term for *poop*. Corinne and Mosley were more than boss and assistant. One glance at them, one quick reading of their posture, the angles of their gazes and the undeniable comfort level between them told him that.

She'd been in his bed last night, he reminded himself. And last week. She'd stood before a storm with him. She loved his baby.

Two months ago, the sight of a woman he desired talking intimately to another man wouldn't have irked him. He would either have competed for her or blown her off. But he didn't want to blow Corinne off, and he wasn't certain he had the strength to compete for her. He'd gone from being a carefree bachelor to a single father in one fateful instant, and the changes his life had undergone since then left him insecure. He had to ration his energy. He had to preserve his love for D.J., who needed it more than Corinne.

As for Levi, he could do without love for now. He'd done without sleep in the past month and a half, without order, without his old routines, without his sister. He wanted Corinne, desired her, longed to spend night after night—and day after day—with her naked in his arms. But what he wanted didn't matter as much as D.J. did.

If she was going to landscape Mosley's patio... Whatever the hell that signified, Levi had enough of a sense of self-preservation to convince himself he'd be better off if he didn't let himself care.

CHAPTER THIRTEEN

EVERYONE WAS in a cranky mood. Levi's face had darkened with shadow in the time she and Gerald had conferred. Gerald was in a snit. And D.J. was fussing and whining as plaintively as he had the first time she'd met him, when he'd been teething.

Maybe Levi and Gerald had sore gums, too. Corinne didn't know. She *did* know that if they didn't cheer up soon, she'd be tempted to augment their teeth pain by giving each of them a fat lip.

"That's the baby?" Gerald had demanded to know, once he'd dragged her away from Levi to the far corner of the house's foundation.

"Yes, that's the baby. I told you Levi had a baby."

"But it's just—it's just an ordinary baby. I mean, what's so special about it?"

"It's a *he,* not an it," she corrected him. "What are you doing here, Gerald? Did you come to check up on me?"

"I came to check up on my house," he said indignantly, then faltered and gave a sheepish shrug. "And you. I'm worried about you."

"Why?" She held her arms out from her sides, displaying herself. "As you can see, there's nothing to worry about. I'm perfectly fine."

"So what's going on? Are you having an affair with Holt?"

Was it that obvious? She hadn't realized Gerald was observant enough to notice beard burns or flushed cheeks or—well, whatever transformation she might have undergone by becoming Levi's lover.

She didn't want to discuss Levi with Gerald at the edge of a construction site. For that matter, she didn't want to discuss Levi with him at all. But he was her friend, and at least part of his annoyance was due to her having denied their friendship by not confiding in him.

There were plenty of other things she'd never told him, though. She'd never shared with him more than the most superficial details of her childhood. She'd never let him see how her parents' multiple marriages and divorces had scarred her. She had never told him about her pet cat, about how devastated she'd been when her father had given Muffy away.

One of the things she appreciated about Gerald was that he never wanted to share the intimate details of his life or know about hers. He didn't demand the kind of openness Levi invited. She could not imagine lying in bed with Gerald, feeling troubled and having Gerald murmur, "Tell me about it."

She used to think that kind of detachment was exactly what she wanted.

"Levi and I are close," she told Gerald now.

He raked a hand through his hair. Sunlight bounced off the lenses of his glasses, shielding his eyes from her. "When did this happen?"

Suddenly. Strangely. She couldn't explain it to Gerald. She didn't want to—and that made her sad. While she and Levi might be close—more than close—she'd been close to Gerald a whole lot longer. She wasn't prepared to welcome him into the special world she and Levi and D.J. had found together, but she wasn't willing to shut him out, either.

"Why don't we all get some lunch and talk," she suggested.

"About what?"

She couldn't guess if Gerald was deliberately giving her a hard time or just being literal. "About your house," she suggested. "About your new car. About the baby."

"It looks like a pretty ordinary baby," Gerald muttered, glancing over at the stroller. Levi stood next to it, his arms crossed and his expression glowering. He cut a tall figure in the clear midday light, his dark hair mussed, his shoulders broad. His jeans fit his long, lean legs as if they'd been custom-tailored to his physique. She let her gaze linger for a moment on his strong thighs, his narrow hips. A totally inappropriate pang of desire tugged at her.

"The baby is a *he,* not an *it,*" she repeated, forcing her attention from Levi to D.J., who looked disgruntled, as well. Maybe he was an ordinary baby. She didn't know enough babies to judge which were average and which were stellar. All she knew was that she and D.J. empathized with each other on some primal level, that D.J. made her want to sing lullabies, that when she held him in her arms she felt peaceful inside.

"I don't get it," Gerald argued. "I mean, you and a baby? You told me it wasn't a biological clock thing. If it's just that you're hot for the architect and you're accepting the baby as part of the deal, that would make sense to me."

That would make sense to Corinne, too—but it wasn't how things had happened. She'd been aware of Levi's appeal from the first moment she'd met him, but only in an objective way. Her first real connection had been with D.J. If not for that evening when she'd sung to him, she might not have made love with Levi.

"The thing is…" Gerald turned back to her, and the movement of his head allowed her to glimpse his eyes before the sun's glare washed across his eyeglass lenses again. He looked perplexed. She'd presented him with a formula he couldn't calculate, a proof that didn't end in QED. "You're like me, Corey. We aren't into all that soft, gooey baby stuff. In all the time I've known you, I have never once seen you get warm and fuzzy."

"I know." She sighed. "But this time it's different. For some reason, D.J. is different."

"D.J.?"

"The baby. His real name is Darren Justice, and he—"

"That's okay," Gerald cut her off. "I don't really want to hear some long, touching story, all right?"

"Have lunch with us." She heard an edge of pleading in her voice. It was important to her that Gerald understand, or at least accept, that something had changed inside her. Whether the change was permanent she couldn't say, but she wanted him to acknowledge it. "We'll talk. You'll get to know Levi and D.J. a little better, and maybe this will start to make sense to you."

A wry smile quirked his mouth. "Does it make sense to you?"

She smiled back, just as wryly. "No."

"Are you in love with Holt?"

"I—" She swallowed and looked away. Love had never made sense to her, either. Yet when she gazed back at Levi and felt not just a physical urge but a need to be with him, a soul-deep yearning to touch him and kiss him, to hear his low voice, to feel his breath against her cheek... Was it love when two people could get a baby out of his car seat and into a stroller so smoothly, without conferring about it, without planning or even talking? Was love about being on the same wavelength, moving to the same rhythm, wanting the same thing? Even when all they wanted was a baby safely strapped into his stroller?

"I'm not sure I know what love is," she admitted, as honest an answer as she could give.

He nodded. "All right. Let's have lunch."

Smiling, she beckoned him to follow her back over the rutted dirt to where Levi stood and D.J. sat. As soon as she neared them, D.J. began powering his feet, kicking and swinging them in circles. They were bare, and his toes were tiny pink nubs, smooth and soft. "Hi," she said brightly.

Levi scrutinized Gerald and then turned to her. His smile was halfhearted and subarctic.

"We're going to have lunch," she announced, wishing she could pull Levi aside the way Gerald had pulled her aside, and talk to him, and maybe thaw him with a kiss. Although why she had to thaw him was beyond her.

"Lunch?" He arched one eyebrow.

"Is there a restaurant anywhere nearby?" Gerald asked. "I could go for some Chinese food."

Levi angled his head toward D.J. "He's got to get home. He's been cooped up in a car all morning— except for now, when he's cooped up in his stroller."

"Why don't we pick up some food and bring it back to your house," Corinne suggested, adding, for

Gerald's sake, "Chinese, if you'd like." Whatever was broken between these two men, whatever was bugging them, she was going to take care of it, fix it up, make it right. That was her job.

A job she used to love but right now resented. In the past, she'd always hastened to step into the role of the fixer. But today, she didn't want to solve Levi's and Gerald's problems, whatever they might be. If they believed themselves rivals for her affection, she'd just as soon they dealt with their competition themselves. *She* didn't think they were rivals. She adored them both.

"Fine," Levi said crisply. "We'll get Chinese food and eat at the house." He spun around and stalked to his car. Reaching across the driver's seat, he popped open the tiny glove compartment and pulled out his cell phone. "How spicy do you like your food?" he asked.

"Very spicy," Corinne said.

"I hate spicy food," Gerald said simultaneously.

Levi's left eyebrow rose again. He punched in a number—"I have the best Chinese restaurant in town on automatic dial," he explained—and then turned his back on them so he could converse with the restaurant uninterrupted.

Gerald eyed D.J. with a blend of curiosity and apprehension. D.J. shrank back against the curved canvas of his stroller seat. His eyes narrowing on Gerald, he thrust a thumb into his mouth and sucked pensively.

"I don't get it," Gerald muttered.

"Get what?"

"He's a *baby*."

She hunkered down in front of the stroller so D.J.

could view her at eye level. "We're going to go home in just a few minutes," she told him, wondering if he considered that good news—wondering if he could even understand what she was saying. "This man is Gerald. He's my colleague. This—" she gestured toward the concrete and lumber shaping the outline of a house "—is going to be his home once it's built. Your uncle is building it. Uncle Levi."

D.J. removed his thumb from his mouth but kept it handy, resting against his plump lower lip. "Lee-baa."

"That's right," she agreed. "Levi."

He considered her for a moment, then reached out, aiming for her nose. She leaned back in time to escape his fingers. "Lee-lee-lee!"

"We're going home," she repeated, straightening up.

Gerald was staring at her. "That was enlightening," he said, sarcasm coating every word.

"Okay. You don't like babies."

"Neither do you."

"Except for this one."

Levi disconnected his phone and turned to them. "Let's go. I have to detour to the restaurant to pick up our order. Mosley, do you know where I live?"

"No."

"Why don't you go with him, then," he suggested to Corinne. "D.J. and I will meet you at the house."

Strictly practical, she assured herself. He wasn't implying that he didn't want her in his car. He was simply figuring out a strategy to make sure Gerald didn't spend the next hour driving in circles around Arlington.

"Okay," she said. "We'll meet you there." She

tried to hold his gaze with hers, but he eluded her, busying himself with the task of unstrapping D.J. and transferring him from his stroller to his car seat.

The sun had reached its noon height, and she felt its heat seeping through her hair to her scalp. It added to the tension gathering behind her eyes and rapping against her temples.

She didn't want to fix everything. She didn't want to make things right. She wanted Gerald to be her friend and Levi to be her lover, and she didn't want to have to explain anything to either of them.

The Corinne she'd been a few weeks ago would have gladly arranged a lovely luncheon where all the ruffled male feathers could be smoothed out. But that Corinne was gone. The Corinne of today wanted to snatch D.J. and disappear long enough for Levi and Gerald to resolve their antagonism themselves. Let them reach a consensus on the glass wall in the kitchen of Gerald's damned house, on the fireplace in the bedroom—even on the landscaping around the free-form poo-poo. Let them be guys together, butting heads until they discovered they both had unbreakably thick skulls.

Meanwhile, she and D.J. could go to the zoo and eat ice cream. Or mashed bananas.

It was a nice fantasy. The reality was that she had to climb into the elevated cab of Gerald's macho new SUV—a telling contrast to Levi's macho sports car. The reality was that she had to settle onto the stiff leather seat, inhale the distinctive new-car smell and figure out a way to survive what was certain to be a tension-filled lunch.

HE'D ORDERED sweet-and-sour chicken and Szechuan beef. And a large tub of fried rice. People could eat whatever they wanted.

He was acting like an ass, and it bothered him. He wasn't used to feeling possessive. It was like a quivering alertness running through his body, a wariness regarding a man about whom he'd never entertained a single negative thought. Gerald Mosley was a client. He and Corinne had known each other and worked together for years—of course they'd be friends. Meanwhile, Corinne had spent last night in Levi's bed. Why was he feeling so threatened?

He'd never experienced jealousy before. Never. He hadn't been jealous of his siblings who'd been his parents' favorites; he could have been among the favored if he'd yielded to his parents' rigid views. Nor had he ever felt jealousy toward classmates who got higher grades, friends who got prettier dates, any of those challenges that were supposed to bring out a man's primitive warrior instincts. He could fight for what mattered, but chest thumping had never interested him.

Just that morning, he'd been thinking of Corinne in terms of marriage. As he unloaded the cartons of Chinese food on the kitchen table, careful not to step on D.J., who was practicing his crawling moves on the kitchen floor, he remembered that odd, exhilarating whimsy about marriage—and he also remembered the way she and Mosley had gone off to confer in private. And where the hell were they now? He'd stopped for food on his way home; they'd supposedly been driving straight here. They should have arrived ahead of him.

He heard the rumble of Mosley's pumped-up vehicle out in the driveway. "They're here," he informed D.J. none too graciously. Some host he was going to be.

Get over it, he ordered himself. Corinne had told him she had no other boyfriends. Mosley was her pal, nothing more.

The thing was, Levi didn't want to be just her lover. He wanted to be her pal, too. He wanted to be everything to her—the man who made her laugh, made her think, made her come.

Damn it. He seemed to have gone and fallen in love.

"I'm in trouble, buddy," he whispered to D.J. "And I think it's your fault."

D.J. gave him a wet grin, showing off his front teeth, and let loose with a barrage of meaningless syllables.

"Thanks for the advice," Levi muttered, abandoning the kitchen in response to the chiming doorbell.

He tried to read Corinne's expression for a clue to what she and Mosley had talked about on their drive over. But her face gave nothing away. Her eyes were luminous, her lips slightly pursed. She looked, if anything, a bit tense. "Sorry it took us so long," she apologized. "Gerald wanted to see a little of Arlington."

"Corey has spent a lot more time in town than I have," Mosley added.

There was that nickname again. She'd never asked Levi to call her Corey. It irked him that Mosley received that personal privilege.

"Lunch smells good," she said, preceding Mosley into the house.

"I'm figuring we can eat out on the porch," Levi suggested.

"Fine. Where's D.J.?" Before he could answer, she vanished into the kitchen. Her lilting chatter drifted through the house to him: "Hey, D.J. How's it going? Ooh, you feel damp. What do you say we change your diaper."

D.J. screeched with pleasure.

Levi glanced at Mosley, who appeared dumbfounded. He was a smart man—it took a certain degree of intelligence to make a multimillion dollar fortune—but the idea of Corinne's changing D.J.'s diaper, and doing it cheerfully, was apparently more than his high IQ could absorb.

After a few seconds, Corinne swept back through the entry with D.J. in her arms, gleefully swatting at her hair. Without sparing a look for either Levi or Mosley, she ascended the stairs with the kid.

"Well," Levi said, staring up the stairs as if he could will her speedy return. "Can I get you a drink?"

"Sure," Mosley said, his gaze also fixed on the vacant stairway.

Levi started for the kitchen. Mosley followed him. Levi produced a couple of beers from the refrigerator, displayed them for Mosley and handed one over when Mosley nodded. He wished he could revive the feelings he had for the guy in December, when they'd first started negotiating on the house. Back then, Mosley had been a client with an open mind and an open wallet; back then, Levi had been a bachelor with no dependents and no desire for any.

Everything was different now, thanks to the invasion into his life of the two people upstairs.

He couldn't help but view Mosley from his new perspective. Mosley was still a compact man with generously wavy hair and an adolescent fashion sense. His smile seemed benign, his eyes honest. Whatever negatives Levi saw in him were caused by his own resentments, not by anything Mosley had said or done.

"What's with the baby?" he asked as he wrenched the cap off his beer.

"What do you mean?" Levi busied himself arranging serving spoons, forks and plates on a tray.

"She's changing a diaper. What's that all about?"

"I guess it's about her not wanting D.J. to get a rash on his butt."

Mosley shook his head. A vague, airy laugh escaped him. "When did she ever give a hoot about a baby's butt? She's tough. She's smart. Baby rashes never registered on her radar screen before." He sipped some beer and shook his head again. "I don't get it."

Levi felt a pang of sympathy for Mosley. "I think it has something to do with D.J. himself."

"What? Not to insult him, he's just fine as far as babies go, but what is it about him that makes Corey care about rashes, all of a sudden?"

Levi drank some beer, his eyes level on Mosley as he tipped the bottle back against his lips. Swallowing, he set the bottle on the counter and shrugged. "She feels some kind of kinship with the kid. Maybe it's because she didn't have a solid relationship with her parents, and he's a baby who has no real parents at all. All he's got is an uncle." He lifted the tray and beckoned with a nod for Mosley to follow him out onto the screened porch.

The air out there was warm and fragrant, heavy with the scent of rain-washed foliage. Levi set down

the tray, gestured toward a chair and folded himself
into another chair, gripping his bottle by the neck.
Mosley sat, as well.

"The thing of it is," Mosley began, then took another sip of beer. He looked dismal, his face poised
as though he were about to sneeze. "I mean, she and
I never discussed it in so many words, but I always
just assumed she'd be sharing the house with me."

That brought Levi up short. He remembered her
arguments with him over the initial design for the
house. She'd been passionate, full of conviction, as if
arguing for her own sake as much as for Mosley's.
But he'd never actually thought—certainly not once
he'd made love with her—that she had a personal
stake in how the house came out.

He took another long, slow drink, buying time to
collect his thoughts. "Okay," he drawled once he'd
lowered the bottle. "Do you and Corinne have some
kind of understanding?" He really hoped they didn't.
He couldn't bear to think Corinne had lied to him
about any involvements back in New York.

"No, it's not like that. It's…" Faltering, Mosley
picked at the label on his beer bottle. He worked his
thumbnail under a corner and pried it free of the glass.
"We never really talked about it. It was just kind of
there. Corey and I are two of a kind, that's all."

"Two of what kind?"

Mosley glanced up and smiled sheepishly. "Mis-
fits."

Levi couldn't suppress a bark of laughter. "I'm a
misfit, too. Who isn't?"

"Yeah, well, it's just—neither of us ever date. We
don't have lives, you know? All we ever had was
work and each other. And work *was* each other."

But now Corinne had something more. She had Levi and his nephew, a baby to whom she was so attached she was taking fifteen minutes to change his diaper instead of socializing with men of her own generation.

"Do you love her?" he asked Mosley.

"Of course." Mosley's answer shot out so quickly Levi wasn't sure how seriously to take it. "You?"

He couldn't answer glibly. To him, speaking the words would be committing to them, hammering the truth of them into place like a nail straight through the heart of a two-by-four.

He pictured her upstairs, smoothing D.J.'s diaper across his belly, sliding his shorts back into place and lifting him into her arms. He pictured her feeding him, peering into his eager face, lifting him to the window so he could see outside, crooning "Hush, little baby, don't say a word…"

He remembered how turned on he'd been by her, watching her sing to his baby.

"Yeah," he confessed.

Mosley sighed. "It's not like she and I are…well, you know."

Sleeping together, Levi surmised—and the notion relieved him. Even so, he felt a kinship with Mosley. Both of them were in love with her, each in his own way and for his own reasons. "That doesn't mean your love for her is less valid than mine," he said generously, all the while thinking, *Please, let her love me for real. Let her love for me be more valid than her love for Mosley.* "If it makes you feel any better, I don't think she intended to get involved with me. Our first few encounters weren't exactly warm."

"She was fighting you over the details of my

house,'' Mosley recollected. "She was really bothered by that big window in the kitchen."

"The wall of glass?"

"She thought it was way extravagant. Pretentious and useless."

"It's going to look terrific."

"I thought it was pretty cool, actually. I'm glad it survived in the final design." Mosley poked at another corner of the label with his thumb. "She mentioned something about how you think the inside should be outside and vice versa."

"That's the general idea." Before Levi could go into greater detail concerning his philosophy of architectural design, he heard footsteps nearing the porch from inside. Corinne and D.J. appeared at the sliding door, and Levi leaped from his chair to open it for her.

D.J. announced their arrival with a barrage of gibberish. "Baa-baa! Baa-lee-lee!"

"I couldn't have said it better," Levi concurred, smiling for D.J. while he searched Corinne's face for a sign of her mood.

"D.J.'s hungry," she said mildly, giving nothing away. "So am I."

"Then let's eat." Still smiling, still wishing with all the power in him that whatever existed between him and her was love, real love, true love, a love that could encompass everything he needed and wanted in his life—he headed inside to get the food.

THEY TALKED about the house. They talked about construction techniques, roofing materials and Rick Bailey's neurotic beagle. They talked about the irascible CEO of Bell Tech and Gerald's impetuous purchase of the Range Rover that morning. The men drank their beers, while Corinne nursed a glass of iced tea and D.J. scooted around the porch in his walker.

Three guys, she thought, observing them as they filled the air around her with their presence, their energy. Three guys and she loved them all—she, who had never believed herself truly capable of love.

She wondered what D.J. was thinking. Did he carry any memories at all of his first few months? Levi had told her his sister had shared a house with other artisans. Were their lunches like this, a group of unrelated but intricately connected adults gathered around a table, talking half the afternoon away? Did they discuss cars and multimillion-dollar deals, the chintzy practices of some builders who used particleboard instead of plywood to save money and installed insufficiently large hot-water tanks?

Did it matter what they'd talked about? D.J. probably couldn't understand a word of it. His vocabulary seemed limited to "lee-lee" and "baa-baa," with an occasional "bo-bo" mixed in. Oh, and his brand-new phrase, "poo-poo-poop."

She tried to imagine him thirty years from now, seated at a table with his friends, surrounded by the faint scent of soy and tangy ginger. In her mind he looked like Levi, tall and ruggedly chiseled, his face a sculpture of harsh angles, his shoulders broad and his hands leathery. His voice would sound like Levi's, a low, slightly husky drawl, and like Levi he would think before he spoke. He would talk about whatever his passion was, and his eyes would be simultaneously dark and bright, lit from within.

She wanted to be there to see it. Thirty years from now, she wanted to know that D.J. had grown into a strong, confident man like Levi. She wanted to help bring him to that point.

If Levi let her... She wanted to be a part of D.J.'s life forever.

THERE WERE MORE PEOPLE than usual on the porch, but he didn't care. He was in his walker and the woman was close by. She'd taken him upstairs and changed him and talked to him, telling him things in a sweet voice that wasn't singing, but he didn't care.

He loved her smile, and the softness of her hands.

She'd brought him down, and he'd eaten apple-sauce and small chunks of cheese and a bottle, and then he got to roll around in his walker while the grown-ups talked.

Mostly the men talked. She watched them, and she watched him. He wished he could tell her how happy she made him, just by being close. He wished he knew the words to say it. For days she was gone. But then she came back, and it was like the sky opening wide, filling the world with light.

He wanted her to stay. He wanted her to be a part of his life forever.

CHAPTER FOURTEEN

LEVI USED TO measure his time in terms of work: how far along a house was toward completion; how much time until a proposal was due or a bid needed to be submitted; how many weeks until he could take his annual vacation in California, visiting Ruth.

Now time's measurements were completely transformed. Days were marked in what new things D.J. had learned, what he had accomplished, how much he'd grown. One day he might taste a peach for the first time, or gnaw on a hard chunk of pizza crust. Another day he might throw a ball with both hands. Yet another day, Levi might discover a new tooth cutting through his pink upper gum.

Weeks were measured by Daddy School classes. He attended religiously, every Monday night. He sat in the community room at the YMCA while Allison Winslow discussed digestive problems in babies, dysfunctional sleep patterns, the pros and cons of flash cards and all manner of child-related topics he would never have wasted a thought on if not for D.J.

Nights were measured by Corinne: five nights without her, two nights with her. Every Friday, the late-afternoon train would carry her from New York City to Arlington, and they'd enjoy two intense weekend days of what looked to Levi an awful lot like a family. He and D.J. and Corinne would do things together.

They'd take long walks pushing D.J. in his stroller, or attend a free evening concert on the lawn in front of the Arlington Public Library—the performers had been a mediocre brass band playing John Philip Sousa marches at pathetically sluggish tempos, but since he hadn't had to pay for tickets, Levi hadn't had a right to complain.

Some weekends, they'd rent movies and eat popcorn. One Saturday night he'd hired Tara from across the street to baby-sit and taken Corinne to Reynaud, where they'd lingered for two and a half leisurely hours over a gourmet feast.

Corinne would tell him about her projects with Mosley in New York, and he'd tell her about the office complex in Boston for which his partner Phyllis was the primary architect. And once D.J. was in bed, he and Corinne would go to bed, too.

He couldn't get enough of her. He would spend those five weeknights alone, thinking of her, dreaming of her, counting the seconds until her head would once again rest on his pillows, her body beneath his. Or above his. He'd realized early on that she was not the most experienced lover in the world—but she was willing to try anything, willing to trust him. They experimented with new positions and laughed when things didn't quite line up, when they tumbled off the couch or wound up resembling drowned rats after a particularly adventurous outing in the shower. One night, they'd tiptoed down to the porch and made love there, bathed in the fresh evening air and serenaded by crickets.

By the end of July, he began to tire of the long, lonely stretch from Sunday night to Friday afternoon, when she was in New York. Other Arlington residents endured daily commutes to their jobs in Manhattan; it wasn't a trip he would wish on the woman he loved, but maybe he and Corinne could work something out that would enable her to spend at least one more night a week in Connecticut. If she found a job closer to Arlington or quit working altogether, he would gladly support her, but he doubted she would care for that. She loved her job and relied on it. For her entire life, until that past June, she'd believed her career was the only dependable aspect of her world, the only thing she would dare to love.

Besides, Mosley meant a lot to her. Levi was willing to accept that, now that there was no more talk about her moving into Mosley's weekend retreat once construction on it was completed. "I never thought about a home," she'd told Levi just last week, during one of those wonderful moments when they'd finished making love and were simply lying together in bed, holding hands and whispering. "A house was a place where you lived. It was a building, a roof over your head. I didn't know what a home was, because I never really had one."

"Do you have one now?" he'd asked, almost afraid to hear her answer.

She'd gazed into his eyes, her lashes a thick, dark frame around her silvery pale irises. "Do I?"

He'd thought about the way she'd tucked D.J. into his crib, nestling his teddy bear next to him and stroking the blanket smooth over him, and the way she'd come to Levi's bed. The way she brought him fresh bagels from the city and prepared coffee in his coffeemaker as if she were in her own kitchen. The way her toothbrush stood next to his in the porcelain rack above the sink.

"If you want it, yes, you do have a home," he'd said.

Her smile had told him that if she wasn't exactly ready to have him raise the subject of love—long-term let's-get-married love—she wouldn't flee from him with her hands clamped over her ears simply because he'd broached the subject. He'd thought about taking her out for another dinner at Reynaud, then decided that if they were going to deal with such a significant subject as marriage, they'd be best off talking about it at his house. He'd make dinner, just as he'd made dinner the first evening they'd spent together. Marinated steak on the grill, a good wine, the fragrance of the woods beyond the porch. Home. That was the best place to talk about home.

She would be on the four-thirty train Friday afternoon, and he tried not to think about it. His week was a long one: Monday, Jamie McCoy had commissioned him to design a new extension for his house. At Daddy School Monday evening Jamie's wife, Allison, had lectured on time management, and Levi had thought that, what with Martina Lopes taking care of D.J. from eight-thirty until five-thirty every day, he ought to be managing his time a lot better than he was.

If he didn't spend so much of it thinking about Corinne, he'd be able to accomplish a lot more.

Tuesday he'd brought D.J. with him to his weekly poker game. The guys were all so glad he was making the games they didn't mind D.J.'s presence. Evan's daughter, Gracie, fussed over D.J., and her elder brother seemed thrilled that D.J. distracted her so she wouldn't pester him. While the children played in the family room, Murphy donned his attorney cap and interrogated Levi until he confessed he was thinking about asking Corinne to make a more concrete commitment to their relationship. "Buy her a rock," Brett advised, to which Evan had added that if Corinne loved D.J., Levi shouldn't have to bankrupt himself buying jewelry to persuade her to get serious. Tom Bland said he'd investigate her finances, an offer Levi politely refused.

Wednesday, a man named Travis Justice showed up at Arlington Architectural Associates, looking for Levi. Sharon buzzed Levi in his office to let him know. "He says he needs to see you," she reported. "He wouldn't tell me what it's about."

Levi knew no one named Travis Justice. Maybe the man was a potential client, though Levi couldn't guess why he would refuse to tell that to Sharon. He stared at his computer monitor, which held a simple rendering of the blueprint of Jamie McCoy's house, and tried to calculate his time. Besides the McCoy project and his continuing oversight of Mosley's house, his colleague Bill had requested his input into a renovation of a landmark building across the street from the train station in town. That would take a bit of work—not just in designing the renovation but also in dealing with all the bureaucratic agencies that entered the fray whenever the word *landmark* was mentioned.

Still, he needed to bring more work into the firm. With Allison's time management guidance still fresh in his mind and his nanny in place, he ought to be working at high gear, the way he'd been before D.J. had invaded his life.

D.J. Darren Justice.
Travis Justice.

A dawning realization plunged through him, hard and heavy, leaving a gaping tear in his soul.

Don't jump to conclusions, he warned himself—in vain. He'd already jumped.

"Levi? Are you still there?" Sharon's voice emerged through the phone receiver.

"Yeah. I'll see him. Send him up." He disconnected the phone before Sharon could question him, and rose to his feet. Standing before his window, he gazed out at the overcast July afternoon and took a deep, bracing breath. He would be fine. This would be okay. He'd proved himself capable of handling everything fate threw at him; he could handle this.

And maybe he was wrong. Maybe Travis Justice was only another New York millionaire looking for an architect to create a weekend retreat for him on the west side of town, with all the other New York millionaires.

He fingered his necktie, which dangled loose around his collar. His sleeves were rolled up, his shirt limp. He saw no point in tidying up. People didn't have the same expectations of grooming in an architect that they had in a banker. He looked like what he was: someone who'd been working hard all day. Keeping thoughts of Corinne from undermining his concentration was perhaps even harder work than devising an organic expansion for Jamie McCoy's already expanded house.

A knock on his door drew him from the familiar view of trees and traffic outside his window. He sucked in another deep breath and crossed the room.

As soon as he opened the door and came face-to-face with the man on the opposite side, he knew. Ruth had told him the man was handsome, and he wouldn't argue the point. But it was his chin in particular, a chin much more triangular than the square jaws of the Holts, that confirmed his guess. In the past two months, D.J.'s chin had begun to emerge from the roundness of his baby fat—and it wasn't square.

"Levi Holt?" the man asked. Clad in an expensive-looking silk T-shirt and slim-fitting black slacks, his brown hair trimmed in the sort of punkish fashion that could be attained only in a pricey salon, he appeared, if anything, more nervous than Levi felt. He chewed on his lower lip, and his right hand, circled by a silver bracelet, fidgeted at his side.

"Come on in," Levi invited him, stepping aside and waving him into the office. He estimated he had only a few years on the man, but he felt immensely older. He wasn't sure why, unless it was that his hair and clothes weren't so stylish and his only jewelry was a utilitarian wristwatch on a plain leather band.

"I'm Travis Justice," the man said as Levi shut the door.

Levi extended his hand. Travis's palm was icy.

Levi admitted to himself that he had as much right as his visitor to be nervous. But someone had to stay calm. Someone had to make sure the next ten minutes made sense.

"I—um—I was a friend of your sister," Travis said.

Levi eyed him up and down. He could make this easier by revealing that he knew who Travis was and why he'd come. But he saw no reason to make it easier. He wanted to find out what kind of man Travis Justice was, and one way to do that was to observe him under pressure.

"I only found out a few weeks ago that she'd died. It really—I mean, I'm so sorry."

Levi nodded.

"I was up in Mendocino and I stopped by her place. I wanted to see her again, but her friend Sandy—did you know Sandy? They shared a house with some other people up there. In Mendocino."

Levi felt a little sorry for him. "That's right," he said helpfully.

"And Sandy told me about Ruth's—what was it, a stroke?"

"An aneurysm."

"Yeah, that was it. I knew it was something with the circulation in her brain, and it just—I mean, my God." He shook his head. His sorrow seemed genuine.

Levi considered offering him a seat, but if he did, the boy—and he really did strike Levi as more a boy than a man—might collapse in a welter of tears. He didn't want to spend his afternoon comforting him.

"I feel terrible," Travis confessed. "She never told me—I mean, I had no idea…"

"No idea?"

"I mean, she should have told me. About the baby, I mean."

Levi said nothing. He couldn't refute Travis. Ruth *should* have told him.

"And I don't even think Sandy was going to tell me, either, but that guy—the one who made belts? He lived in their house, too, and something slipped out— I don't remember what." He shook his head again.

Levi waited.

"I'm not a deadbeat, Mr. Holt. If Ruth had told me, I would have owned up to my obligations. It's just, you know, I was heading up to Vancouver, scouting sites for a movie, and Ruth sent me on my way. I mean, I just—we both just sort of assumed it was going to be one of those things, you know? A happy memory, nothing more.''

Levi remained silent. He had no idea what to say. ''So glad we've finally had this chance to meet?''… ''So glad my sister was a happy memory for you?''

''If she had told me, I would have been there for her. I swear.''

''I believe you.''

''So, maybe I'm a few months late. But I'm here. Sandy didn't want to tell me where you were, but that guy at the house, the one with the belts, well, he convinced her I had a moral right to know. I considered phoning you, but then I thought maybe it would be better for me to come here so we could meet in person.''

''Okay.'' Everything Travis said was right, it was proper, it rang true. Levi ought to be more cordial, but his words froze in his throat. When he let his mind sneak past the reality that Ruth's onetime lover was standing in his office, he glimpsed things he didn't want to see: the crib in his spare bedroom. The walker in the kitchen. D.J. in the walker, zooming back and forth and burbling joyfully.

''So, I'm here,'' Travis said, his gaze sad but steady. ''I'd like to see my son.''

''Of course.''

Travis clearly hadn't expected such quick acquiescence. He paused to collect himself, then stood a little straighter. ''Where is he now?''

''He's at home with the nanny.''

Travis nodded, then swallowed. "What's his name?"

Levi was besieged by more visions—D.J. in his bath, in his high chair, gazing through his window at a night sky strewed with stars. D.J. on Levi's shoulder, leaning back to stare at Levi, grinning and flashing his milky teeth. D.J. figuring out how to crawl across the kitchen floor.

D.J. in Corinne's arms, settling sweetly into her embrace as she sang him that lullaby he loved.

"Everyone calls him D.J.," Levi answered. "His real name is Darren Justice. Ruth gave him your name."

HE WROTE OUT the directions to his house and asked Travis to come at five-thirty. But after Travis left the office, Levi was helpless to get any work done.

He told himself D.J.'s father's arrival in Arlington was a good thing. It reassured him that the man with whom Ruth had a fling wasn't an ass. If he hadn't done the right thing before, it was only because he'd been ignorant of the consequences of that fling. Levi had thought from the start that Ruth ought to inform the father, but she'd stubbornly refused, wanting the baby all to herself.

Her decision hadn't been fair to Travis.

Levi couldn't find anything to criticize about the man. His hair and clothing were a bit too chic, but he worked for a film company, and people in Hollywood were probably used to edgier style. His attitude was anything but edgy, though. He'd been soft-spoken, humble, obviously overwhelmed by what he'd accidentally learned. In his position, Levi doubted he could have handled things any better.

But still… Now that Travis was here, what would he want?

Levi supposed he'd find out at five-thirty.

He prowled his office until his circular pacing made him dizzy. Then he slumped in his chair, leaned back, closed his eyes—and was barraged by more images of D.J., his sounds, his smell, the stickiness of his hands after he ate, the taut skin of his belly. The sleepless nights. The frantic juggling. The days Levi had spent trying to work with D.J. perched in his arms, screaming in pain from teething.

Opening his eyes, he saw that the blueprint of Jamie McCoy's house had been replaced on his monitor by a swirling, colorful screen saver. It made him as dizzy as his circular pacing had.

He was never afflicted by dizziness. Screen savers and walking in circles shouldn't make him feel as if the ground were slipping and shaking, the earth trembling, his consciousness teetering on the understanding that once the tremors stopped he might no longer recognize his surroundings. He used to tease Ruth about living in the land of seismic threats, but he was the one enduring a massive earthquake right now.

He was used to being strong, guiding Ruth through her assorted crises and ordeals. But he needed guidance now. He could call his lawyer—but he didn't really care about the legalities of the situation. He was D.J.'s legal guardian, so named by D.J.'s mother. Nothing that had occurred in the past half hour could change that. At least, he didn't think it could.

In any case, what he needed wasn't an attorney but a friend, someone who could give him emotional guidance. He lifted his phone and punched in Corinne's office number. She would tell him everything was going to be okay. She'd tell him D.J. was lucky to possess the genes of a decent, dutiful man. She'd assure him that D.J. was loved and cared for, and everything would turn out fine.

The secretary who made up the third member of their consulting company's three-person staff answered the phone. "I need to speak to Corinne Lanier," Levi said. "It's Levi Holt."

"Oh, hi, Levi." That she knew who he was, even though he rarely phoned, gratified him. It meant that Corinne talked about him, that he was significant enough in her life for her to discuss him with colleagues. "Corinne isn't in right now. Can I have her get back to you?"

"Sure. Tell her to use my cell phone number." He had no idea where he'd be when she tried to call him, but he doubted it would be his office. The drafting table, the corkboard, the vertical blinds, even the walls were making his head ache.

He hung up, packed his file of notes on the McCoy house into his portfolio and left the office. Sharon intercepted him at the bottom of the stairs. "Is everything all right, Levi?" she asked.

She was dressed in a daffodil-yellow outfit—yellow-and-white striped shirt under a ridiculously abbreviated yellow jumper. He wished he had his sunglasses.

"Everything's fine," he assured her.

"Who was that guy? A client?"

"No."

"He didn't exactly shout 'Arlington,' if you know what I mean. Definite outsider vibes. Charisma, too." She scrutinized him more closely. "You sure everything's all right? You look kind of pale."

"I'm fine," he lied. "I've got to go visit a site, Sharon. I'll see you tomorrow." Before she could question him further, he bolted for the door.

Safely ensconced in his car, he started driving without giving any thought to where he was headed. Maybe the state forest land, where he'd driven with Corinne that Saturday morning a few weeks ago, when the earth had been recently washed clean by a thunderstorm and D.J. had been chirping and crowing in the back seat. The baby seat wasn't in his Porsche now—he'd left it at home in case Martina needed to drive somewhere with D.J. during the day. His back seat looked larger without the safety seat occupying it. It looked empty.

He steered west down Hauser Boulevard, passing the YMCA and the *Arlington Gazette* building, the shopping district, the rectangular blue sign with the big *H* centered on it and an arrow pointing out the direction of Arlington Memorial Hospital. He kept driving.

Beyond the downtown area, commercial buildings were replaced by small houses, which were in turn replaced by larger houses settled on generous lots. He turned down a winding side street, then up the dirt drive and around the stand of trees to Mosley's site.

The crew was hard at work, a half-dozen sturdy men swarming over the construction, hammering the first story's walls into place. Through one section where the exterior wall hadn't yet been built, he could see the interior taking shape, a confusing maze of rooms divided only by vertical studs. The stairway was a series of horizontal planks climbing upward in a slow spiral that framed the towering entry. A large rectangular opening yawned where the front door would go.

The house was growing, he thought, becoming more and more the thing it was destined to be. It wasn't completely formed; he knew changes could still be made to it. But it was fast becoming a reality. Not the house Gerald Mosley had intended it to be, but a house nonetheless, one that would bring him pleasure. One where Corinne would always be welcome, even though she would never live there. She'd told him Mosley was coming to terms with the fact that his assumptions about their relationship no longer held water. "He isn't heartbroken," she'd insisted. "That was the whole thing—that we could be together without our hearts getting involved. I think he's disappointed, but he'll work it through. He's dating a new woman now—I can only hope she's smart enough to keep up with him."

His house would be smart enough. It would fill with sunshine, with moonlight, with the soothing warmth of a fireplace and the clean austerity of a glass wall. It would grow into a home, and even if it wasn't exactly what he'd envisioned when he'd first conceived the idea, it would bring him pleasure.

Just like a child, Levi thought, remaining in his car and watching through the windshield as the crew labored on the first-floor walls. A child was conceived and born, expectations changed, but the people in charge of raising that child did what they could to make him grow up smart and wise. They gauged each new step, each development: the ability to sit, the ability to crawl, those first teetering attempts to pull himself to his feet. They brought him along as his vocalizing evolved from wails to gibberish to distinct syllables that conveyed actual meaning.

At the start of the project, people did whatever they could to help the baby grow into a strong, healthy adult. But there was no blueprint, no floor plan. No diagram that determined the precise distance between upright beams, the way there was with a house. No formula to incorporate the details. There were books, there was Daddy School, but there was no guarantee, once the project was under way, that the child would be a part of the home his guardians had created.

Levi had done everything he could for D.J. Sometimes he'd done it reluctantly, sometimes resentfully—and sometimes openly and eagerly. But he'd done it, knowing it was his job, his burden, his honor.

Now D.J.'s father was here, and Levi no longer knew how his house was going to turn out.

CORINNE FINALLY got home a little past eight. The Bell Tech people had just signed an extension of their contract, and they'd insisted on taking her and Gerald out for drinks to celebrate. Gerald hadn't been in the most celebratory mood—he still despised the Bell Tech executives—but he'd behaved himself, downed a gin and tonic and made small talk. Corinne had nursed a glass of merlot, which had ultimately given her a headache, one of those tight throbbing circles at the center of her forehead.

Rather than returning to her office, she'd headed for her apartment, stopping to pick up a tray of sashimi at the take-out Japanese restaurant around the corner from her building. She rode up the elevator, her purse slung over her left shoulder, her foil-wrapped dinner in her right hand, her key and her mail in her left hand and right foot sliding out of her low-heeled leather pump and then back into it as the elevator glided to a halt at her floor. She strolled down the hall to her apartment, juggled the mail and the tray while unlocking the door and stepped inside. Letting out a deep sigh, she kicked off her shoes, set down the tray in her closet-size kitchen and moved to the bathroom to pop some aspirin.

Only two more days and she'd be up in Arlington—a thought that worked on her headache more effectively than the painkilling tablets she washed down her throat with a glass of water. Only two more days and she'd be with Levi and D.J. in a world both peaceful and full of activity, a world where she didn't have to wear business shoes and ride elevators and make nice to clients her boss couldn't stand. A world where she could sleep in Levi's arms and wake up to the cheerful clamor of D.J. just down the hall, announcing that he was ready for the day to begin.

She stripped out of her suit, wrapped a soft cotton robe around her and padded barefoot to the kitchen. While she ate her sashimi, she thumbed through the newspaper—a morning paper, all its news was out-of-date by now, but she needed something to occupy her mind and the television would only exacerbate her headache. The silence of her apartment helped to dull the drumming inside her skull. But it also reminded her of how alone she was.

Only for two more days. Then she'd be with the Holts. Man, woman and child, just like a real family.

She couldn't believe this had become her new dream. At one time she'd adored the silence, the lack of interference by people she might or might not be related to tomorrow, the spats and tantrums and tearfests her parents and their spouses and her assorted stepsiblings indulged in. She'd loved not being dependent on anyone but herself for her own happiness.

But now, her greatest happiness came from Levi and D.J. She loved the noise, the bustle, the sound of her own voice lilting in a lullaby.

By the time she was done eating, the silence of her apartment was actually annoying her.

She wandered to her bedroom, stretched out on the bed and lifted the cordless handset of her phone. She had programmed Levi's number into the machine, but even if she hadn't, she knew it by heart.

He answered on the third ring. "Hello?"

"Hi, Levi—it's me."

"Corinne." There was a long pause. "I thought you were going to call on my cell phone."

She frowned. "Was I supposed to?"

"It doesn't matter. I left you a message at your office to call me on the cell phone."

"I'm sorry, Levi. I didn't get it. What's up?"

"I can't talk now."

His voice, she realized, sounded crisp and cool. Not exactly as if something were wrong, but not as if everything were right, either. "What happened?" she asked, then felt a sharp clutch in the vicinity of her heart. "Did something happen to D.J.?"

"As a matter of fact..." He sighed. "I really can't talk right now, okay?"

"What?" Panic rippled through her in icy waves. "What happened? Is he okay?"

"He's okay," Levi said, still in that frosty voice. "I have a guest right now."

"Who?"

"D.J.'s father."

CHAPTER FIFTEEN

*HOME FELT DIFFERENT with the new man in it. D.J.
didn't know who the man was, or why he kept staring
at him. The new man's hands weren't as big as Levi's.
They were smoother, too—not like a woman's hands,
but softer than Levi's.*

*He wanted the new man to leave, and he wanted
the woman to come back. When she was gone he
missed her so badly it was like a hunger in his belly.
Levi could hold him and feed him and do all kinds of
things for him, but he never sang the lullaby. Only
the woman did that.*

*Maybe the new man would sing to him. But D.J.
didn't expect it. The man seemed too shy, too fright-
ened. He only watched.*

SHE EMERGED from the train Friday afternoon. Her
nerves were pulled tight and her heart kept thumping
unevenly. Usually, the hour and a half train from
Manhattan was a time for her to unwind, exhale, let
the week's tension seep from her, emptying her so
she could fill up with Levi and D.J. But this time, she
didn't unwind and exhale. The closer the train pulled
to Arlington, the more anxious she grew.

She couldn't believe D.J.'s father had just materi-
alized in Arlington eight months after his son's birth.
What Levi had told her made a certain kind of sense:

"You can't blame him for not showing up sooner. Ruth never told him she was pregnant. They'd both agreed that their affair wasn't going to lead to love and marriage. Ruth had been fine with that. She wanted the baby and she didn't want Travis, so she never told him. It's not his fault."

"Maybe not," Corinne had allowed, "but still, after all this time... To just show up at your office and say, 'Hi, I'm D.J.'s father.' What gives him that right?"

"His genes. His sperm. He *is* D.J.'s father, Corinne."

"A father isn't just genes and sperm." She'd argued as if she were some sort of expert, as if she were the product of an ideal upbringing in which her parents fulfilled their roles with utter mastery. "A father is someone who burps a baby and feeds him and walks the halls with him in the middle of the night. You're D.J.'s father as much as this—this Travis person is."

"Who's to say Travis wouldn't have been burping D.J. and feeding him and walking the halls with him if he'd known D.J. existed?"

"Maybe he would have, and maybe not. The thing is, you did."

"And the other thing is, Ruth named him after Travis. His name is Travis Justice, Corinne. She named her son Darren Justice. She was acknowledging D.J.'s father, admitting that the guy existed, that he was an important part of the situation."

"Important enough for a name. Not important enough to walk the halls with him at night."

Levi had sighed. "Look, Corinne, Travis is a nice guy and he's trying hard to do the right thing, which—given the fact that Ruth denied him some essential information—is pretty noble. He'd be within his rights to turn his back on D.J., to pretend he'd never learned he had a son. Ruth shut him out, so why not? But instead, he tracked me down and traveled all the way here from Los Angeles to meet me and see his baby. He's putting some effort into this.''

"So he's still in Arlington?"

"He's planning to stay awhile. You can meet him this weekend if you want."

Corinne didn't want to meet Travis Justice. She knew she wasn't being fair to him, knew everything Levi said in the man's defense was true—but she didn't want to meet this stranger who claimed that his ties to D.J. were as significant as Levi's.

But there she was, bracing herself as the train rolled into the Arlington station, the wheels squealing against the rails and the car shuddering to a halt. She pulled her bag from the overhead rack and squared her shoulders, determined to make the best of a difficult situation. She would be with her two favorite guys; everything would be okay.

Out on the platform, she scoured the milling throngs in search of Levi and D.J. Towering over most of the other people, Levi was easy to spot. He was alone, though. D.J. wasn't on his shoulder or seated in his stroller parked beside his uncle's long legs. As pleased as she was to see Levi, his now familiar smile, his thick, windswept hair and his dark, soulful eyes, she felt a small but real stab of disappointment that D.J. wasn't with him.

No, not disappointment. Fear. Dread.

Forcing a smile, she wove through the crowd to him and accepted his hug. He brushed her mouth with his in a light kiss, a promise of what awaited them later that night. Usually, his simple kiss of greeting was enough to send an erotic thrill through her. Not this time, though. Not when she didn't know where D.J. was or what was happening to him.

She wanted to ask Levi how D.J. was, but thought the first words out of her mouth shouldn't be about him. So she said nothing, only swallowed her panic and nodded her thanks when Levi took her bag from her. He laced his fingers through hers as they left the platform for the parking lot. His hand felt so hot against hers—and she realized that was because her hand was icy.

She risked a glance over her shoulder as Levi helped her into the passenger seat of the Porsche. D.J.'s car seat wasn't strapped to the upholstery the way it normally was. She tried not to cringe, but by the time Levi settled behind the wheel, her cheeks were cramped from her false smile and her heart was aching from all the possible explanations for that missing car seat.

She couldn't hold back any longer. "Where's D.J.?" she asked.

Levi inserted the key into the ignition but didn't start the car. Instead, he twisted to look at her. "He's with his father."

"Where? At your house?"

"Travis has a room at the Arlington Inn. He asked to take D.J. for a couple of hours today. We can swing by there and pick him up on our way home, okay?"

"Okay." Her smile at this answer was genuine, accompanied by a flash of tears. D.J. was only visiting with his father. He'd be coming home with her and

Levi. Home for him was Levi's house, not a room at the Arlington Inn with someone he didn't even know.

Levi touched the key but didn't turn it. His gaze remained on Corinne, searching, questioning. "I know this whole thing is strange," he conceded. "But everything in D.J.'s life has been strange. His mother dying so young was tragic—but also strange. My getting custody of him was strange. That his father tracked me down shows the kind of man he is. I think D.J. is lucky to have his father in his life."

His tone was casual, but she heard chiding in it. He was lecturing her. He knew she was upset, and he was telling her she ought to be reasonable.

And he was right. D.J. was her lover's nephew, period. He was a usually sweet, occasionally crabby baby who'd lost his mother and taken up residence with Levi. His father certainly had a more legitimate claim on D.J. than she did. Where the baby was, and with whom, was not her business. Her anxiety was completely unreasonable.

But the pain in her chest swelled, devouring her from the inside. She didn't want D.J. to be anywhere but with her and Levi, seated in his car seat, kicking his feet and chattering incoherently. Maybe she had no rights, but she had feelings, longings, love for that wonderful little boy.

Levi had taught her the meaning of home, of love, of trusting in both. But D.J. had taught her the beauty of lullabies.

After a long silence, Levi revved the engine and pulled out of his parking space. "You're quiet," he commented.

"I know."

"Travis and I are feeling our way through this

thing. I'm not saying any of it is easy. Bringing D.J. home with me three months ago wasn't easy, either. But it's all going to work out all right.''

"How do you know that?''

"Because Travis and I both have D.J.'s best interests at heart.''

She couldn't refute that. Levi would do what he believed was best for D.J., and she had no reason to doubt that D.J.'s father would, too.

Still, the car seemed woefully empty without D.J. in it. Her arrival in Arlington seemed empty. She had yet to wrap her arms around D.J., inhale his baby scent, feel his damp breath on her cheek and his hands patting her hair. Until she saw him, her heart would feel a bit empty, too.

When she'd first taken a room at the Arlington Inn last June, she'd thought it a welcoming building, its colonial architecture charming and its broad windows beckoning. Now, in the hazy heat of an August evening, the sprawling clapboard inn looked forbidding to her, cold and aloof. She knew she was getting carried away, letting her emotions distort her perspective, but she couldn't help herself.

After parking in the front lot, Levi ushered her inside. He gave Travis's name to the desk clerk, who phoned his room. No one answered.

Oh, God. What if Travis Justice had absconded with D.J.? What if Levi had been a fool to trust him? What if he was a kidnapper, or worse?

What if Corinne never saw D.J. again?

She felt only a little foolish when, across the lobby, one of the French doors leading out to the pool swung open and a man carrying D.J. entered. The man had expertly groomed hair and a sharp, almost pretty face, with hollow cheeks and a long, narrow nose. His apparel was sleek and elegantly casual, and he looked only slightly awkward holding D.J., who was squirming and mumbling, attempting to face forward so he could see where they were going. One lunge brought his head around enough to spot Corinne, and he let out a cry and squirmed even harder.

Without stopping to think, she raced across the lobby, her arms outstretched. "D.J.! Hello, my sweetie! I missed you at the station!"

She was scarcely aware of Levi and the father exchanging a look as she eased D.J. out of the man's arms and into her own. He nuzzled her neck and she kissed his hair. He let loose with a wondrous assortment of syllables and giggles. His bare feet left wet spots on her shirt.

"I dipped his feet in the pool," the man said, more to Levi than to her. "It was hot and I thought he might like that."

"Did he?" Levi asked, sounding genuinely curious.

Corinne wanted to knock their heads together. What had the man been thinking, to dangle a baby over a pool? What if he'd sneezed and lost his grip? D.J. could have fallen into the pool! Or if the water had been cold, he might have been chilled. How could this so-called father have done such a boneheaded thing?

And why wasn't Levi scolding him for it?

"Hey, buddy," Levi addressed D.J. "Did you like the pool?"

D.J. answered with happy gibberish.

"I've been wondering about when to take him into a pool," Levi said. "I asked the Daddy School

teacher, and she said anytime, as long as a grown-up
held him the whole time. She said those baby swim
classes weren't a good idea, but he could be held in
a pool if he enjoyed it. Some kids do, some don't.''

''I think he did.'' The man sounded modest, uncertain in a way that would have been endearing if
Corinne had been disposed to think kindly of him.

Belatedly, Levi introduced them. ''Corinne, this is
D.J.'s father, Travis Justice. Travis, this is my friend
Corinne Lanier.''

''I'm D.J.'s friend, too,'' she said before planting
a kiss on the crown of D.J.'s head.

''Well, yeah, I can see that.'' Travis held out his
right hand, and Corinne shifted D.J. into the curve of
her left arm so she could shake hands with the man.
D.J. rested heavily on her elbow. He'd grown so
much in just the couple of months she'd known him.
All those mashed bananas and boiled carrots, all those
bottles of formula… He must weigh close to twenty
pounds by now. Corinne would have to ask Levi.

''Listen, Travis,'' Levi said, ''we're going to take
off. Corinne just had a long train ride. I know she'd
like to go home and freshen up.'' Corinne hid her
smile. The train ride hadn't been that long. Levi was
just eager to get her and D.J. away from the father
and take them home. She appreciated his tact—and
his sensitivity to her. He knew she didn't want to
hang around in the lobby of the Arlington Inn, making
small talk with Travis Justice.

''Okay,'' Travis said. ''So, I'll be by tomorrow?''

''Sure.''

If she'd been inclined to smile before, that last
exchange doused her happiness. Why was Travis going to be by tomorrow? She was here for the week-

end. She ought to be allowed to enjoy a couple of days with D.J. and Levi, without the intrusion of some West Coast interloper.

"I need the car seat," Levi added.

"Oh, yeah—I've got it in my car."

His car? He'd been driving with D.J.? He *could* have kidnapped the child if he'd wanted.

But maybe he didn't want to. Maybe he wanted to visit with his son and then go home. And Levi, being the kind of man he was, would allow him to enjoy that visit without interference.

They all trooped through the hotel's front door together. Corinne walked straight to Levi's car with D.J., while the men crossed the parking lot to another car. The asphalt felt sticky beneath her feet, and the evening air was thick and muggy. D.J. rested his head in the crook of her neck and murmured something unintelligible.

"I know," she agreed, just to make him feel better. "They're getting your car seat and then we'll go home."

"Oh-oh."

"That's right. Home."

Levi strode across the lot, carrying D.J.'s car seat and tossing a quick wave to Travis, who veered back to the hotel's front door. Deftly juggling both the seat and his keys, he managed to unlock the car, shove forward the passenger seat and wedge D.J.'s seat into place behind it. D.J. let out a rousing hoot. He loved riding in the car.

Reaching around, Levi took D.J. from Corinne and eased him into his seat. Then he unfolded himself from the cramped space of the car and straightened up in front of her. His eyes searched her face, and for

one moment she forgot about D.J., forgot about his
father and his car seat and the steamy August evening
settling around them. All she could think of was Levi,
so steady, so capable. So secure. So unlike the people
she'd grown up among, her loved ones, on whom she
could never depend.

She could depend on Levi. For her, that was an
arousing notion—a man who could love her, who
could ignite a fire inside her with his touches, his
kisses—and could still be there the next morning, the
next day, the next week. His steadiness, his serenity,
his confidence turned her on in a way even his kisses
couldn't.

She loved him. She knew it, and she knew it wasn't
his kisses that had made her fall in love with him.
They were wonderful, sex with him was unspeakably
marvelous—but she'd fallen in love with him because
he was a rock, solid and steady even as wild tides
and rapids churned around him. He was a man who
could have an infant dumped on him, and without
complaint he would bring that infant home and take
care of him. He was a man who would take classes
to become a better father for the child. He would surround the child with books and toys, a crib and a
walker and a boat-shaped tub for baths. He was a man
who thought before he spoke, who listened, who designed buildings that could protect the people inside
them while letting the outdoors inside.

He was amazing. And she was in love.

She would have said so, too—even though they
were standing in a parking lot in the waning light,
with the drone of rush-hour traffic cruising past the
hotel—but before she could speak, D.J. cut loose with
a bleat of impatience. Levi grinned, stepped away

from the passenger seat and helped Corinne into it. She heard him open the tiny trunk and toss her bag inside, and then he joined her in the car.

The silence that accompanied them home was friendlier and more peaceful than the silence that had risen between them when they'd first left the train station. Corinne was feeling better now with D.J. in the car. Everything was fixed, back in balance, arranged the way it ought to be. And in truth, the car wasn't exactly silent. Throughout the drive, D.J. provided a running commentary in his own unique language.

At the house, they worked in tandem to get her bag and D.J. out of the car. These were their Friday rituals; they didn't need to confer. Corinne carried D.J. inside, discreetly poking her finger into the leg opening of his shorts to check his diaper, and Levi lugged her bag into the house. While Corinne went upstairs with D.J. to change his diaper—it was always damp, and she didn't know why she even bothered to check it—Levi headed to the kitchen to start dinner. He was a better cook than she was. And in all honesty, she would rather change D.J.'s diaper than cook. Diapering him gave her time alone with him, an opportunity to prove her mettle as a caretaker, a few minutes to bond and giggle with him and feel as if she were an indispensable part of his life.

He chattered enthusiastically while she taped a dry diaper onto his bottom. He was full of news for her; she wanted to believe he was filling her in on the entire week. Since baby talk struck her as meaningless, she responded in a straightforward way to his prattling. "Is that so?" she asked as she smoothed the diaper tapes at his waist. "Are you sure it happened that way?"

"Lee-lee ga baa-baa!"

"I think you're pulling my leg," she muttered, then gave his leg a playful tug. "Just like that."

"Ga-lee-lee!"

"Yes, well, that's easy for you to say." His shorts back in place over his diaper, she lifted him off the pad on the dresser that Levi had set up as a changing table. He eagerly wrapped his arms around her neck, still pontificating on all manner of nonsense. Together they descended the stairs to the kitchen.

The room was empty, but she spotted Levi outside on the deck, lighting the grill. Smiling, she lowered D.J. into his walker and he sped off. Everything felt normal to her, proper, perfect. Travis Justice might as well have been a figment of her imagination. She and Levi and D.J. were home now, and all was right with the world.

Levi came back inside. He gave Corinne a breezy kiss on his way to the refrigerator, from which he removed a tray of skewered chunks of swordfish. He set it on the counter, then turned to face Corinne and gave her a longer kiss, a deep, lazy kiss that both relaxed and excited her, made her move against him and think that, as tasty as those swordfish shish kebabs looked, a few minutes in bed with Levi would satisfy other, stronger appetites of hers.

But he broke from her, smiled again and grabbed the tray. Not until he was back on the deck, arranging the skewers on the grill, did she realize that they weren't talking much.

They always talked a ton when she arrived from New York. He would want to know all about her

week, and she'd want to know about his. He'd ask
her how Gerald was doing, chuckle with her over
Gerald's most recent outings with women, promise
her that someday Gerald would find a woman suited
to him and predict that Gerald was going to seduce
that woman by building a fire in his master bedroom
fireplace. Corinne would interrogate him about the
house and about his other projects. She'd want to
know how this or that proposal was coming along,
how it exemplified his theories of design, what input
his partners and associates were providing and
whether a bid was likely to succeed. She'd complain
about how crowded and noisy Manhattan was at this
time of year, and he'd boast about how calm and quiet
Arlington was in comparison, the air fresh, the small
city surrounded by orchards and rolling, forested hills.

But tonight, she didn't care about his work projects,
not the way she usually did. His kisses and smiles
couldn't erase her sense that something was awry in
their world, its rotation not quite smooth, the atmosphere not quite pure. Electrical currents buzzed in-
visibly in the air until it seemed to crackle, making
the hairs on her arms quiver in warning.

"Travis Justice," she whispered, her gaze following Levi as he turned the skewers on the grill, then
stared out at the woods behind his house. "Travis
Justice is what's wrong."

But he'd be gone soon, she assured herself. He
lived in California. Surely he'd have to go back there
eventually. And then the atmosphere would settle
back to its normal tranquillity, and she and Levi and
D.J. would regain their balance.

She pulled a bottle of chardonnay from the refrigerator, uncorked it and filled two goblets. She knew

her way around his house as well as around her own apartment. He was always encouraging her to help herself to whatever she needed or wanted, use his dishes, pour wine, think of his house as her home. Usually she did. Tonight, however, there were those eerie currents in the air.

Trying to ignore them, she carried the glasses out onto the deck. D.J. zoomed toward the door, but she circled back inside to lead him to the screened porch, where he could cruise around in his walker without hurting himself. Then she rejoined Levi on the deck, lifted her glass and took a sip of the dry, cold wine.

"There's a salad in the fridge," he told her.

"I don't care." Corinne used to be circumspect, but loving Levi had made her less cautious, more willing to take chances. "Levi, what's going on? Why aren't you talking to me?"

He opened his mouth and then closed it. He wasn't going to deny her accusation or contend she was crazy to suggest anything was wrong. That was one more reason to love him: he didn't play games, didn't pretend things were fine when they weren't, didn't act as if her intuitions were silly.

"I thought maybe we ought to have dinner first," he said.

Apprehension bubbled up inside her. "It's Travis, isn't it. His being here—it's causing problems."

"Not problems," Levi said carefully. He turned the skewers once more, studying the chunks of white fish to make sure they were grilling evenly.

"Then what?"

"He wants custody of D.J."

Her heart stopped for a fraction of a second, then resumed its steady beat. "Well, he's not going to get it. Your sister named you D.J.'s legal guardian. Her will—"

"I've already talked with Murphy about this," he said, cutting her off. "My lawyer. He told me a birth father has legal rights in a situation like this."

"But you have legal rights, too," Corinne said firmly. If she spoke with enough conviction, maybe that would make it true. "Your sister named you D.J.'s guardian in her will. She was D.J.'s mother. Her wishes have to count for something."

"They do," Levi agreed. He lifted the skewers and placed them on the platter, then shut off the grill. "But Travis's wishes also count for something. He's D.J.'s father. And the only reason I even became D.J.'s guardian was that Travis had been excluded from D.J.'s life."

"Well…" She scrambled for a better argument. "If he'd been any kind of a decent guy, he wouldn't have fooled around with your sister and then disappeared. If he'd stuck around, if he'd exercised any responsibility with her instead of saying, 'Thanks for the good time, I'm outta here,' he would have known about D.J. He isn't blameless."

"No. He isn't." Levi sipped some wine, his eyes dark and penetrating as they searched Corinne's face. "That's not the point, though. The point is, he's D.J.'s father and he wants his son."

"Great. I want smaller feet and more free time. We can't always get what we want."

"Corinne." He perched his glass on the deck railing, then gathered her free hand in his. "I think he should have custody of D.J."

She'd misheard him. Misconstrued his words. Surely he hadn't said what she thought.

When he continued to study her face in the pink dusk light, she laughed. It was absurd, allowing a pretty boy from California to take custody of the magnificent little child scooting around the screened porch of Levi's home. "You're joking, aren't you?" she asked when he didn't join her laughter.

"No."

"But—but D.J. is—I mean, you've been raising him, and—"

"And it wasn't my choice. I took him in, I struggled, I screwed up my professional meetings—" at that reference to their first encounter, he permitted himself a faint, humorless smile "—and I took classes just so I could figure out what the hell I was doing. It wasn't my plan to become a bachelor father to my nephew. It wasn't my lifelong dream. It was the outcome of something very, very bad. My sister died, and this was how everything shook out."

"But—" She silenced herself, unsure what to say. It had never been her lifelong dream to become involved with a bachelor father. She'd never given much thought to babies at all, and when she'd first met Levi, she'd been annoyed that his obstreperous baby was interrupting their meeting.

How had things changed? When had she realized that reality's astonishing surprises could take precedence over lifelong dreams?

"I think it would be good for D.J. to know his father. I'll always be his uncle. He'll always have me. But his father wants to raise him. How can I stand in his way?"

"Easy. You can fight him. Talk to your lawyer some more. There's got to be a way."

"Corinne." Levi sighed. "If it were me, if I'd fathered a child I hadn't known about, and then learned the truth eight months later, I would want that child. I'd want to raise him. And I'd fight—yes, with lawyers, with money, with my fists, if necessary. I'd fight anyone who tried to keep me from my child. That's a father's right. Travis has rights here. I can't in good conscience keep him from D.J.'' He squeezed her hand. ''We're working together, trying to make the transition smooth. I don't want to be his enemy in this. I'm D.J.'s uncle. I want what's best for D.J.''

''Sending him to California with a total stranger—you think that's what's best for him?''

''Sending him to California with his father.''

Tears wadded into a soggy lump inside her throat. This wasn't her business, she told herself. It wasn't her battle. It wasn't her baby.

But the thought of visiting Levi each weekend and not seeing D.J., not holding him, not singing to him, not feeling that fierce surge of love and protectiveness and giddy, playful joy at watching an innocent young child become acquainted with the world...

She couldn't bear the idea of it.

Even worse, she couldn't bear the understanding that Levi would let such a thing happen, would let a stranger take D.J. away, would bow to fate the way he'd bowed to it when he'd learned of his sister's will.

She couldn't bear the thought that the man she loved would give away the baby she loved.

She simply couldn't bear it.

CHAPTER SIXTEEN

SHE LEFT EARLY the next morning. The night before had been hot and sticky—so muggy he'd had to keep the windows shut and the air conditioner running. After making love, they'd lain together in bed, listening to the chilly hiss of the ventilation system. The sex had been great—hot, powerful—but he'd sensed a certain desperation about it, something he couldn't define or explain.

"I don't know what's wrong with me," she'd whispered when he asked if she was okay. Her eyes had been glassy, her skin unnervingly cool against his. "I'm sorry, Levi—I wish I understood it, but I don't."

Now she was gone, and he didn't understand anything, either. She hadn't even let him drive her to the station. She'd arisen at dawn, told him she had to go home and phoned for a cab. He'd choked down a cup of coffee with her, remained downstairs while she tiptoed into D.J.'s room to bid him goodbye and then walked her out to the cab. Warm mist hovered above the grass. Today would be even hotter than yesterday, the sort of day that left one waiting for a thunderstorm to sweep through—praying for it.

She'd apologized again, promised to phone him, touched his lips with hers and then disappeared into the shadows of the cab's interior. He watched as the car drove away and the mist settled back down along the ground, a dense gray blur.

D.J. was chanting in his crib when Levi trudged back into the house. The cheerful babble wafted down the stairs to him, alerting him that the baby wanted to escape from his crib. But Levi needed more coffee, more time—more air. He needed to think. And one thing he didn't need, right this minute, was an energetic little boy with an empty stomach and a full diaper.

He poured a fresh cup of coffee for himself and carried it out to the porch. The morning air pressed against the screens with its smothering heat and dampness, but it was better than the processed air inside. Five minutes he'd give himself, and then he'd go back in and check on D.J.

In the not-too-distant future, he'd be able to sit out on the porch sipping coffee for as long as he wished. He wouldn't have to time himself, wouldn't have to live his life in incremental moments, always wondering if D.J. was all right, if D.J. needed him, if there was something he ought to be doing for D.J. at that exact moment. He'd be the one freed from the crib—his own invisible cage of responsibility and obligation.

He'd miss D.J., of course. As the kid's uncle—and only true tie to his mother—Levi would always be a part of D.J.'s life. But the day-to-day job of raising him would belong to Travis.

The prospect saddened him, but fighting Travis for custody wouldn't be fair, either to Travis or to D.J. A boy deserved his father. And no child deserved to be split in two by bickering adults. Levi knew his Bible. He knew about Solomon's decision to cut a

child in half, and about the love that had motivated
the true mother to cede her child to her rival in order
to save her baby's life. Levi would cede the child
because it would do D.J. no good to be split between
a West Coast father and a New England surrogate
father.

He would have explained all this to Corinne if
she'd let him. He'd tried last night, but she'd shut
down. She hadn't wanted to hear.

This had been the weekend he'd planned to discuss
marriage with Corinne. He cursed at his timing, his
lousy luck. He never would have expected that she'd
react to the custody situation the way she had. He'd
thought she would sympathize with him, assure him
he could remain in D.J.'s life—long distance but still
central to the boy, the way he'd been close to Ruth
even though they'd been three thousand miles apart.
He'd figured Corinne would comfort and support him
through a difficult decision. He hadn't imagined her
weeping after they'd made love, insisting she wasn't
angry but was unable to name the cause of her dis-
tress, lying rigidly next to him throughout a long,
troubled night and departing before the stars had completely faded from the sky.

If he wanted to exert himself, he might come up
with some explanations for her behavior. But he'd
already come up with the most obvious explanation:
if he didn't have D.J., Corinne didn't want him.

He never would have guessed she'd turn out to be
a woman like the ones he'd been warned about, the
sort who became attracted to men because they had
children. The first few times they'd met, she'd seemed
annoyed by the baby. It wasn't until that weekend that
she'd come to Arlington uninvited, as if driven by

some need to know Levi better—and D.J. She'd fallen for D.J. gradually, just as she'd fallen for Levi.

And now she'd fallen away. Without D.J., Levi no longer mattered to her.

He cursed again. His coffee was too hot and his five minutes were up—and he no longer trusted his judgment. He'd been so wrong about Corinne, so crazily, painfully wrong. And as a result, he was going to lose both her and D.J., just months after he'd lost his sister.

A weak man would be demolished by all that loss. Levi wasn't sure how strong he could be. He supposed he was going to have the opportunity to find out.

"THIS WOMAN is—what? A father-school teacher?"

"Daddy School," Levi corrected Travis. They were in his car, D.J. strapped into his child seat behind them, traveling through Arlington to Jamie McCoy's house.

Travis was worried about his parenting skills. "I'm twenty-five years old," he'd told Levi while they sat in the air-conditioned kitchen, drinking coffee as D.J. spun circles around them in his walker. "I've never changed a diaper in my life."

"Neither had I, before I got D.J.," Levi had assured him. "Whatever you can't figure out on your own you can read up on. Or you can take a class."

"What kind of class?"

That was when Levi had gotten the idea of phoning Jamie McCoy and seeing if his wife, Allison, the brilliant Daddy School teacher who'd taught Levi so much, would be willing to meet Travis for a private tutorial. "We're just hanging out today," Jamie had informed him. "It's too muggy to do anything. So come on over and we'll all do nothing together."

"Allison teaches classes on fathering skills in a program called the Daddy School," Levi explained as they drove through the swampy afternoon heat. "She and a friend of hers started this Daddy School. I heard about it from a friend of mine, a divorced father with custody of his kids. Allison's a neonatal nurse at Arlington Memorial Hospital. She knows her stuff, particularly when it comes to babies."

"Okay." Travis looked only slightly mollified. He was wearing another silk T-shirt, and Levi considered warning him that silk was an impractical fabric to wear in the presence of young children. If Allison didn't mention it, Levi would give Travis a lesson on machine washable clothing.

"I mean, I just feel way over my head," Travis muttered.

"No kidding." Levi smiled wryly. "That's how I felt when I came home with D.J., too."

"What happened to your lady?" Travis asked, apparently done discussing D.J. for now. "I thought she was going to be here for the weekend."

"She had to go home," Levi said, trying to ignore the pain and anger that sliced through him when he thought of Corinne, of how he'd counted on her, how she'd let him down. Before his mood could turn from blue to black, he reached Jamie's driveway and steered up it to the house. He nodded for Travis to get D.J. out of his seat, then winced as Travis struggled to reach over the folded front seat and wrestle D.J. out of the straps that secured him. D.J. fussed a bit, swatting at Travis and poking him with his foot.

What Levi could have done in ten seconds took Travis two whole minutes.

But he had to learn. Levi had learned by doing; Travis might as well learn by doing, too.

They knocked on the door and Jamie answered, dressed in a navy-blue cotton T-shirt that had seen better days and a pair of green athletic shorts. "Come on in," he welcomed them.

Once the cool air of the foyer enveloped them, Levi performed the introductions. "Jamie, this is Travis Justice, D.J.'s father. Travis, this is Jamie McCoy. You might have heard of him. He writes a syndicated newspaper column about men. It's called *Guy Stuff*. Your column is carried in one of the Los Angeles papers, isn't it?"

"*Guy Stuff?*" Travis exclaimed. "Hey, I used to read that column."

Jamie laughed, refusing to take offense. "*Used to? *Why'd you stop?"

Travis smiled sheepishly. "Well, it was really funny until you started writing about babies and fatherhood and all that."

"Oh." Jamie exchanged a quick look with Levi. "I'll tell you, Travis, it would be a good idea for you to develop a sense of humor about babies and fatherhood if you're planning to take that little guy home with you." He scruffed a hand through D.J.'s fine hair. "No way a man can survive the fatherhood gig without a sense of humor." He led them into the house, calling out, "Allison? Your tutee has arrived."

Allison greeted them in the brightly lit kitchen. She held several sheets of paper stapled together, and she waited until Levi had introduced them, and Travis lowered D.J. to the floor, before handing the papers to her student. "Here are some reading suggestions, books about early childhood development. Also a checklist of items you're going to need to have on hand for your baby. The most important item on that list is a pediatrician," she said, pointing it out.

The two of them settled at the kitchen table, and Jamie ushered Levi into the den. "You want a drink? I've got beer, iced tea, lemonade, water—"

"No, thanks." If he were a heavy drinker, he'd want to be chugging whiskey straight from the bottle right now, but hard liquor had never appealed to him.

Jamie's daughter appeared in the doorway. "There's a baby in the kitchen," she announced, hands on hips and head tilted as if she deeply resented having not been informed of this visit.

"That's Levi's little boy," Jamie said, then caught Levi's eye and corrected himself. "His nephew, actually. You can play with him if you want."

"I don't want to play with a boy."

"At his age, his being a boy hardly matters," Jamie informed her.

"I'd rather have a baby girl. Can I have a baby?"

"Maybe when you're thirty," Jamie answered, "and only after I've fully vetted the guy you want to have it with."

"Daddy, you're so silly," she scolded him. "I don't want a guy. I just want a baby." With a sigh, she turned and stomped out of the den.

"She reminds me of my sister," Levi muttered. "She didn't want a guy, either. Just a baby."

"And that's the guy she didn't want?" Jamie motioned in the direction of the kitchen with his head.

"That's the guy."

"Do you think he's got what it takes? Not to father

a child—I mean, we know he's got what it takes to do that. But to be a father.''

"He's got what I had when I took custody of D.J.—the desire to do the right thing.''

"You think that's enough?''

"It was enough for me.''

"I think maybe it takes more than just desire to be a good father,'' Jamie argued. "It even takes more than top-level instruction from a Daddy School teacher.''

"All right—a sense of humor,'' Levi added.

"And patience. And a healthy ego. The ability not to care if you're making an ass of yourself.'' He glanced toward the kitchen and snorted. "A lack of regard for good grooming.''

Levi chuckled. "The silk shirt worried me a little, too.''

"And the fancy hair, and the pricey sandals. A guy who cares that much about looking cool had either better have a wife on hand to deal with the baby, or a full-time nanny. He's got a job, right?''

"He works for a production company in Hollywood.''

"So he's going to have to hire a nanny.''

"I don't know. That'll be his problem,'' Levi said, although his heart seized at the possibility that Travis might not be as good at hiring a nanny as Levi had been. What if he hired someone who wasn't up to the task? What if D.J. didn't like her? What if he missed Levi and cried nonstop? What would Travis do?

How would Levi stand knowing that D.J. might be crying on the other side of the country, and he could do nothing to console him?

He'd thought he would have Corinne to help him

through this. He'd been trying to put a positive spin on it, knowing he was doing what he had to do. But he'd counted on Corinne to back him, to help him through the sadness of losing a baby he'd grown to love.

She'd abandoned him.

And that hurt even more than losing D.J.

GERALD SWUNG INTO Corinne's office, carrying two lidded plastic trays of take-out food. "One chicken quesadilla with rice," he said, placing one of the trays onto her blotter with a flourish. "One cheese enchilada special, extra mild," he continued, settling into the visitor's chair across the desk from her and putting down his meal. He dug into the deep pockets of his cargo pants and removed two cans. "Diet ginger ale for you, and Orange Crush for me."

"Thanks." Corinne would have found it odd that her boss was the one racing out for dinner when they had to work late—but he had more energy than she, and was more easily distracted. While he'd been out of the building procuring their food, she'd finished proofreading the new contract the Bell Tech people had agreed to. It was a good contract. It had an especially lovely payment schedule.

But unlike Gerald, she wasn't feeling triumphant. A huge payday couldn't cheer her up. Nothing could.

"I had the worst date of my life this past weekend," Gerald reported as he snapped off the lid of his tray.

"Really?" She forced herself to care. She'd much rather discuss Gerald's social life than think about her own.

"This woman was gorgeous. Blond, short, a little

plump in the right places. Mensa-smart. We went to the planetarium and decided the show was too commercial. Then we went out for espresso and pastries and she didn't once say, 'I really shouldn't' before digging into her cheesecake.''

Corinne picked at her rice and attempted an interested smile.

"I took her back to her apartment. We made out for a while, and then we stopped because we both sort of felt we should go out a few more times before we got carried away."

"I'm waiting to hear what was so bad about this date," she goaded him.

"It was awful, Corey. I enjoyed every damned minute of it. I didn't feel superior to her. I didn't feel intimidated by her. She scraped the cheesecake from her fork with these beautiful white teeth… It was absolutely awful."

"One of us is not making sense," Corinne muttered. "Why was it absolutely awful?"

"I'm in love."

She sighed and twirled the tines of her plastic fork in the melted cheese of her quesadilla. "Why is that awful?" she asked, even though she could come up with plenty of answers herself.

"It's easier not being in love, Corey. It's risk-free. I used to love it when I assumed you and I would wind up together. It would have been so easy, you know? We could work together, we could eat takeout together, we could spend weekends at the house in Arlington together, and we'd never have to get carried away or out of control or—I don't know, whatever happens when you fall in love. I'm scared."

"You could get hurt," she suggested.

"Exactly."

"Or you might hurt her."

"Which I really don't want to do, because I'm in love with her."

"She could do something that disappointed you so deeply you couldn't stand the pain." Corinne heard the scratchy emotion in her voice. She hoped Gerald didn't notice.

He did. Lowering his fork, he leaned forward, angling his face so he could peer into her eyes. "What happened? Did something go wrong between you and Levi this weekend?"

"Yes." She couldn't lie to Gerald. She didn't *want* to lie. He was her best friend, and she'd been feeling so wretched since she'd left Levi's house Saturday morning. Now it was Monday night and she only felt worse.

"What, Corey?" Gerald reached for her hand and gave it a squeeze. "What happened?"

"He did something that disappointed me so deeply. It hurt. So I hurt him."

"Ah." He kept his hand folded around hers, warm and soothing. "What did he do?"

"He gave up custody of the baby."

"You're kidding! Who'd he give it to?"

"The baby's a *he,* not an it. And he gave him to the birth father, who only just found out he had a son and wanted custody of him."

Gerald mulled that over. "Sounds like Levi did the right thing."

"I know." She quit trying to hide her tears. A few slid down her cheeks, and she wiped them with a napkin that said Paco Rico in bright-orange letters. "That's the worst part of it, Gerald—he did the right thing. I should have praised him for his courage. I should have admired him for his sacrifice. But all I could think of was that he was giving away D.J. I love D.J."

"More than you love Levi?"

"No." She let out a damp, shaky sigh. "But when Levi told me he was giving up the baby, I felt as if I were falling out of love with him. I thought, he should have fought to keep D.J. He should have refused to give him up."

"Would that have been the best thing for the baby?"

"Probably not." She sighed again, so deeply her lungs ached. "It would have been selfish. But it was what I wanted him to do."

Releasing her hand, Gerald leaned back and forked a bite of enchilada into his mouth. "You know what I think?"

"What?" She had never imagined she'd be asking Gerald for advice on romance, but she was desperate.

"I think you've got a problem with that biological clock thingy. I think you want a baby."

So much for expecting any useful advice from him. "It's not that at all," she snapped impatiently. "Maybe I can imagine myself having a baby some-day, but no—this was specifically about D.J. There was just something about that one special baby."

"I didn't see it." Gerald shook his head. "I met the kid, and sorry, but I just didn't see anything special about him."

"Don't apologize. It was something between D.J. and me. Something magical. I never felt about other babies the way I felt about him. He made me sing."

"Jeez. I'm glad I missed that."

"I happen to have a very nice voice. But I'm not often inspired to sing. D.J. inspired me." She let out another deep breath and nudged her plate away, sorrow sabotaging her appetite. "I still can't believe Levi gave him up to that—that skinny hotshot twerp from California."

"Well, if he's the baby's father—"

"I know. But I love the baby. He doesn't even know the baby. How can he love him?"

"You women drive me crazy," Gerald griped. "You complain when fathers *don't* take responsibility for the babies they create, and now here's a father who *is* taking responsibility, and you're putting him down. Do you think he'd be a better man if he hadn't shown up and taken responsibility?"

"No," she conceded. "But I'd have been a happier woman."

"Well, maybe your happiness isn't the most important thing here."

She jerked her head up. She and Gerald were always honest with each other—but rarely so honest that the words stung. His statement was like a slap on the cheek. She felt her skin tingling with heat from it.

"And I'll tell you something more, Corey," he continued, pulling Corinne's barely touched dinner toward himself and scooping up some rice with his fork. "You're only making yourself more miserable by turning your back on Levi. You lost the baby—even though he was never really yours to lose. So what's to be gained by losing Levi, too? What's the point of making yourself feel even worse?"

She sipped her ginger ale and sank back in her chair, wishing the upholstery were softer, wishing it would swallow her up. "One of the things I loved about Levi was how devoted he was to D.J., how hard he worked to make a good life for him. The first time I met him—met them both—" her voice cracked as she recalled that morning at his office "—he canceled a meeting with me because D.J. was teething. He wanted to give his full attention to making D.J. feel better. At first I was ticked off, because he was screwing up my schedule. But then I realized how wonderful he was, putting a baby's comfort ahead of everything else. Taking that baby's pain away. Trying to make up for the tragic loss that baby had suffered. Accepting a complete upheaval in his own life to accommodate this tiny little invader. That kind of selflessness and dedication... That's why I fell in love with him."

"And—what? This past weekend, you discovered he wasn't so selfless and dedicated?"

"I thought he would fight for the baby. He was D.J.'s champion, and I thought he'd stick by that baby no matter what. Everything always changes in my life," she lamented. "My parents used to come and go, my stepparents, my addresses, even my cat."

"You had a cat?" Gerald's eyes grew almost as round as the frames of his eyeglasses.

She ignored the question. "All I ever wanted was a stable home, something that wouldn't change. It would be just what I wanted it to be, and it would stay that way. Levi, D.J. and me. A real home. And Levi threw that all away."

"So your complaint is, he wasn't selfless when it came to what you wanted. Only when it came to what he wanted, or D.J. wanted, or D.J.'s father wanted."

A fresh spate of tears filled her eyes, and a few

leaked out. "Oh, God. Levi *was* selfless, wasn't he? He wasn't thinking about me, but he wasn't thinking about himself, either. He was thinking only about what would be best for D.J."

Gerald devoured a chunk of Corinne's quesadilla. "Hey, it's always possible he was secretly glad to give up the baby. Maybe he wanted his bachelor life back."

She dismissed that possibility with a shake of her head. "Levi wanted D.J. to grow up knowing his father. If anyone should understand that, I should. I had all those fathers—more fathers than I wanted—but I couldn't even depend on my own real father. Levi wanted D.J. to have his own real father. Not a step-father. Not a surrogate. Not a substitute. The real thing. For God's sake, I should understand that."

"Okay. So now you understand it. What are you going to do about it?"

"I'm going to let you eat my dinner," she mumbled, dabbing her cheeks with her soggy napkin. "I should go throw myself at Levi's feet and beg him to forgive me for being so thoughtless," she admitted. "He probably won't want to see me, though."

"He's not an idiot," Gerald pointed out, his eyes brimming with affection, the sort of love best friends had for each other. "He'll want to see you."

She glanced at her watch. "It's seven-thirty. I don't know how late the trains run to Arlington—"

"I'll drive you," he offered. "I'm paying a fortune to park that damned Range Rover in the garage of my building. I might as well get some use out of it."

"You'd really want to drive all the way up to Arlington at this hour?"

"Corey. You always fix everyone else's mistakes,

but this time you're the one who made a huge mistake. You never make mistakes. This is probably the first mistake you ever made in your life. I feel privileged to witness it.''

She threw a wadded-up napkin at him, then managed a limp smile. ''If you're serious about driving me, I'm not going to say no. That would be an even bigger mistake.''

''Then let's hit the road.'' Gerald rose, grabbed Corinne's hand and hauled her out of her chair. ''Let's go and see if there's still a home waiting for you in Arlington.''

LEVI HEARD the rumble of an engine and the crunch of large tires on driveway. He wasn't expecting anyone, but he couldn't get up and peek through the window while he was in the middle of changing D.J.'s diaper. D.J. squawked and squealed and attempted risky maneuvers with his feet while Levi scrubbed his bottom clean with a clutch of disposable wipes. He heard the doorbell ring and slid a clean diaper into place between D.J.'s legs. His thighs were losing their fat, he noticed, and his legs were getting straighter. All that exercise—the walker, the crawling, the new trick he'd demonstrated just an hour ago, when he'd positioned himself at the bottom of the stairs and then moved his hands up to the second step, pulling himself to his feet—were turning his legs from baby legs to real legs, legs that would someday run, kick, jump, climb and carry him through the world.

The doorbell rang again, and he pulled D.J.'s pajama bottoms onto him. D.J. giggled and tried to kick the pj's off. Not a great time to play that game, Levi thought.

He wrestled D.J. into the pj's, then snapped the bottoms to the tops so D.J. couldn't push them off. He heard the rumble of an engine again. Whoever had come by was leaving.

Probably someone trying to sell something, he figured. Or someone trying to get him to sign a petition. It was nine o'clock, too late for a delivery.

He hoisted D.J. into his arms and descended the stairs. D.J. made a gobbling sound like a turkey. That morning, Martina had brought him a toy that created animal noises when he pointed an arrow to a picture and pulled a string. At least, they were supposed to be animal noises. As far as Levi was concerned, the noise that emerged when the arrow was pointed at the duck sounded more like a bicycle horn than a quack. The sound that accompanied the dog resembled a truck backfiring. But D.J. had fallen in love with the gobbling turkey.

Levi opened the door, just in case someone had left a package or a flyer.

Corinne was standing on the doorstep.

He stared at her, holding his face immobile while a series of emotions washed through him in waves: joy, fury, resentment, self-protective caution. Love, relief, fear.

She'd left him because she'd only loved him for D.J. Now everything she wanted had come true, and he didn't know whether he could forgive her.

"I'm sorry," she said, and forgiveness began to trickle into his soul.

D.J. shrieked and reached for her, but she didn't acknowledge him. Her gaze locked onto Levi's. "I'm so sorry, Levi. I love you. Can I come in?"

The trickle increased to a gentle flow, but he resisted it. She'd left him. She'd broken his heart. He had to be careful.

D.J. continued to reach for her, but she looked only at Levi. "Sure. Come in. How did you get here?"

"Gerald drove me," she said, entering the house.

Levi glanced down the empty driveway before shutting the door. "He just dumped you on the doorstep and left?"

"If you weren't home—or you refused to let me in, I was going to call him to come and get me. We've both got cell phones. But I thought it would be best if I saw you alone. He drove across town to look at his house."

"It's dark. I hope he doesn't do something stupid like walk around the construction site. He could get hurt."

"He's too smart to do anything stupid," she said, moving past Levi toward the living room, where a lamp filled the air with golden light. D.J. snagged a fistful of her hair as she walked past, and she yelped. "Ouch! Let go!"

D.J. laughed. Levi fought to unfurl his tight little fingers and free her. "I guess you aren't happy to see him," he said thoughtfully. He would have expected her to snatch D.J. out of his arms and crush him in a hug, then to question Levi about how much longer he would have D.J. staying with him, how much longer she could spend with him before Travis took him away.

But she didn't. In the light from the lamp he noticed that her cheeks were tear-stained, her lashes clumped from moisture. She was dressed in a well-tailored navy-blue wool suit, stockings and pumps. Had she come here on business?

No. She'd just apologized and said she loved him. That didn't sound like business.

"I was wrong," she said. "I was wrong to leave you. I thought you were giving D.J. up. It never occurred to me that you were trying to do what was best for him, that you loved him as much as I did."

His stores of forgiveness increased, but he only watched her and let her continue.

"I loved the way we all were when we were together. The way you and I seemed to think alike when we were doing things for D.J., the way we just knew intuitively where we were and who we were and what we were all doing. Like we belonged together."

"I know," he finally said. Her eyes were filling with tears, shining with them. He had to offer her something, some encouragement so she could get through this.

"I've never had the kind of family I had with you, Levi. I know it wasn't that long, but it felt so right. Just the three of us. It felt so true."

"I know."

"And—yes, I hated you for letting it slip away. I'm sorry. Because even after D.J. is gone, you'll still be the best thing that ever happened to me, and I want you in my life."

"D.J. isn't going to be gone," he finally told her.

"I mean it, Levi. I want to be together with you. We can make our own two-person family, can't we? And maybe, in time, we could have a baby of our own, and no one would ever take our baby away—"

"No one is taking D.J. away. He's staying here."

At last his words registered on her. "What?"

"Travis left for California yesterday. Alone."

"Why?"

"He was scared to death. I made him sit down for a couple of hours with Allison Winslow—my Daddy School teacher—and she told him exactly what to expect when he became a full-time single parent. And he panicked. He said he didn't think he could handle it. He broke down and cried."

"Oh, no." She shook her head, appearing genuinely sorry for him. "The poor man. He'd come here with the best of intentions."

"And he left with the best of intentions. He left knowing D.J. would be better off here than in California with him." The shimmer in her eyes was breaking down his resistance. Her nearness, her sincerity, the tremulous softness of her lips as she bared her heart to him... Forgiveness was flooding him now. She was back. She'd said she loved him.

But she still hadn't acknowledged D.J., other than to yell at him for pulling her hair. Evidently, she'd come to Arlington prepared to love Levi alone, without the baggage of a baby. And now the baby had become a part of the deal again, just when she'd accepted that the baby was *not* a part of the deal.

Not only had the baby become a part of the deal, but he'd yanked her hair.

"Travis knows he'll always be a part of D.J.'s life. He can come and visit whenever he wants, as long as he gives me a little warning. And maybe, when D.J.'s older, he can fly out to California to visit his dad. But Travis gave me full custody. He said he'd have his lawyer handle whatever paperwork is necessary."

"He must have been disappointed."

"Disappointed and relieved, both."

"And you?"

"Mostly relieved," Levi admitted.

Her face blossomed into a smile, the first real smile he'd seen since she'd arrived—in fact, the first real smile since her last visit, when she'd been tense and worried about Travis's presence in Arlington.

She was smiling because Levi wanted D.J. Which meant she wanted D.J., too.

"I love you," she murmured, her eyes overflowing. She'd already told him that, but he would gladly listen to her tell him again and again. She opened her arms, wrapped one around him and one around D.J. and rested her head against Levi's shoulder. "I love you both."

He touched his lips to her soft, silky hair. "Welcome home, Corinne," he whispered. "Welcome home."

SHE WAS BACK. She was hugging them, and he knew from the way her arms felt, the way her body pressed close, that she wasn't going to leave anymore.

He wasn't sure exactly what home *meant, but he believed it had something to do with being held, being safe and being loved. He felt safe right now. He felt loved. He was surrounded by the man and the woman, by strength and softness, and neither of them seemed likely to let go.*

This must be home, D.J. thought with a happy sigh.

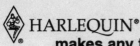

Harlequin invites you to walk down the aisle . . .

To honor our year long celebration of weddings, we are offering an exciting opportunity for you to own the Harlequin Bride Doll. Handcrafted in fine bisque porcelain, the wedding doll is dressed for her wedding day in a cream satin gown accented by lace trim. She carries an exquisite traditional bridal bouquet and wears a cathedral-length dotted Swiss veil. Embroidered flowers cascade down her lace overskirt to the scalloped hemline; underneath all is a multi-layered crinoline.

Join us in our celebration of weddings by sending away for your own Harlequin Bride Doll. This doll regularly retails for $74.95 U.S./approx. $108.68 CDN. One doll per household. Requests must be received no later than June 30, 2001. Offer good while quantities of gifts last. Please allow 6-8 weeks for delivery. Offer good in the U.S. and Canada only. Become part of this exciting offer!

Simply complete the order form and mail to:
"A Walk Down the Aisle"

IN U.S.A	IN CANADA
P.O. Box 9057	P.O. Box 622
3010 Walden Ave.	Fort Erie, Ontario
Buffalo, NY 14240-9057	L2A 5X3

Enclosed are eight (8) proofs of purchase found on the last page of every specially marked Harlequin series book and $3.75 check or money order (for postage and handling). Please send my Harlequin Bride Doll to:

_____

Name (PLEASE PRINT)

_____

Address   Apt. #

_____

City   State/Prov.   Zip/Postal Code

_____

Account # (if applicable)   **098 KIK DAEW**

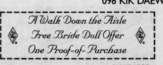

Visit us at www.eHarlequin.com   PHWDAPOP